Broken Hearts

Book Seven of the Barrington Family Series

Chris Taylor

LCT Productions Pty Limited

LCT Productions Pty Limited

18364 Kamilaroi Highway, Narrabri NSW 2390

ISBN: 9781925441116 (eBook)

ISBN: 9781925441123 (Print)

BROKEN HEARTS

Other books by Chris Taylor

The Munro Family Series (in order)

The Profiler
The Investigator
The Predator
The Betrayal
The Deception
The Negotiator
The Christmas Vigil (A novella)
The Ransom
The Defendant
The Shooting
The Maker

The Sydney Harbour Hospital Series (in order)

The Perfect Husband

The Body Thief
The Baby Snatchers
The Final Bullet
The Debt Collector
The Lab Test
The Stolen Identity
The Cliff-top Killer
The Likeable Fraudster

The Sydney Legal Series (in order)

An Accidental Murderer
At the Hand of her Father
A Woman Scorned
Lies and Deception
Ordinary Evil
The Ties that Bind
The Perfect Crime
A Toxic Inheritance
Malicious Love

The Craigdon Family Series (in order)

Callum
Joel
Isabella
Nicholas
Sophia
Flynn

Noah
Logan
Elizabeth

The Barrington Family Series (in order)

Broken Lives
Broken Promises
Broken Bonds
Broken Spirits
Broken Minds
Broken Vows
Broken Hearts
Broken Dreams
Broken Homes

The Fairfax Family Series (in order)

A Cattleman in Disguise
A Cattleman's Quest
A Cattleman's Daughter
A Cattleman's Secret Baby
To Catch a Cattleman
The Doctor and the Cattleman
To Rescue a Cattleman
A Cattleman's Heart
For the Love of a Cattleman

Bachelors and Brides Series (in order)

Matilda
Austin
Farrah
Benjamin
Verity
Denver
Ebony
Tyrone
Willow

Books by Chris Taylor
Writing as
Bella
Christian

This Is Where It Ends Series
(in order)

Jessie's Story
Ryan's Story
Holly's Story
Sarah's Story
Veronica's Story

Love audiobooks? Check out Chris Taylor Books on audio
iTunes Amazon Audible

Join Chris Taylor's Facebook reader group/fan page and be among the
first to receive news of book releases, read and review books prior to release
and other amazing offers.

Join Now!

This book is dedicated to my friend and paramedic extraordinaire, Kim Summers, and to all the paramedics and first responders who put their lives on the line for others. I appreciate all that you so selflessly do to make this world a better place.

And to my husband, Linden, my very own hero. The love of my life, my soul mate. I'll love you to the end of time.

Chapter One

With lights and siren blazing, intensive care paramedic Molly Barrington downloaded the address of the latest accident site from the mobile terminal data and relayed the information to her colleague behind the wheel.

"What do we have?" Benson Pitt asked, his attention focused on the busy city road in front of him.

"A single vehicle accident. One male victim. According to the person who called in the emergency, he's in a bad way. Also, it looks like he's trapped in the vehicle."

Benson acknowledged her comments with a nod. His expression was a mixture of nerves and anticipation. Molly knew the feeling well.

Benson was one of the newer members of their team. He was also one of their most inexperienced. Molly didn't begrudge him that. They'd all been newbies at one time. The best way to learn was on the job and she still had fond memories of the senior paramedic who'd taken her under his wing all those years ago. She was happy to pay it forward. Besides, the more competent Benson became, the more he was an asset to work with. That helped everyone out, including him.

She and Benson had decided at the beginning of their shift that he'd be the driver for the day. His job was to get them to any callout and back again safely and deal with all communications while at the scene. As the treating officer, her role was to deal with the patient.

As they drew closer to the accident site, Molly savored the familiar surge of adrenaline. Her mind was already focused on the description of the scene provided and what decisions she might have to make: the amount of damage to the vehicle; the likely difficulty of getting the victim out; the extent of the victim's injuries; whether he was still alive…

She wasn't surprised to see the crowd of onlookers. Nothing drew spectators quite like an accident, fascinated by their morbid curiosity to view someone else's misfortune. Benson parked perpendicular to the road a safe distance away, helping to block the traffic from the accident scene. The police arrived shortly afterward and set about cordoning off the area surrounding the accident site with blue-and-white checked police tape.

Molly spied a white, late model Toyota Corolla wrapped around a steel power pole. It had suffered extensive damage. The driver's side had taken the brunt of the impact. She glanced at Benson.

"Looks bad," he said, looking a little scared.

She remembered feeling the same way when she was a rookie. She did her best to reassure him. "It's okay. We've got this. You call in our location and update them on what we have. I'll go and assess our patient."

Benson nodded. He switched off the siren but left the beacons on. In silence, Molly quickly pulled on her protective clothing—high visibility vest, helmet, safety glasses, and mask and climbed out of the vehicle. While Benson radioed their exact location and other details of the accident back to their control center, Molly took stock of any potential dangers, including fallen power lines, and then hurriedly made her way over to the wreckage. She nodded in passing to a uniformed police officer who was doing his best to move the crowd back.

Approaching the driver's side, she was relieved to discover the victim was conscious. One side of his face was covered in blood from a large laceration on his forehead, most likely a result of contact with the steering wheel. The front of the car had folded in on itself and was crushed against the driver's legs, along with the steering wheel that now pressed against his chest. Both the driver's and front passenger's airbags had been deployed and further restricted the driver's space. Wanting to reassure him, Molly made eye contact and shot him a friendly smile.

"Hi, I'm Molly. What's your name?"

"Shane. Shane Lucas," he hissed through gritted teeth.

"How old are you, Shane?"

"Thirty."

"Do you know what day it is?"

"Um...Monday...?"

"Where are you?"

"In Caringbah."

"Have you been drinking?"

"No."

"Drugs?"

"No."

"I'm not a cop. I don't care whether you have or not, but I need to know if you've taken anything."

"I don't do drugs."

"Okay. Well, we're going to get you out of there as fast as we can. Can you tell me where it hurts?"

"Everywhere," he rasped.

"Can you be a bit more specific? I can see you've cut your forehead. Where else does it hurt?"

"My legs. My chest. My lungs. I can't breathe."

"On a scale of one to ten, with ten being the worst pain imaginable, how would you rate your pain?"

"Ten."

The driver's side door was buckled. She tried the handle, but the door was stuck fast. The passenger side had also sustained serious damage. There was no way she was going to be able to get either door open without help. She looked at what was left of the driver's side window. The glass had shattered into a million splinters, most of which were embedded in the man's clothes. Shards were also stuck to his face. They glinted in the mid-afternoon sunlight.

She reached carefully around the broken window and checked the pulse in the side of his neck. It was weak and erratic and fast. His skin was pale and clammy. His startling green eyes, though focused, were glazed with pain. With the steering wheel jammed so tightly against his chest, there was also a strong possibility of internal bleeding.

"Can you squeeze my finger?" she asked, leaning in again.

He shook his head. "Can't move. It hurts too much."

She pinched the skin at the back of his neck hard. "Can you feel that?"

"Yes. I think so."

"Good. Just keep breathing, Shane. Slow, deep breaths. That's it. You're doing well."

"When...can you...get me...out...of here?" he gasped.

"Soon. The door's stuck and you're wedged pretty tightly against the steering wheel. We might need to bring in a rescue crew with the jaws of life."

"How long?"

Molly looked around her at the now-chaotic scene. The crowd of onlookers had swelled. People held up their phones, presumably recording the carnage before them. Several more police vehicles had arrived, along with her duty operations manager, Raoul Kumar, dressed in full PPE. She was relieved to see him.

He nodded a greeting as he approached her. "What have we got?"

"Thirty-year-old male. High speed crash into a power pole. Major vehicle deformity. Patient is alert with a GCS of seven," she said, referring to the universal Glasgow Coma Scale that was used to measure a person's level of consciousness. "He's also trapped. We're going to need some help to get him out."

"I'll speak to the police commander and see what we can organize." Raoul switched his attention to the man who remained trapped in the car, his face a mask of pain.

"Hang in there, mate. We're going to get you out as soon as we can."

With that, Raoul strode away, headed in the direction of the police commander. Molly returned to Shane's side and offered him another reassuring smile. She needed to keep him talking. That would not only take his mind off his injuries, but it would also help him maintain consciousness.

"You sound like you have an accent. Where are you from, Shane?"

"Born...in the UK. Came out...backpacking. Liked it so much...I stayed."

"What about your family?"

"Parents still live...in the UK. A sister...in the US."

He grimaced as another wave of pain hit him. She reached for his hand and squeezed it. "Is there anyone we can call? A wife? A partner?"

"No wife. No girlfriend. Just me."

"Okay. But we're going to have to notify someone. Do you have a friend we can contact?"

His answer was swallowed up by a moan of pain. Gasping for breath, his eyes glazed over. His grip on her hand tightened.

"Oh, God. Please. It hurts so much."

"Breathe, Shane. Slowly in and out. As big as you can manage. In. Out. In. Out."

Slowly, the pain in his eyes eased, along with the pressure exerted by his hand. Molly resisted the urge to pull her hand away and flex her fingers. Despite his obvious pain, his grip had been tremendously strong and she wasn't at all certain her fingers were all still working.

"What do you do for a living?" she asked to keep him talking.

"Lawyer."

"Wow," she said, impressed. "What kind of law do you practice?"

"Family law."

"That must get tough sometimes," she murmured.

"Yeah."

Raoul came up to her again and drew her to one side. "I've spoken to the police commander. He's put in a call for the jaws of life. Unfortunately, the closest police rescue team was called out on another job only twenty minutes earlier. Someone's fallen off a cliff at Bondi. They're going to be caught up for the rest of the afternoon. The commander's trying to source another team. It might take a while."

"How long?" Molly asked.

"An hour or two. Maybe more."

Molly's heart sank. Though it wasn't unusual for a specialized police rescue team to take that long to attend an accident, particularly if they were otherwise engaged, it meant that her patient would remain trapped for all that time. It made treating him more difficult and further delayed his transfer to a trauma center where he could receive more specialized medical and surgical care.

"I'll see about some pain relief then," she murmured.

She returned to the car. Shane's expression twisted with pain.

"How long?" he gasped.

"I'm afraid it's going to be a while yet," she answered.

"How long?"

The desperation in his eyes filled her with dread. She hated having to tell him the truth, but she'd never shied away from that, not even when the news was bad.

"An hour or two."

Shane's eyes flared wide with surprise. His expression quickly turned to one of despair. "An hour or two?"

Molly held his gaze. "Yes. The closest team is out on another emergency. We've had to call in a unit from outside the area."

"Fuck."

The quiet expletive held a wealth of emotion. She hurried to boost his spirits.

"They'll be here as soon as they can and then we'll get you free. In the meantime, I'm going to administer some pain relief. Are you allergic to anything?"

"No."

"Are you taking any medications?"

"No."

"How much do you weigh?"

"Ninety-five kilograms."

"When did you last eat?"

"Lunchtime."

"So, a couple of hours ago?"

"Yeah. I guess."

"Do you remember what happened?"

"Yeah. A vehicle ran the red light. Came out of nowhere. Clipped my car and spun me around. I think I flipped. I can't remember. It all happened so fast. Then I slammed into the power pole."

Molly frowned. She'd seen no evidence of another damaged vehicle. But that was for the police to sort out. Her only priority was her patient.

"Can you stretch your arm out for me?"

"No. The pain."

She nodded in acknowledgement. "I understand, but I need to check your blood pressure before I can give you anything for the pain. Are you sure you can't stretch out your arm?"

With gritted teeth, the man tried to do as she asked. It was awkward in the cramped confines of the driver's seat, but inch by inch and with her help, he managed it.

"That's great," she encouraged. She opened her kit and pulled out a blood pressure machine. Wrapping the cuff around his arm, she quickly took a reading. Though it was low, it wasn't as bad as it could be.

She released the blood pressure cuff and tucked it back into her kit. She squeezed his arm reassuringly. "I'll go and get that pain relief. I'll be back in a minute."

Hurrying back to where Benson remained with the ambulance, she slid open the door to access the rear of the vehicle and stepped inside.

"How's he doing?" Benson asked.

"He's conscious, at least. There's a two hour wait on the jaws of life."

Benson winced. "Shit."

"Yeah. I'm going to give him some pain relief."

"Morphine?"

"No. He's not alert enough for that. There's a good chance he has internal injuries. His blood pressure is low, but stable, which is a good sign. I'm worried his level of consciousness might decrease the longer we have to wait."

"So, ketamine then?"

She grinned, pleased at his response. "Yep."

Molly opened a drawer and pulled out IV equipment, along with the ketamine. It would help with the pain without making him drowsy. It was the best option in the circumstances.

She double-checked the medication with Benson and then wrote it up on a new patient notes form, adding Shane's name, age and weight, before climbing out of the vehicle.

"You need some help?" Benson asked.

Molly smiled. "No, but you're welcome to come and observe. The more experience you get dealing with accident victims, the better prepared you'll be for the next one.".

Benson gave her a nervous smile but after pulling on his PPE, he followed behind her as she turned and strode back to Shane's crushed vehicle. The crowd of onlookers had begun to disperse. No doubt the lack of immediate action meant their attention had waned. It also helped that the police were actively encouraging people to move on. Molly was glad. The less gawkers getting in the way, the better. Particularly when the jaws of life arrived.

"Hey, Shane. You still with me?" she asked, leaning in carefully through the window opening to avoid the jagged glass that remained behind.

He gave her strained look. His skin was chalky. "Still here."

"Great." She indicated Benson who hovered behind her. "This is my colleague, Benson. We've organized some pain relief. I'm going to give it to you intravenously. That means inserting a needle into your vein. Are you okay with that?"

"Just do it," he replied through clenched teeth.

Quickly and efficiently, she inserted the cannula into a vein on the back of his wrist. She was relieved that his veins hadn't yet collapsed. That gave her hope that if there was internal bleeding, it wasn't severe enough to affect the volume of blood in his veins.

"How're you doing?" she asked as she taped the cannula in place.

"Never been better." He gave her a lopsided smile.

It transformed his face. She suddenly noticed other things about him. Thick hair the color of ripened wheat. Olive complexion. Vivid green eyes. A strong jaw.

Impatient with the direction of her thoughts, she quickly pushed them aside and focused on her job. She prepared the syringe of ketamine and injected it into him through the cannula port.

"That will take a few minutes to take effect. Keep breathing, nice and slowly. Try and relax."

His heavy brows met in a frown. "You're kidding, right?"

She grinned. "Do I look like I'm kidding?"

Chapter Two

Shane Lucas had never been in so much pain in his life. Not even when he'd come off his motorbike at full speed when he was seventeen and had skidded fifteen yards along the asphalt on the seat of his pants. The road had torn through the leather and had shaved several inches of skin off the back of his thighs. One of his wounds had required a skin graft. But even that was no match for the agony that consumed him now.

He hurt in every part of his body. Every time he tried to move it was like a red-hot poker searing through him. Every breath was agony. He worried about broken ribs, punctured lungs—any manner of injury for that matter. His legs were immobile. His chest was jammed hard against the steering wheel. His face stung from a variety of cuts. Only God knew what other injuries he'd sustained. He was on the verge of panic.

It took a gargantuan effort to rein in his imagination. His head was filled with worst-case scenarios. At least he was still alert. Kind of. That was a blessing. Or maybe not. If he were unconscious, he wouldn't feel the pain. Then again, if he were unconscious, he wouldn't be talking to the pretty paramedic.

Molly. That's what she'd said. It suited her. Glossy dark hair pulled back off her face. Bright blue eyes. Kind eyes. Compassionate. Friendly. She was a nice distraction. Kept him from thinking about the pain. At least a little. Her gentle yet confident voice filled him with hope even as he battled with the pain that raged through his nerve endings and he slowly lost feeling in his legs.

His mind shied away from what that might mean. God, he couldn't stand the thought he might be paralyzed. That would be unthinkable. He'd be better off dead. Maybe God was playing a cruel joke on him? Injuring him seriously enough that he'd never walk again, but not injuring him enough to kill him... No doubt God thought he deserved that kind of punishment and hell—he probably did.

He tried to remember back to the accident, but it was all a bit of a blur. He could remember the lights changing green and accelerating into the intersection before the other car came from nowhere and T-boned him. He remembered seeing a flash of silver. He thought the other car was a 4WD—maybe a Toyota Prado or a Landcruiser. There was no doubt it had been much bigger than his Corolla.

The other driver had come at him fast. There had been nothing he could do to avoid the collision. He'd taken a direct hit to the driver's side. The awful screech of the impact of metal-on-metal still rang in his ears. He was spun around several times before his car took to the air and flipped. Finally, it landed on its wheels, wrapped around a power pole. Thank God he'd been wearing a seatbelt. Then again, if he were now paralyzed, he'd be better off dead.

There was broken glass all around him, filling his hair, covering his clothes. Shards had punctured his cheeks and his bare arms. Warm blood trickled from a cut on his forehead. All in all, he felt like shit. But at least the pain medication appeared to be working. The pressure in his chest had eased, along with the pain in his legs. At least, he hoped the receding pain was due to the painkillers and not something more sinister. Worry once again held him in its grip.

"How are you feeling, Shane?"

Molly was back, regarding him with concern. Her colleague had shifted from Shane's field of vision. He tried for a smile, but it came out as a grimace.

"A little better. Thanks. Whatever you gave me took the edge off."

She smiled, showing a row of even, white teeth. "Good. It should help the pain without interfering with your level of consciousness."

"How much longer?" he asked, trying to keep the anxiety out of his voice. Now that it seemed he was going to get out of there alive, he was keen to get the steering wheel out of his chest and to feel his legs again.

"A little while yet, I'm afraid."

He was filled with a surge of desperation. "I can't feel my legs."

Her lips tightened, but instead of responding, she said, "Tell me more about yourself. How long have you been in Australia?"

He closed his eyes on a stab of irritation. The last thing he wanted to do was talk.

Just bring on the rescue crew and get me the hell out of here...

"Shane?"

He heard the concern in her voice. No doubt she was worried about his level of consciousness. He opened his eyes and sighed wearily.

Fuck it.

He answered grudgingly. "Ten years. Came out on a working holiday. Had a great time traveling around the country, driving tractors, picking fruit, meeting the local women. There's nothing quite like Australian women." He winked and was amused to see her blush. It made her look younger. He wondered how old she was.

Why the hell would you care about that?

"Ah. So, it was the women who made you stay," she said with a grin, her color still high.

She had a nice smile. Despite himself, his irritation began to fade. "That and the weather. Months and months of sunshine. What's not to like?"

"What about your family? Don't they miss you?"

He drew in a breath and was relieved to discover it didn't hurt as much as it had. "Yeah, I guess. But they're both retired now and they're busy doing their own thing. Mom was a high school teacher. Dad was a lawyer."

"Did he inspire you to go into the law?" she asked.

He surprised himself by answering truthfully. "Yeah, I think so. He never put any pressure on me. It was something I always saw myself doing."

"You said you had a sister. What does she do?"

"Harriet's studying fashion design in New York. She says she's never going to leave."

"How old is she?"

"Twenty-five."

Molly's eyebrows rose. She slowly shook her head. "Your poor parents! Neither of their children close by! Not even living in the same country! My parents would hate that!"

The sound of her husky voice was soothing. It also helped distract him from his pain. He closed his eyes again.

"Let me tell you about my family," she said brightly.

He swallowed a groan. He didn't want to hear about her family. He didn't want to continue their conversation. Period. All he wanted was to wallow in self-pity and rage silently against God for not putting him out of his misery and taking his life, if indeed he'd been paralyzed. The possibility continued to freak him out.

Why? Damn you! Why?

Oblivious to his dark thoughts, the pretty paramedic kept talking. "For a start, there are nine of us. I have six brothers and two sisters."

Despite himself, her words caught him by surprise. He opened his eyes and frowned. "Nine?"

She grinned cheekily. "Yep."

"Six brothers? Are you kidding?"

She laughed. "I'm afraid not."

"I can't imagine what that was like growing up."

"Loud. Boisterous. Crazy. But so much fun. I'm actually a triplet."

He blinked. "A triplet?"

"Yes. One boy, two girls."

"Oh. So, I take it you're not identical," he said dryly.

She laughed. The husky sound of it washed over his battered body, bringing a moment of relief.

"Oh, Shane. You're too funny."

"Glad I could make you laugh."

She smiled. "Tell me about your sister. Do the two of you get on?"

He shrugged and then winced with pain. "Sure. I guess. As much as any siblings."

"That's great. All of us get along, too. That doesn't mean we don't enjoy a good argument every now and then, but there's a lot of love between us."

The tenderness that had crept into her voice told him a lot about how she felt about her siblings. It irritated him that he liked that she cared about them so much. He still wanted to end the conversation. He didn't want to hear any more about her perfect family and how much they all loved each other, but she prattled on.

"The best thing is, we all still live in Australia. Most of us live in or around Sydney. One brother lives in the country about six hours' drive away from here. The rest of us get together fairly regularly for family dinners at our parents' house. They live about ninety minutes south of Sydney."

Shane refrained from commenting, but he couldn't prevent the wonder that flooded through him. He could hardly comprehend getting together regularly with his family for dinner. Though he and his sister were close enough, they'd both been keen to leave home and strike out on their own.

The fact they'd made their lives on different continents was an indication of how they didn't need to live close enough to see each other even occasionally.

He loved his life in Australia. He couldn't ever imagine returning to live in the UK just because his parents were still there. Or to move to the US to be close to his sister. Then, without warning he was hit with a wave of homesickness. It had been more than three years since he'd last been to the UK. Though his parents had visited him in Australia a couple of times over the past decade, it had been even longer since the whole family had been together. He hadn't been aware of missing them, but it was at times like this... When he hurt in every part of his body. When he wasn't sure what the prognosis would be. When he didn't know if he'd ever walk again...

The yearning for his mom hit him like a sledgehammer. He gasped aloud from the impact. Molly's face immediately reflected concern.

"What is it, Shane? Where does it hurt?"

Tears of pain and helplessness burned in his eyes. "Everywhere."

"Oh, Shane. Hang in there, buddy. We're going to get you out soon."

He stared up at her, pleading with his eyes. "How bad is it?"

She regarded him somberly. "It's hard to say. The fact you're still conscious is a good sign. Until we get you free, I can't do a proper assessment."

"What's going to happen when they remove this steering wheel? What if it's controlling the bleeding and when they release the pressure, I end up bleeding to death?"

"That's not going to happen."

She said it with so much certainty, he believed her. Staring into her clear blue eyes, he took courage from her confidence.

"Specialist retrieval teams have already arrived to help," she continued. "They're just waiting for the police rescue team to arrive with the jaws of life. Once they've removed the door and the steering wheel and any other barriers to your release, my partner and I will move in and do whatever needs to be done to stabilize you for transportation. Then we'll get you to the hospital."

He looked at her, wanting to believe her. No matter that only a short time ago he was damning God for not letting him die. Now he was eager to take reassurance from the hope and conviction in her voice.

"Okay, time for twenty questions," she said with a smile, interrupting his thoughts.

He groaned. "Twenty questions?"

"Yes. I ask you a question. You give me an answer. Then you get to ask a question."

He wanted to turn her down; to tell her straight out he wasn't interested in playing stupid games. But her face was alight with good humor and anticipation and he found himself responding instead.

"If I ask you a question, will you answer it?"

She grinned. "That depends."

He felt her smile all the way to his gut. Reluctantly, he grinned through his pain. "On what?"

"On whether I want to."

"Oh. I see. So do I get to choose whether I answer or not?"

"Of course not."

He chuckled and then grimaced as pain rippled through his chest. "Australian women. You don't play fair, Molly."

She shrugged and smiled again. "You wouldn't be the first person to accuse me of that. You ought to be there when I play Monopoly. Let's just say I can get a little competitive." She winked.

Despite his pain and his dark mood, his belly clenched with instinctive desire. Before he could contemplate that any further, she cleared her throat and clapped her hands.

"Okay, so are you ready to play?"

"Do I have any choice?" he grumbled.

"None at all! I have a captive audience!" She gave him a triumphant grin as he groaned in response.

"First question: What's your favorite color?"

He looked into her eyes. "Blue."

Her cheeks turned pink. She looked away momentarily, appearing flustered. She cleared her throat.

"Favorite song."

"That's easy. Anything by Cody Johnson."

Her eyes widened with surprise. "You like Cody Johnson?"

"Dear Rodeo..." he managed in a passably good imitation.

She grinned. "Oh, my goodness! You really *do* like Cody Johnson."

He widened his eyes in mock innocence. "Would I lie to you?"

"Okay, next question."

"Hang on. It's my turn now."

She smiled. "Right. Go ahead."

"The name of your first boyfriend."

He wasn't sure she was going to answer. Then she said, "Wayne Stanford."

"Did you kiss him?"

She held his gaze. "Yes."

"Did you like it?"

She screwed up her nose. "I was twelve. Not so much."

He laughed and then gasped as pain ripped through him again. Despite everything, he realized he was enjoying their conversation.

"My turn," she said. "What's more important? Love or happiness?"

"Who says you can't have both?" he shot back.

She shook her head. "Nope. You have to choose. Love or happiness?"

He thought for a while. "Happiness."

Her eyes went wide. "Not love?"

"What good is love if you're unhappy?"

She gave him a searching look. "Interesting. I guess I'd like to think if I was in love, that would make me happy. Have you ever been in love?"

"No. Have you?"

She shook her head and averted her gaze. "No."

Before he had time to further contemplate her answer, she spoke again. "Okay, first person you had sex with."

He started in surprise. She gave him a cheeky smile. He hadn't expected her to get so personal. This was getting interesting. "Marley Matthews."

"How old were you?"

"Sixteen."

"Were you in love with her?"

"No. I already told you I've never been in love. But I wanted to have sex with her."

Her eyes flared with emotion. "Was she in love with you?"

"I think so."

"And you didn't think to tell her you were only there for the sex?"

He deadpanned her. "I was sixteen."

"How long did you date her?"

"Who said anything about dating?"

Her mouth turned down. He could tell he'd disappointed her. Somehow, he wished he'd been able to give her a different answer. Then again, he was being honest. If she didn't want the truth, she shouldn't have asked the question. He'd never pretended to be an angel.

"My turn," he said. He kept his gaze on hers. "First lover."

Her cheeks turned crimson. She wouldn't meet his eyes. "Pass."

"Oh, come on!" he protested. "That's not fair."

"I already warned you I don't play fair." She smiled to soften her words.

Unable to help himself, he smiled back. Their gazes locked. Something indefinable passed between them, a connection as real and as startling as a spark of electricity. He could tell she'd felt it too. Her blue eyes darkened. Her mouth parted on a quick intake of breath and she looked slightly confused. The knowledge that she was just as affected as he left him feeling good, despite the constant pain. Somehow, she'd managed to make him forget about it for a few minutes. He could kiss her for that. He focused on her mouth. Full bottom lip. Soft and plump. Sensuous. So ripe for the kissing...

As if aware of the direction of his thoughts, she cleared her throat again. "Okay, let's keep going. Favorite holiday destination."

Okay, so now she's going to play it safe... He sent her a knowing look but answered anyway.

"That's easy. The Great Barrier Reef."

She nodded. "I've heard it's beautiful."

He looked at her in surprise. "You've never been?"

"No. In fact, you've probably seen more of my country than I have. After graduating from university, I went straight into full-time work. I haven't had the luxury of doing much sightseeing."

He thought about all the places he'd traveled while he'd been backpacking around Australia. He'd spent time in every state, except for Tasmania. From the tropics of Queensland to the dry deserts of Western Australia. The diversity had been spectacular and mind blowing. Each state was different and all had something to offer him. He wondered if he'd ever get to travel like that again.

Not if you're in a wheelchair...

The thought came from nowhere and snatched his breath. At the same time, a pain so severe it made him cry out ripped through his chest. He gasped, but it only made things worse. Molly was right there beside him, her expression filling with concern.

His eyes were now so heavy he could barely keep them open. The woman in front of him went blurry. He could only just make out her features.

"Shane? Stay with me, mate."

He heard the elevated anxiety in her voice, but there was nothing he could do to stave off the encroaching darkness. The pain swirled through him, surrounding him, draining him. He wanted desperately to keep his eyes open so he could keep looking at her, but he was fast losing the battle. He was gripped by a pang of disappointment.

He didn't want to die after all.

Chapter Three

"Patient is now red label!" Molly shouted, looking about her for help.

Benson came running over, along with Raoul.

"What's wrong?" Benson asked.

"He's lost consciousness," Molly supplied.

"What happened?" Raoul asked.

"I don't know. We were just talking. Then he cried out in pain. God, I hope it isn't a blood clot."

Her fingers were pressed against the pulse in Shane's neck. It was so weak. She quickly applied the blood pressure cuff and took a reading. Her heart sunk. It had also fallen dangerously low.

"We need to get him out of here," she said.

"I'll get an updated ETA on the jaws of life," Raoul muttered and strode away.

"What can I do?" Benson asked, his eyes wide.

"Nothing. Until we get him out of there, we can't do anything. We can't even administer CPR the way he is."

Benson looked grim. Molly hated the feeling of helplessness that threatened to overwhelm her. This wasn't the first time she'd been in a life-and-death situation with a patient, but somehow with Shane there was an added layer of desperation. He was more than just another accident victim. They'd connected, weaved a fragile bond. She didn't want to lose him.

She leaned farther in through the shattered window, ever mindful of the glass. His skin was a sickly pallor. His breathing shallow and uneven. She checked his blood pressure again. Dread filled her stomach. It had fallen even lower.

Urgency swept over her. It was all she could to do maintain a professional calm. "I need some help over here!" she yelled. "Where the hell is everyone? We need to get this man out."

And then chaos erupted around her. The police truck carrying the jaws of life had finally arrived and rescue police hurried toward her. They quickly surrounded the car as she stepped out of the way, giving them the room they needed to do their job. Until Shane was released from the car, there was nothing else she could do.

She found Benson and Raoul standing a short distance away. Both men watched solemnly as the rescue team got to work, removing the driver's side door first before they cut away the roof. It was discarded to one side and a hydraulic ram brought in to lift the dashboard and steering wheel away from Shane's body. Endless minutes ticked by. Molly stood by, feeling helpless, praying for him to hang on.

Finally, he was clear enough from the wreckage that they could move back in and attend to him. Benson hurried to bring forward the stretcher. Molly crouched beside Shane. His eyes remained closed. His skin was now chalky. She felt for his pulse and was relieved when she found it. Weak and erratic, but still there.

"Shane! Shane! Can you hear me?" She slapped his cheek. To her relief, he slowly opened his eyes.

Shane woke to excruciating pain.

I'm still here, still breathing... Thank you, God...

He ignored the feeling of relief and tried to focus on what was going on around him. The sun beamed in on him where the roof of his car had once been. The driver's door was also gone. The dashboard and steering wheel were no longer pressing in on him, but he still couldn't move. It was like he was glued to the seat.

Panic surged through him. He looked around for Molly and found her. She was crouched low beside the car, staring at him. Her expression was tense, her cheeks were pale. Concern darkened her blue eyes. When she realized he was awake, her expression changed. She gave him a strained smile.

"Hey, Shane. You're back with us. How do you feel?"

"Terrible," he managed.

She smiled again. "We're going to get you out of here. Just hold in there, okay? Big, slow breaths."

He tried to do as she asked, but it hurt too much. The red-hot poker was back, and it was burning a hole in his chest. Whatever she'd given him for the pain had worn off.

"It hurts," he gasped.

"I know, Shane. We're working as fast as we can."

He wanted to tell her he wasn't worth saving, especially if his legs didn't work, but somehow, he couldn't form the words. The face of her colleague once again filled his vision.

Molly spoke again. "Shane. You remember my partner, Benson. He's going to help me get you out of there."

From the corner of his eye, Shane spied a stretcher. It had been brought down to his level. It looked like a simple matter to slide across onto the mattress, but the effort was beyond him.

"Can't," he croaked.

"That's all right, Shane. You don't have to do anything," Molly reassured him. "Benson and I are going to move you. But first I'm going to give you another shot for the pain."

With that, she fiddled with his hand. Cold liquid slid into his veins. Within minutes, the pain had subsided enough that he could breathe again.

"Oh, God. That's good stuff." He sighed.

Molly smiled and patted his forearm. "Okay, Shane. We're going to move you now." She looked at her partner. "On three. One. Two. Three."

"*Arghhhh!*" The involuntary cry of pain was ripped from his body. The paramedics lifted him out of the car and settled him down on the gurney. If he thought the pain had been bad before, now it was unbearable.

"More!" He gasped. "The pain. Please. I need more."

Tears slid down his cheeks. He was beyond feeling embarrassed. All he wanted was to be rid of this agony.

"I can't give you more right now," Molly replied calmly. "You're doing so well, Shane. Big, slow breaths. That's it. We're taking you to the hospital. They'll be able to give you something else for the pain there."

Her calm and professional manner helped contain his panic. He tried not to think about the fire that coursed through his body or the kind of injuries that could cause such agony. As he was loaded into the back of the ambulance, he held back another cry of torment. Though he could tell Molly and her partner were trying their best to minimize the jostling, it wasn't possible to load him without some movement. Each bump was torture.

"Sorry about that, Shane. Keep hanging in there," Molly encouraged.

He was beyond words. It was all he could do to keep breathing through the pain. They worked around him quickly and efficiently inside the vehicle, strapping him in securely, checking his cannula, starting an IV. It was obvious they'd done this sort of thing before. The knowledge brought him a measure of comfort.

On a ragged sigh, he closed his eyes again. There was nothing he could do but put himself in their hands and pray for the nightmare to be over. As the darkness descended once again, he let himself be consumed by it with barely a whisper. The pain receded.

Thank you, God...

Shane's eyes drifted closed and Molly knew he was once again on the verge of losing consciousness. A wave of urgency washed over her. His skin was so pale it was almost translucent. He was cold and clammy to the touch. She'd hooked him up to the monitor and now had a constant read on his vital signs. His blood pressure remained alarmingly low.

Benson had climbed behind the wheel. He started the ignition and called out to Molly.

"All good to go?"

"Yep. Step on it. He needs to get to the hospital. Pronto."

With lights and siren blazing, Benson did just that, radioing ahead with details of their patient. The Emergency Department staff were on hand when they arrived and went to work like a well-oiled machine. As the ambulance pulled into the ambulance bay and Molly and Benson wheeled Shane through the plastic doors, doctors and nurses appeared from nowhere and surrounded the gurney. Molly brought the ED doctor up to speed on Shane's condition, including providing a brief description of the accident, injuries she'd observed, his vital signs and what pain relief she'd administered. Shane was transferred onto another bed and taken straight to X-ray.

Suddenly, Molly's part in the emergency was over. Her shoulders slumped with relief. They'd managed to get Shane to the hospital still breathing. The adrenaline flooding through her veins slowly eased. She drew in a deep breath and tried to recalibrate.

"I'll attend to the gurney," Benson offered and wheeled it out of the way where he could wipe it clean and change the sheets in anticipation of their next patient.

"Thanks," Molly said. "I'll deal with the paperwork."

Finding the nurse who'd taken over charge of Shane's care, Molly went through the details of the accident she had to hand.

"Any drugs or alcohol in his system?" the nurse asked.

"He said no. I couldn't smell any alcohol on his breath and he didn't appear to be under the influence of drugs."

"Allergies?"

"No."

"Next of kin?"

"None in Australia. He told me he'd moved here from the UK. His parents are still there. He has a sister in New York. That's all I know."

She thought back to their conversation. The twenty questions game. She actually knew more about him than she'd let on. Okay, so they hadn't gotten to twenty questions, but she'd found out some interesting things about him in that short time. His favorite color, holiday destination, first lover...

She couldn't believe she'd asked him something so personal. At the time, she hadn't given much thought to her questions. She'd just been trying to keep him from sliding into unconsciousness. She'd been surprised he'd told her about his first sexual experience. She sure as hell hadn't been prepared to share hers. And then his intriguing answer to her question about love and happiness...

It was too bad they hadn't met under different circumstances. Not only was he good looking, but he was also interesting. Despite the pain, his green eyes had shone with intelligence and good humor. He'd told her he was a lawyer. He was an altogether attractive package and one she would have enjoyed exploring further under different circumstances.

For now, he was seriously injured, possibly on the brink of death. If he'd suffered internal injuries, there was always a chance they wouldn't be able to stem the flow of blood in time. Despite all the advancements in modern medicine and early intervention, some patients still lost their battle. She was acutely aware of the time it had taken to extricate him from the wreck and get him to hospital. She could only hope and pray they'd given him enough time to beat the odds.

"You ready?"

Benson appeared behind her. She turned and nodded. "Yep. All done. Let's get out of here."

Time to go back to the station and wait for the next call.

Shane was swimming through molasses. Like the time he'd jumped off a cliff about fifty feet above a deep, natural pool in the middle of the Western Australian desert. He'd hit the water hard and had sunk down, down, down. He'd panicked when he realized how deep he'd gone. Kicking frantically, he'd fought to find his way back up to the top, plowing desperately through the water. By the time his head broke the surface, his chest had been on fire, his lungs burning for air. He felt that way now.

Every part of him hurt. There was an elephant sitting on top of his chest. He tried to breathe, but it was too painful. There was also something on his face. An obstruction in his throat. He wanted to claw at it, but he couldn't find the strength to lift his arms. He must have made a sound, but he couldn't remember speaking.

Suddenly, someone was there, talking to him in low, soothing tones. *Molly?* He couldn't tell. At the same time, he was filled with disappointment that he was still alive. He'd wanted to get his death over and done with and square things off with God. But it seemed God wasn't ready to clear the slate yet. He was still alive.

Great.

In the background, he heard the beeping of machines and the hum of conversation. It all sounded so far away. Then something cold slid into his veins and the pain began to fade, along with everything else. He surrendered once again to the darkness.

Molly tossed her keys on the hall table and pulled off her boots. She dropped them on the floor and padded in stockinged feet down the corridor of her apartment. She walked into the open plan living and dining room and with a weary sigh, threw herself down on the couch. The last couple hours of her shift had passed quickly, with another two callouts. Thankfully neither had involved anything so traumatic nor with such high stakes as a serious car accident. Still, she was pleased the day was over. She was beat.

All afternoon, her thoughts had kept returning to Shane. There was no doubt he'd been in bad shape when she'd left him at the hospital. The nurses had been prepping him for surgery even before she and Benson had cleared the ED. She hoped he was doing okay. She had no way of knowing the extent of his internal injuries, nor how much damage had been done to his legs. All she could hope was that he'd pulled through the surgery and was on the way to making a full recovery.

She wasn't sure what it was about this patient that stood out for her among the hundreds she'd treated over the course of her career. She'd attended plenty of car accidents. Sure, not all of them were so drawn out or required specialist police rescue teams, but a few of them had. And yet those patients hadn't left much of an impact past the time she'd delivered them safely to the ED.

What is it about this guy that has me still thinking about him? It's strange...

Even during the trauma of his accident and the excruciating pain, he'd managed to maintain a sense of humor. Though she'd sensed some darkness in him, they'd talked, quipped, and a few shared confidences. Or at least he had. She'd chickened out. But they'd had a connection, something intangible, but which had felt real.

It was stupid, really. He was a stranger. Just another patient who'd crossed her path. She wondered if she was projecting feelings on him that only existed in her mind. The fact she was even thinking along those lines surprised her. She'd always shied away from love. Despite the fact her parents had been married nearly thirty years and were still devoted to each other, her mother's life hadn't always been so rosy.

Evelyn Barrington had once been in love with a scoundrel. From what Molly had figured out, Henry Craigdon had been rich, spoiled, and entitled. He'd gotten her mother pregnant and had then abandoned her. All she'd meant to him was a bit of fun. He'd never once acknowledged his biological son, Christopher. Not even on his deathbed. That rejection had screwed up Molly's half-brother for a long time.

Her mother had been all of twenty when Henry abandoned her. She was left to raise her son on her own. Times had been tough. She'd worked two jobs to keep food on the table. Then she'd met Molly's dad.

Christopher had been ten when Evelyn met Frank Barrington and though the young boy had taken some time to warm to his new stepfather, Christopher was finally in a good place. A lot of that had to do with his new wife, Lexi. It just went to show how love could make a difference in the world.

But what if it all went wrong? Molly's mother had been desperately in love with Henry Craigdon and yet that hadn't made a difference to him. He'd used her for his own pleasure and then discarded her without another thought. Molly was wary of taking such a risk with her heart. That was the main reason she was twenty-six and had never been in love.

She'd freely admit that after watching so many of her siblings fall in love, she was tempted to give it a try, but the wariness was still there. Besides, there were plenty of nights when she stayed out late and kicked up her heels and was thankful she was single and could party the night away without considering anyone else. At those times, she was glad she was on her own. But when everyone around her, including two of the triplets, had found enduring love, she couldn't help but feel she was missing out on something and that maybe, just maybe, she should find the courage to give love a go.

She'd dabbled in the dating websites. She'd even gone on a few blind dates with other hospital employees. Nurses, doctors, a fellow paramedic. Once, Benson had set her up with one of his cousins. The man was a builder and worked for a large contractor and though he'd been easy going and pleasant on the eyes—tall and muscular as only someone who did hard physical work for a living could be—there had been no spark. No connection. Nothing to excite her, or to get the butterflies swarming in her stomach and the blood rushing through her veins. And that was important.

That was the problem with online dating. It was impossible to know whether there was any physical attraction when you were "getting to know someone" through a screen. There had been plenty of times she'd found a guy who ticked all the boxes on paper, who should have been her perfect match, and when they'd come face to face, there hadn't been the slightest hint of a spark. On those occasions, she was honest enough to admit she'd been relieved, but it had also felt like a waste of time and that was one thing she hated to do.

At least, that's how she justified her decision to steer clear of the dating apps for now. She'd had enough bad experiences to reinforce her opinion that finding true love was tough.

Maybe I'm not meant to find my soul mate. Maybe I'm meant to go through life alone? Maybe it's for the best?

No. She didn't believe that. She only had to look at her brothers and sisters to see how finding love had changed their lives. Out of her eight brothers and sisters, there was only her and her sister, Hannah, who hadn't fallen in love. Oh, and maybe her adopted brother, Vaughan. She hadn't seen or spoken to him for so long, who knew what was going on with him, but the point remained the same. At least seven of the Barrington siblings had found love. The odds appeared to be in her favor, but was that what she really wanted?

Her triplet sister, Charlotte, who was nauseatingly in love with her fiancé, Grayson Thorpe, had encouraged her not to give up.

"You'll find it one day, when you least expect it," Charlotte had told her when Molly had raised the topic. Charlotte didn't seem to understand when Molly tried to explain she didn't particularly care for love.

"How can you say that?" Charlotte had asked, aghast.

Molly had merely shrugged.

"You wouldn't say that if you knew how wonderful it feels," Charlotte insisted.

Molly had remained silent. As close as she was to her sister, she didn't feel like sharing the reasons that kept her from actively pursuing love. After all, it was a little crazy to keep harking back to their mother's experience. Things had turned out well for Evelyn Barrington in the end.

So, what's holding me back? Fear. That's what.

There, she'd admitted it. Not that it made much difference. It didn't change the way she felt. And even if it did, finding love was hard, no matter how easy her siblings made it appear.

Sex was one thing. There was no shortage of men to sleep with if she were so inclined. That wasn't the point. She'd never been into casual sex. That's why she was still a virgin. Before she made love to someone, she wanted understanding, trust, commitment, security, and yes, love. Or at least some kind of mutual respect and affection. Call her old-fashioned, but that's how she felt.

Is that too much to ask? To expect?

So where did that leave her and the connection she'd felt, albeit it briefly, with Shane? She made a sound of disgust in the back of her throat.

Don't be a ninny. He's a stranger. A patient I treated... Nothing more. Time for some reality...

In an effort to force him out of her mind, she climbed off the couch and headed into the kitchen. She grabbed a bottle of Chardonnay from the fridge and poured herself a glass. To her annoyance, her thoughts once again drifted to Shane.

It was ridiculous to think he might have noticed a connection. He'd been almost delirious from pain. At one stage, he'd lost consciousness. Okay, twice. No doubt any kind of "connection" she'd imagined had more to do with the life-and-death situation they'd been facing, rather than some instant, meant-to-be *thing*. Besides, they didn't even know each other. She knew the barest of information about him. He'd viewed her through a prism of pain.

But there was something about him that drew her. Maybe it was the fact that he was seriously injured and all alone. No family in Australia and he hadn't mentioned any friends. She wanted to check up on him, see how he'd gotten on. Whether he'd come through the surgery...

Am I being ridiculous? I've no interest in falling in love...

And then she shook her head, smiling ruefully. My, what an active imagination she had! They were almost strangers. Who said anything about love?

But she couldn't shake the need to see him again. The feeling was so strong, it took her by surprise. What did it matter if they were as good as strangers? What did it matter if he thought it weird? He might never regain consciousness. He might never even know she'd been back to see him.

But checking in on him was something she needed to do. She knew herself well enough to know this weird feeling compelling her forward wouldn't just go away on its own. She'd faced down many impossible situations. She'd never been a quitter. In fact, she did her best work against the odds. She'd always been that way. That's why she'd been attracted to such a high-stakes career as an intensive care paramedic. Battling life-and-death situations. Doing all she could to beat the odds.

The thing was, fear of falling in love or not, she wanted to get to know Shane Lucas better. She wanted to explore the tenuous connection she'd felt with him. So, what was stopping her? She knew where he was. Where he would be for at least a few weeks. Maybe more, depending on the extent of his injuries.

And why shouldn't she visit him? He didn't have any family in Australia to keep him company. She could help lift his spirits. Encourage him to think positively. Be a friend. Those things she knew for certain how to do. And they were safe. She could be a friend and still keep her heart intact.

Their twenty questions game had been fun. He'd been reluctant at first, but then he'd really gotten into it. They'd gotten personal so quickly and yet, it hadn't felt uncomfortable like she would have expected between strangers. Of course, being caught in a traumatic situation often had the effect of bringing people together quicker than what could ever be achieved in real life.

Real life.

The words echoed in her mind. She sipped at her wine and contemplated them, frowning. Rescuing someone from a life-and-death situation wasn't the usual real life for most people. Emotions were high on both sides. Attributing feelings of connectedness to a man who'd been in excruciating pain and was worried about living or dying was real enough, but it wasn't real life. Those kinds of emotions couldn't be trusted. They were a product of an urgent situation that could have gone very badly wrong at any moment. Just another reason why she should feel comfortable extending her hand in friendship.

In fact, the more she thought about it, the more it seemed ridiculous to think they'd communicated on a deeper level. She was simply the person who'd provided a lifeline for him to cling to as he'd battled overwhelming pain in a battle to survive. And that was a good thing. It gave her the confidence to fulfil her desire to see him again without making things complicated. She'd offer him friendship. Everyone needed friends, especially someone in Shane's predicament.

By the time she'd finished her third glass of wine, she was eager to see Shane Lucas again. She didn't have to worry about falling in love. They were going to be friends. Something told her he needed all the friends he could get.

Chapter Four

S hane slowly roused to the sound of beeping. He opened his eyes, momentarily disorientated by the mask on his face. He tried to push it away. Pain tore through his body. He was brutally reminded of where he was and why. The light was dim, making it hard to identify objects in the room. Muted conversation filtered through the steady beeping. He realized the beeping was coming from him, or more accurately, from the machine attached to him.

The wheezing of the oxygen mask was almost in concert with the beeping. He swallowed. His mouth was dry and his lips were cracked. At least the obstruction in his throat had been removed. He no longer felt like he wanted to gag.

He made another effort to move, this time more cautiously. Though the pain wasn't as bad as the first time, it gripped him with enough ferocity that tears sprang to his eyes. Where was Molly? He needed some of her magical pain medication that had at least taken the edge off. Or maybe it was Molly herself who'd helped him through that?

He could still see her shining blue eyes, her glossy dark hair, her smile. His angel of mercy. The woman who'd helped save his life. Too bad his life wasn't worth saving. Though it seemed God had other ideas.

He still didn't know the extent of his injuries. He hadn't been conscious long enough for anyone to give him a summary of the damage he'd sustained. But he could tell from the pain that wracked his body that the news wasn't good.

He still couldn't feel his legs. They were elevated in some kind of strange contraption comprised of rope and pulleys. He tried to lift them, but it was useless. No matter how hard he willed for them to move, they remained where they were. Then he focused on trying to wriggle his toes. Once again, his body stubbornly refused to cooperate. The effort left him weak and helpless. He bit down hard on a sigh of self-pity. As he drifted back to the darkness, he thought fleetingly of his guardian angel.

Molly... Sweet Molly... I need you...

And then he was reminded of just how unworthy he was to be given another crack at life. How his life had gone so far off track. He'd told Molly he was a lawyer. He supposed that was still true, but he hadn't told her about the other... The part that even now still filled him with shame. If she knew who he really was, what he'd done, she wouldn't have looked at him like he was a good and decent guy, like she was interested in what he had to say and wanted to know more.

No, Molly deserved better. She might be his angel of mercy, but he couldn't see her again.

Molly pressed the buzzer to activate the intercom outside the ICU ward and waited for someone to answer. Twenty-four hours had passed since she'd brought Shane to the hospital. She was rostered on a night shift, due to start at 1800 hours. She'd elected to take a few minutes beforehand to check in on him.

The intercom crackled to life. "ICU."

On a sudden wave of nervousness, Molly cleared her throat. "It's Molly Barrington. I was the paramedic on duty yesterday afternoon when Shane Lucas was brought in. I was wondering how he's doing?"

"Molly! What a surprise! It's Belinda. I'll buzz you in."

Molly sighed softly with relief, glad to discover a familiar nurse was on shift. Belinda Baxter was a good friend of Zoe Parker, the psychologist who'd recently begun dating Molly's brother, Lincoln. Molly had met Belinda only a few weeks earlier, when the four of them had gone out for dinner at a local bar.

The double doors to the ICU swung silently inward. Molly stepped inside. She was already dressed for work. Her rubber-soled work boots made no noise on the linoleum. She spied Belinda seated at the desk behind the nurses' station and walked over to her.

"How's he doing?" she asked.

Belinda grimaced. "He's stable at least. He sustained damage to his intestines and his spleen. There was a lot of internal bleeding. The doctors managed to stem the flow and he's had a blood transfusion."

"What about his legs?" Molly asked. She held her breath as she waited for the answer.

Belinda shook her head. "Multiple leg fractures. He now has several screws, wires and pins holding his bones together."

Molly grimaced. "Ouch. Poor guy."

"Yeah. The good news is there's no damage to his spinal cord."

Molly breathed out on a sigh of relief. "That's great news."

Belinda nodded. "You're right. He's got months of rehab to look forward to and all the agony that comes with that, but at least he has the chance to walk again." She paused. "I can't find much about his family and there isn't a contact number for a next of kin. Do you know anything about him?"

Molly thought briefly of the crazy, tension-ridden two hours of playing twenty questions in a bid to keep his spirits buoyed. "Not really. His parents live in the UK. He has a sister in New York. No family here."

Belinda compressed her lips. "I was hoping to call someone. It doesn't seem right that he's here so badly injured and no one who cares about him knows about it."

Molly nodded in agreement. "I'd certainly want to know if one of my brothers or sisters was in the ICU."

"Right."

"Is he conscious?" she asked.

"No. Earlier today, we put him in an induced coma. We administered as much pain relief as we could, but it wasn't making much difference. He kept going in and out of consciousness and each time he woke, he grew agitated. The doctor thought it best to knock him out for a while until his body has a chance to start to heal and we can get a better handle on his pain."

"Is he intubated?" Molly asked.

"No. So far he's holding his own."

Molly breathed out in relief. "That's good news. Can I see him?"

Belinda looked surprised but nodded. "I guess so. Sure. He's in bed three."

Molly braced herself for coming face to face with Shane again. It was one thing to deal with trauma while she was in work mode and running on adrenaline. It was quite different to look upon that same badly injured individual in the quiet and calm surroundings of a hospital ward. Particularly when she had no official role to play other than as someone concerned for his recovery and even that role was tenuous at best. They were almost strangers. She was an interloper. He should be surrounded by family, by people who knew him well and loved him.

He lay pale and still on the hospital bed. His eyes were closed. An attempt had been made to clean up his face. The shards of glass had been removed from his cheeks and the cuts and lacerations had been painted over with iodine. A dressing had been taped across the deeper laceration on his forehead. Both legs were heavily bandaged and were elevated on pulleys. Molly drew up a chair and sat beside him. After a moment of hesitation, she reached for his hand.

"Hey, you. How're you doing?" she whispered.

Of course, there was no response and she hadn't expected one. His breathing remained slow and even. She let her thoughts wander. She thought about the things he'd told her. His family, his travels, his decision to settle in Australia. That he worked as a lawyer and specialized in family law. That he only had one sister. They'd covered a lot of ground in their short time together, but there was still so much she was curious to know.

What was it about him that drew her? He wasn't the first patient she'd sat with, talked to during a tricky rescue, but somehow things felt different. Maybe it had something to do with his striking good looks and the intelligence and humor she'd seen in his vivid green eyes. Maybe it was that weird connection.

Whatever it was, she wanted to explore it. A firm believer in fate, right now, it seemed to her like fate had brought them together. She wanted to be his friend.

She continued to talk to him about her day, the weather, her work colleagues, that soon she'd be starting a night shift which nearly always meant she and Benson would be run off their feet with callouts. She'd thought she'd feel silly talking to someone who could neither hear her nor respond, but she was strangely content. And there was always the slight possibility he could hear her and might take some comfort from her presence.

After a few minutes, a glance at her watch confirmed it was time to go. With a final squeeze of his hand, she reluctantly set it back down on the mattress.

"I'm praying for your speedy recovery, Shane," she whispered. "This isn't over yet. You need to get better so we can get to know each other and have some fun."

She gave him a small, whimsical smile and then turned away. Farewelling Belinda with a brief wave, Molly left the ICU. As she headed out of the hospital, her thoughts turned to the night ahead.

Shane floated in an ocean of warm water. He'd never been so relaxed. The sun was pleasant on his face. The water cushioned his body, keeping it afloat. Seemingly without any effort, he glided through the light waves, drifting ever closer to the woman's voice.

Is it Molly? Is that who I can hear?

He tried to turn his head to catch a glimpse of her, but the effort was too great. Maybe it was the drugs? Maybe this was all a dream? Though the water was crystal clear and the blue sky overhead was sparkling, his thoughts were hazy, like he couldn't quite get his brain to work. It was like he was watching himself from a distance through a distorted prism. Nothing was quite what it was.

Then there was a touch on his hand. Soft. Warm. Comforting. It was her; he was sure of it. His angel. She spoke to him in soothing tones, her gentle voice washing over him, calming him. He wanted to respond, to urge her to join him in the water so they could float away together. But then reality asserted itself.

He wasn't the man she thought he was. He didn't deserve an angel like her. Life had chewed him up and tossed him back, damaged beyond repair. He had nothing to offer her. He'd lost everything. He could no more wish for the attention of someone like Molly than he could wish to turn back the clock.

With a feeling of hopelessness and overwhelming despair, he sunk back below the water and into oblivion.

It had been two days since Shane had been put in an induced coma. Two more days she'd gone to the ICU after her shift ended to sit by his side. She still had a crick in her neck from when she'd fallen asleep in an awkward position the second time she'd visited, waiting for him to regain consciousness. The hospital chairs hadn't been built with comfort in mind.

The doctors had eased back on his medication. He was expected to regain consciousness at any time. A lot of the swelling in his legs had gone down. Soon they'd put him in plaster. She hoped they'd gotten on top of his pain, or at least made it bearable.

She wasn't sure if he knew she was there, but she liked to think he did. There had been studies done on coma patients who, once they'd regained consciousness, recalled hearing loved ones speaking to them, singing, playing music. She hoped this was true for Shane. After all, he had no one else. Just his crazy paramedic stalking his recovery.

Once again, she hoped he didn't think it weird that she'd been visiting him. It would be mortifying if he felt like that. She'd have to come up with a ready excuse, just in case.

How many other patients have I visited after rescuing them?

The thought made her squirm. Okay, so she'd never sat at the bedside of one of her patients before, but she'd enquired after them on occasion and once she'd met with a woman she'd revived after a heart attack. Surely, that counted. She cared about people, especially those she'd assisted during some of the worst moments of their lives. Surely, she was allowed to feel curious about how they'd fared after she'd left them in the ED?

"We finally made contact with Shane's parents," Belinda said quietly coming up to the bed. She checked his vital signs and made notations on his chart.

Molly glanced up from where she sat beside him. "That's great news! I'm so glad! At least his loved ones know about the accident and might be able to hop a plane and visit him."

Belinda shook her head. "I'm afraid not. They're elderly and in no condition to make the long plane journey. At least, that's what his mother said. She was shocked to hear what had happened and was quite distraught. We assured her he's doing well. She wishes there was something they could do…"

"That must be terrible for them! To know their son's seriously injured and be unable to be by his side."

Belinda eyed her quizzically. "He's lucky he's got you."

Molly refrained from answering. She still wasn't sure she should be there, but knowing he had no one else was just another reason to stay.

"We agreed to keep his parents informed with regular updates. At this stage, there isn't much to tell. We'll know more once he comes out of the coma and is responsive."

"He told me he's a lawyer. What about his employer, or work colleagues? Is there some way to contact them?"

"There was nothing in his wallet to indicate where he might work. Did you ask him?"

Molly shook her head. "No."

She looked at Shane who lay quietly asleep. His skin was still chalky, but the cuts and scrapes on his face were beginning to fade. It was good to see the healing process had begun.

Shane came slowly awake. He opened his eyes and stared up at the ceiling.

Where am I?

He turned his head slightly to one side. Bulky dark shapes came into focus. A machine with blinking, colored lights. An empty hospital bed. And then everything came crashing back.

The accident... I'm in hospital... Thank God the pain's receded...

With an effort, he looked around the room. Eight or so beds were arranged in a semi-circle around a well-lit nurses' station. The sound of telephones ringing and machines beeping belatedly registered. And then he looked at his legs.

He gasped. They were strung up on pulleys. He'd forgotten the earlier glimpse he'd had of the strange contraption. It felt like eons ago. Panic rushed through him. What kind of damage had he done to them that required him to be strung up like that? He made a sound of distress in the back of his throat.

A familiar face emerged in his field of vision. The beautiful paramedic... So, he hadn't dreamed her. She leaned over him, a mixture of concern and relief on her face.

Molly...

"Shane! Oh, my goodness! You're awake!" Then she turned away from him and called out to someone he couldn't see. "Belinda! Hurry! He's awake!"

A nurse appeared in front of him and smiled. "Welcome back, Mr Lucas. My name's Belinda. It's nice to see you're awake."

She shifted until she stood beside him and shone a torch in his eyes. Then she pricked him with a pin: his arm, his hip, his exposed toes.

"Ouch!" he reacted each time.

Both the nurse and Molly beamed.

"That's great, Shane! It doesn't appear you've suffered any nerve damage," Molly said, still grinning.

He ought to feel grateful, but there were still so many unanswered questions. How badly had he been injured? What the hell was going on with his legs? How long would he be there? What was the paramedic doing at his bedside?

He had tubes coming out of his hand and another one in his side. An IV pole with several bags of fluid stood beside his bed, along with the beeping machines. Something of his bewilderment must have showed on his face. The nurse...was it Belinda...started to speak.

"You gave us all quite a scare, Mr Lucas. You suffered some internal injuries and there was a fair amount of bleeding. We gave you a blood transfusion. The tube in your side is draining away the excess fluid. Thankfully your internal injuries are healing well. We've been keeping up your nutrition and fluids intravenously. Your legs are probably in the worst shape."

"How bad?" he rasped and then braced himself for her response.

"Fractured femur on the right. Fractured tibia and fibula on the left. You're going to be sore and sorry for a while, but you'll mend," Belinda replied cheerfully.

He held his breath, hardly daring to ask the question. "No spinal damage?"

She held his gaze. "No. The surgeon inserted several pins, wires, and screws. They'll be removed later," Belinda explained. "For now, the bones are being held in place by the pulleys. It's important to keep your legs straight until the bones have had a chance to begin to heal. I'll let the doctor know you're awake. No doubt he'll be along to give you a more thorough rundown on your injuries."

Molly grinned. "Don't worry. I'm sure you'll be up and walking before you know it."

He stared at her and frowned. Her sunny disposition irritated him. He knew enough about fractures to realize it would take months of rehab to get back on his feet and that would surely come with a lot of pain. Even then, there was no guarantee he wouldn't end up with a permanent limp. He guessed he ought to be grateful he'd survived the accident, but right at that moment, he found it hard to feel thankful about anything.

He glared at her. "For Pete's sake, who are you? Pollyanna? And what the hell are you doing here?"

A flush stained her cheeks. She opened her mouth as if to speak, but nothing came out. She half-turned away from him, but not before he saw the hurt in her eyes. He cursed. He hadn't meant to lash out at her. No doubt she'd only stopped by to see how he was. He hadn't forgotten how supportive she'd been during his rescue. If it hadn't been for her and her ceaseless chatter, he might have gone mad from the pain.

"Oh. I-I'm sorry," she stammered, glancing briefly in his direction. Her cheeks were crimson with embarrassment. "I'll go."

She bent down to collect her handbag. He felt like a heel but refused to take anything back. What the hell was she doing there? She wasn't his family. They weren't even friends. She was the paramedic who'd helped rescue him. What was wrong with her that she *wanted* to be there? Was she some weirdo? Someone who got off on talking to strangers in hospital beds?

He sighed wearily. That wasn't fair. They weren't exactly strangers. In fact, they'd shared more personal information than he'd exchanged with anyone in years. Perhaps that's why he felt so irritable? He wasn't used to anyone wanting to get close to him, let alone a beautiful woman.

As she started to walk away from him, he surprised himself by calling out to her. "I'm sorry. Don't go." His voice was low and weak and far from convincing.

She paused and bit her lower lip, looking undecided. He cleared his throat and tried again. "Please. Stay."

This time his words had the desired effect. Though she averted her gaze, she slowly returned to his bedside and regained her seat.

Belinda hovered at the end of his bed. "How's your pain on a scale of one to ten?"

He thought for a moment. "It's okay. Maybe a three."

The nurse nodded. "Three's good. Let me know if it gets worse. The doctor's written up some pain medication if you need it. And don't wait until it's unbearable. Best to stay on top of it."

He sighed. "Thanks."

"I'll go and call him now and let him know you're awake," she added before turning away.

Once they were alone again, Molly glanced in his direction and just as quickly looked away. He was filled with a surge of guilt.

"I'm sorry for being a prick. I shouldn't have spoken to you like that."

She shrugged off his apology. "I get it. You've just woken up after being hit by a car. You're entitled to feel grumpy." She paused and then added, "How *do* you feel?"

He grimaced. "Like I was hit by a car."

She chuckled. He managed a slight grin. Her expression lit up at the sight of it. He was reminded again how beautiful she was.

So, it wasn't just in my imagination... She really is that beautiful...

"I spoke to the police," she said. "A witness described a Toyota Landcruiser driving fast through the intersection. Two tons of metal and steel coming for you at speed is not for the faint of heart. You took a direct hit to the driver's side. You were lucky to survive."

He stared at his legs. "I don't feel so lucky. To tell you the truth, I feel like shit."

"But you're awake and breathing. I'm sure your family will be pleased about that."

He frowned in alarm. "Hell. My parents. They must be so worried. Do they know...?"

"Yes. The hospital staff were able to contact them. You must have had their details on you."

He nodded. "A card in my wallet."

"Well, I'm glad you're on the mend. Now that you've regained consciousness, they'll be able to shift you out of the ICU and into the orthopedic ward." She glanced at the empty bed beside his. "You'll probably have better company there. And food."

Her cheeky wink was followed by a smile and to his surprise, he once again found himself responding. He looked pointedly at the bags of clear fluid that hung from the IV pole. "You're right. Anything would be better than this liquid diet."

As if on cue, his stomach rumbled. Then another thought occurred to him. "How long have I been here?"

Chapter Five

Molly's breath escaped in a silent sigh of relief. Whatever mood had gripped Shane earlier seemed to have passed. He was back to his usual self. Well, at least what she assumed was his usual self. She didn't know whether cheery or grouchy Shane was the norm.

"Three days," she said. "You were taken to surgery as soon as you arrived in the ED and they've kept you in an induced coma pretty much ever since to try and aid the healing process. Apparently, you were getting agitated every time you regained consciousness."

He accepted her response without comment. She was still a little embarrassed about being there. What would she say if he asked her the question again? That they'd formed an inexplicable bond during the ensuing drama of the accident? That she wanted to be his friend? That sounded crazy even to her.

She realized in that moment she hadn't really thought things through. She hadn't really considered he might not welcome her presence or think it strange.

What sort of ninny am I? Of course he'd think it strange. Even I think it's a bit strange...

She was starting to feel incredibly foolish, not to mention embarrassed. She should just wish him well with his recovery and get the hell out of there while she still had her pride intact. With that thought motivating her actions, she pushed her chair away from his bed and stood.

He frowned. "Where are you going?"

She flushed. "I... I have to go." She looked down at her uniform.

"Are you heading to work?"

She flushed again. "No. I... I finished my shift an hour ago."

"And you came here?"

His penetrating look sent a fresh wave of heat across her face. "No, no. I was already here. At the hospital. I just thought... While I was here... I'd check in on you."

He gave her an inscrutable look. She wasn't sure if he believed her and she didn't blame him. She'd always been a terrible liar.

"Thank you," he said.

He sounded so sincere, she blushed again and looked away. "Th-that's okay. I was just doing my job."

"You did more than your job. You kept me alive. Without you, I might have given up. The pain was so bad... Hell, I *wanted* to give up. But you kept pulling me back, forcing me to listen, to respond. Forcing me to hang in there. I owe you a lot."

She shrugged off his praise. "It wasn't just me. There were a whole team of rescuers involved. Everyone played their part. It was just unfortunate it took so long to get you out."

"However you try to explain it, Molly, I'm grateful for what you did. There might have been a hundred people involved, but you're the only one I remember. I even dreamed I heard your voice."

Yet another wave of embarrassment exploded across her cheeks. She was sure he hadn't meant anything by his comment, but regardless of her earlier self-castigation, she couldn't help the little leap of optimism in her chest.

Hopeless!

"It's good of you to check up on me. No doubt you've had a busy day." He frowned. "It *is* daytime, isn't it?"

She smiled, glad to be on less slippery ground. "Yes. It's about eight in the morning."

His frown deepened. "I thought you said you just finished work?"

"I have. I was on a night shift. Two day shifts, two night shifts. Followed by five days off. That's the roster."

"Is this the first time you've called in to see me?"

She flushed again but answered him honestly. "No. I came up yesterday and the day before, too."

His green eyes filled with curiosity. "Why?"

She'd expected the question, but she was unprepared just the same. Keeping her gaze averted, she explained.

"You have no family here. I couldn't leave you in the hospital all alone. I... After the time we spent together at the accident, I..." She cast around for something to say that wouldn't make her sound like an idiot.

He stared at her. "You what?"

She veered away from telling him the truth. If she mentioned their weird connection, he'd think she was stark raving crazy. And maybe she was. Instead, she gave a self-deprecating laugh. "I thought you might like some company. Medically induced coma notwithstanding."

She laughed again in an attempt to make light of the situation and was relieved when he chuckled.

"Did you talk to me?" he asked.

She nodded. "Yes."

"Sing?"

"What? No!"

He looked mock disappointed. "You didn't sing?"

"No, I didn't sing. I don't sing for anyone."

His eyes twinkled. "Not even in the shower? Come on, everyone sings in the shower."

"Not even in the shower," she said firmly.

He grinned. "Too bad. I might have woken up sooner if I'd heard you singing."

"More likely you would have run for the hills to escape the sound," she quipped and grinned back at him.

She was heartened by the casual back and forth that seemed to come so naturally to them, as it had at the scene of the accident. This was what being friends was all about. Casual conversation, hanging out, trading jokes.

Yes, I can do friends. This is nice. No pressure, just two people getting to know each other. Now, it's time to get out of here... I don't want him to get the wrong idea. Besides, there's no coming back from being considered a stalker.

Once again, she stepped away from the bed.

Shane frowned. "You're leaving?"

"Yes. I need to get home. I have a million things to do."

His face fell. "Of course. Well, thank you for coming. It was nice to see you again. And thanks for looking out for me in the absence of my family. I can't imagine I'll be seeing them anytime soon."

"It was my pleasure. I'm glad to see you're doing so well. In a few more months you won't know yourself."

"I hope so. As soon as I'm able, I'd like to take you to dinner to thank you for everything you've done."

Molly flushed with pleasure, but she refused to read anything more into his words. He simply wanted to express his gratitude. That's all it was.

"There's no need for that."

His green eyes captured hers. "Yes. There is. It's settled. As soon as I'm back on my feet, I'm taking you to dinner. No more arguments."

She shrugged helplessly. "Well, if you insist."

He grinned. "I do."

"In that case, I'm going to start researching the most expensive French restaurant I can find."

He laughed. "You like French food?"

"It's my favorite."

"Then French, it is."

She grinned, once again enjoying their banter. But it was time to go. She collected her handbag from the table beside his bed and then turned back to him to bid him farewell.

"I guess that's it then," she said.

He frowned. "Will you come back and visit me again?"

She bit her lip in indecision. "Do you want me to?"

As she looked at him, his expression changed. It was like a shadow falling over his face. He turned his head and averted his gaze.

"No. I think it's best if we finish things here. There are things about me you don't know. I appreciate everything you did for me, but please don't drop by again."

Molly stared at him in confusion. *What just happened?* A few moments ago, they were sharing lighthearted conversation. Now he didn't want her to visit again. What the hell? Feeling a little hurt and a lot confused, Molly stumbled blindly for the exit.

Shane cursed long and loudly and tried to reassure himself this was for the best. Better to hurt the woman now than to string her along and devastate her when she discovered the truth. As much as it hurt to send her away, it would hurt more if he encouraged her attentions. He needed to remember that.

He cursed again. He felt like punching something, legs in traction notwithstanding. Strung up on the pulleys, he could barely move anything. The pain had begun to make itself known again. He felt like shit, aching in every part of his body. He pressed the buzzer for the nurse. He needed some medication.

Waking to discover Molly at his bedside had surprised him. She was the last person he'd expected to find there. He couldn't imagine it was part of her duties to check up on him after she'd delivered him to the trauma center. And yet that's what she'd done. Twice.

Her reasons intrigued him. Maybe she liked him. Her actions went beyond mere professional courtesy. If he were honest, he liked her too, and that was the problem. He was no good for her. She didn't know anything about him. At least, not the things that mattered. The things that had irrevocably changed his life for the worse. There were very few people who knew the truth. His parents and his sister and a small number of his colleagues. That's it. He'd taken responsibility for his actions and had paid his debt to society, but that hadn't removed the shame. He stared up at the ceiling.

That's why You should have just let me die...

Molly obviously had a kind heart and cared for people. She was certainly a glass-half-full kind of girl. Miss Pollyanna. His first impression hadn't been wrong. What was wrong was that she clearly wanted to spend time with him. Worse, he wanted to spend time with her.

Because, goddamnit, he did! All the reasons why he needed to keep his distance, to hold her at arm's length... None of those made any difference to the way he'd started to feel. He was all alone in a country where he'd come close to losing his life and he'd found someone who he connected with in a way he'd never connected before.

Forgive me for wanting to spend time with an angel...

He might hate himself when he finally came to his senses. When the pain and the medication and aftereffects of the coma had worn off and he could see the world more clearly.

But right now, he wished he hadn't pushed sweet Molly away. He might be the worst kind of asshole, a selfish prick, but he wanted to bask in her sunshine for just a little longer...

Except that would be so selfish and I already told her not to come back...

The nurse appeared and he asked for some pain killers. He also asked if she could get a message to Molly.

"Tell her I'd like to see her again," he said.

The nurse shot him a quizzical look but agreed to do as he'd asked. She returned a few moments later with a syringe. She injected a clear substance into his cannula. He felt the cold rush through his veins.

"That should help," she said.

Almost immediately, his eyelids grew heavier. He felt himself relax. The light around him dimmed. With a sigh, he gave up the fight and lost himself in oblivion.

On her first of her five days off, Molly spent the first part of her day doing laundry, cleaning her second-floor apartment from top to bottom, including the windows and washing her car, all in an effort to keep her mind off Shane. By the time she met up with her sister, Charlotte, for lunch, she was wired so tightly she thought she might combust. When Charlotte innocently asked her what was wrong, Molly's self-imposed restraint cracked.

"Is it that obvious?" she asked with a grimace.

"I shared our mother's womb with you, remember? You can't hide anything from me."

Molly tried for an answering smile but failed miserably. Charlotte's concern morphed into a frown.

"Molly? What's going on?"

"It's nothing. Trust me. I'm upset about nothing."

"Quit being a brat. Something's going on. Now, talk to me."

With an exaggerated sigh, Molly did what Charlotte asked. Though she kept Shane's name out of it, she told her sister about the patient she'd helped and how she'd thought they'd had a connection.

Charlotte grinned. "I'm impressed, Molly. I've never heard you express the slightest interest in a man before. To tell you the truth, I'd wondered if you might be batting for the other team."

"Why would you think that?" Molly asked, surprised.

Charlotte laughed. "You must admit, you haven't been very forthcoming in the man department. I mean, have you even had a boyfriend?"

Molly flushed, but defiantly held her sister's gaze. "No, but what does that have to do with anything? I finally found a guy I kind of like and he sends me packing. He doesn't even want to be friends! What an insult!"

"Maybe he doesn't see things the same way you do. You did say he was unconscious for some of the time you were together and the rest of the time he was suffering from a lot of pain. Perhaps his memories from that day aren't quite as rosy as yours."

Molly compressed her lips and nodded. "You're right. We barely know each other. How could I expect him to want to be friends? No wonder he went all weird on me. He probably thought I was a crazy woman."

Charlotte chuckled. "I'm sure you're being too hard on yourself. I can't imagine any hot-blooded male turning down the opportunity to be your friend, or more. But this guy's been seriously injured. He's hardly thinking straight. He's probably trying to get his head around everything that's happened, including his long-term prognosis. He has a lot going on. I think you should cut him some slack. Maybe leave him be, at least until he's had a chance to come to grips with his present situation."

Molly sighed. "You're right again. The whole idea was ridiculous. I mean, connection or not, I'm certainly not looking for a boyfriend, so why bother hanging around? I thought we might be able to strike up a friendship, but it's obvious the only thing he feels for me is gratitude and even that isn't enough for him to want me to stick around. The best thing I can do is accept that and move on."

Charlotte sent her a sympathetic look that Molly waved away. "Don't look at me like that, Charlotte. I'm fine. Like I said, I'm not looking for a boyfriend. For heaven's sake, who wants to fall in love?"

Charlotte's answering smile was so sweet and luminous it almost pained Molly to see it. It was obvious her sister didn't feel the same concerns as she did when it came to love. Charlotte was so in love with her fiancé, Grayson Thorpe, it was sickening.

That didn't mean Molly wasn't happy for her. She was glad her sister had found love. Just because it wasn't for her didn't mean she couldn't appreciate the happiness it brought others. Her parents were a prime example of that.

Deftly moving the topic of conversation to Charlotte and Grayson's recent engagement, she and her sister spent the next hour reminiscing about the joint celebration Charlotte and Grayson had shared with their brother, Trace, and his fiancée, Cassie. It had been a fun family affair held at the Barrington Estate outside of the small town of Broken in the southern highlands. The only thing to mar it was the absence of their adopted brother, Vaughan, who'd been holed up in Bali for the last five months. Nobody knew why.

After farewelling Charlotte and heading back toward home, Molly's mind once again strayed to Shane. Tightening her hands around the steering wheel of her Mazda, she groaned aloud her frustration.

This is ridiculous! Why am I still thinking about him? Listen to Charlotte and leave him well alone. That's the best thing for everyone.

It had been so embarrassing when he'd demanded to know why she was there. A reasonable question. Even Belinda had been surprised to see her there. Molly still wasn't certain how Shane had managed to persuade her to stay. And equally confused when he'd changed his mind.

"*Arrghh,*" she groaned again. The whole thing was doing her head in.

The sound of an incoming call distracted her from her thoughts. She tapped the screen and answered.

"Hello?" "Molly? This is Belinda Baxter."

Molly blinked in surprise and then immediately tensed. "Belinda? How's Shane?"

"He's fine," the nurse said hurriedly. "But he *is* the reason for my call."

Molly frowned. "Oh?"

"Yes. He asked me to pass on a message. He wants you to come visit him again."

Molly's frown deepened. "What? He did?"

"Yes."

"Why?"

"I don't know. That's all the information I have. Like I said, I'm just passing on a message."

Molly thanked Belinda and ended the call. She stared blindly out the windscreen, her thoughts in turmoil.

Why would he ask Belinda to do that? Why did he change his mind?

First, he likes me, then he doesn't. Now he wants me to come see him again, right when I'd decided to bring this whole embarrassing episode to an end. What do I do? I kind of like this guy—as a friend, of course. I like being around him. He's smart and funny. He makes me laugh. But am I being a fool? What would Charlotte say?

Molly pulled up at a red light and spent the couple of minutes while she waited sifting through the pros and cons. Charlotte would tell her to steer clear, at least until the guy had been given the chance to clear his head. She understood that. He'd been badly injured. That was going to take some coming to terms with. But she really wanted to see him...

Why had he asked her to visit again? Was it because he was lonely and maybe even a bit scared and had no one else close by? She thought they had a connection, that they could become good friends, but what if that was only in her imagination? Having him embarrass her again wasn't high on her "to do" list. Even worse was that he might read more into her eagerness to visit him. What if he thought she was romantically interested in him? Oh, hell. She could do without *that* complication.

But I really want to see him again...

And that was that.

The light turned green and she depressed the accelerator. Before she could change her mind, she switched her course for the hospital. She parked in the visitor's carpark. Slinging her handbag over her shoulder, she locked her car with the remote and started across the pavement.

The closer she drew to the main entrance the more her anticipation grew. It was ridiculous how nervous she was. The butterflies swarmed in her stomach. It was a bit daunting how quickly she'd become invested in him and the hope they could be friends. She wasn't sure she could cope with another rejection.

Whoa! Slow down... I hardly know this guy... I'll give him one more chance. If he turns weird or nasty or if I get any inkling he doesn't want me to be there, I'll leave. Simple as that.

Nothing ventured, nothing gained. She didn't want to be left wondering. She'd never been a coward and she wasn't about to start now. Drawing in a deep breath, she took the lift to the ICU and pressed the buzzer on the intercom with resolve.

"ICU," a disembodied voice answered a moment later.

"Hi. It's Molly Barrington. I'm here to visit Shane Lucas."

"I'm sorry. He's been shifted to the orthopedic ward."

"Oh, wow, That's... That's great news. Thank you."

Molly's heart lightened as she headed to the orthopedic ward. Though she was hopeful Shane would continue to improve, the fact he'd improved enough to leave the critical care ward so soon was a good sign. Walking up to the nurses' station in the orthopedic ward, she asked after him.

"He's in room ten, straight down the corridor on the right," the nurse behind the desk told her.

Molly thanked her and headed in the direction the nurse had indicated. The door to room ten was open. She knocked briefly, walked inside and then pulled up short. Shane already had a visitor. Even more startling, it was somebody she knew.

"Oh, my goodness! Flynn Craigdon!"

At her surprised outburst, Flynn turned to face her and smiled. "Molly Barrington! What are you doing here?"

She stepped farther into the room and gave him a brief hug. "I could ask the same thing of you!"

Shane lay in the bed, propped up on a mountain of pillows. His legs were once again raised with pulleys. The bandages had been removed and replaced with bright, white plaster casts. He was looking from one to the other of his visitors with a bemused expression.

"You two know each other?" he asked.

Molly chuckled and came closer to the bed. She was pleased to see some color back in Shane's cheeks. Already he looked so much better.

"You could say that," she replied. "Flynn's my half-brother's cousin."

Shane frowned and shook his head. "Say what?"

Chapter Six

Flynn laughed. "Don't worry, Shane. You're right to be confused. Christopher Barrington's biological father was my uncle."

"And Christopher is my half-brother," Molly added. "We share a biological mother."

Shane continued to look confused. Taking pity on him, Molly changed the subject. "What brings you here, Flynn? How do you and Shane know each other?"

Flynn smiled. "We work together at Sydney Legal. At least, we did."

Molly turned back to Shane. "That's right. You're a lawyer."

"Yeah. At least, I used to be." He flicked a gaze toward Flynn and then looked back at Molly. "I... I haven't practiced for a while."

"That needs to change," Flynn declared. "You're a damned fine lawyer. It's time you took back your job!"

"How did you know Shane was here?" Molly asked.

"I saw it on the news. Recognized the car." He turned to look at Shane. "Hell, mate. You gave me an awful fright. I took one look at that wreck and thought you were done for."

Molly shook her head, still coming to terms with the fact Flynn and Shane not only knew each other but had worked together.

"Talk about a small world," she murmured.

"Yeah," Shane muttered.

Flynn looked at Molly. "You haven't told me how *you* know Shane? I know for one you don't work with him."

Molly laughed. "You're right about that. But we did meet through my work. I attended the scene of his accident. I transported him to the hospital."

Flynn whistled. "Well, I'll be."

"She did more than that," Shane murmured. "She helped save my life."

Flynn winked. "Wow, what a coincidence! What do they say? Six degrees of separation? What are you doing here now?"

The question took Molly by surprise. Flustered, she took refuge in the floor and mumbled, "I just wanted to see that Shane was doing okay. All his family live overseas."

"Yeah, sure," Flynn replied. "Well, good for you, Molly. Going above and beyond. I always knew you were a decent girl."

They shared a smile. Molly snuck a glance at Shane. She was relieved to see that he appeared relaxed.

"You're looking better," she said. "And they shifted you out of the ICU. That's a good sign."

"Yes. Though it still hurts everywhere, they tell me I'm going to make it."

"There will be plenty of difficult days ahead," she warned him quietly, "but every day will bring you that much closer to walking out of here. Be grateful for that."

He looked at her. A shadow passed his face. "Oh, I'm grateful all right."

Except he said it in such a way that made her think the opposite. She narrowed her eyes at him. "Glad to hear it. I didn't do all that work keeping you alive for nothing," she said sternly.

Shane glared right back at her.

Flynn looked from one to the other and chuckled uneasily. "Well, I can see you have all the company you need, mate. I'm glad to see you looking so well. Apart from the legs, that is. But they'll mend. Like Molly says, the most important thing is that you made it. After all you've been through, I'm glad." He stepped closer to the bed and lowered his voice. "You've always been a fighter, mate. You've got this."

Shane's face transformed and his eyes filled with emotion. When he spoke, his voice was husky and just as low as Flynn's.

"Thanks, Flynn. You've always been a good friend to me. Stuck by me. I can't say that about everyone."

Molly saw Flynn swallow and nod. He squeezed Shane's hand, patted his shoulder, then stepped away. "You take care, mate. All you need to do is concentrate on getting better. One of these days, we'll enjoy a beer together."

Shane smiled weakly. "I'm going to keep you to that."

Flynn saluted him. "You bet." He glanced at Molly. "Has anyone heard from the police? Have they caught the asshole who did this?"

Molly shrugged. "Not as far as I know." She looked at Shane. "Have the police been to speak with you yet?"

"No. The nurses told me they stopped by when I was in the ICU, but I was too out of it to answer any questions. Hopefully, now that I'm conscious, they'll be back. I'm hoping there might be some CCTV footage of the accident captured by a camera on one of the nearby shops."

Flynn nodded, his expression grave. "You're right. Someone needs to be held accountable. They could have killed you. There's no way they don't know they hit you. The least they can do is come forward and accept responsibility."

The two men exchanged a long look Molly couldn't interpret. She smiled to lighten the mood. "In the meantime, you can concentrate on getting better. Positive thinking will help you more than you think. The power of the mind is an amazing thing."

Flynn rolled his eyes and chuckled. "Here you go, Molly Barrington. Talking that new age nonsense again. You should find some different books to read."

She gave him a look of mock outrage. "It's not new age nonsense, Flynn! A lot of what they say makes good sense. And for your information, I didn't get it from a book. I listen to several podcasts. You ought to try it for yourself someday."

Flynn merely smiled. "Yeah, yeah, yeah. Maybe in the next lifetime. Anyway, it was good to see you again, Molly. You take care. And let me know if this guy starts giving you cheek. I'll be back to sort him out."

Molly laughed and gave Flynn a quick hug goodbye. "Thanks, Flynn. It was good to see you, too. Give my love to Jayde," she said, referring to Flynn's new wife.

"Will do."

With that, he left the room and they were alone. Molly's thoughts scattered like the wind. She cast around for a safe topic of conversation and came up blank.

It seemed Shane wasn't in a hurry to fill the silence either. His expression darkened. He closed his eyes and turned his face away from her. Her heart sank.

"What is it, Shane? What's wrong?"

He took a while to answer. When he did, she started at the harshness in his tone.

"You should leave."

With an effort, she held her temper. "I only just got here. You asked me to come."

"I'm no good for you."

"How about you let me be the judge of that?"

His sigh was world-weary. "You don't know anything about me. I'm rotten to the core."

She pulled a chair up to the bed and sat down. "Why would you say that?"

He slowly turned to face her. His eyes were dark and tortured. "You don't want to know," he muttered.

"Try me."

The silence stretched between them. It was obvious he wasn't going to answer. She sighed. "Why did you ask me to come back and see you again?"

"Because I wanted to see you, dammit!"

His voice was hoarse with a mixture of anger and pain. Her heart clenched. There was a lot more going on with him than she'd realized.

She deliberately lightened her tone. "You make that sound like it's a bad thing."

He turned away again. "You don't know anything. Please, you need to leave." His voice was muffled against the pillows.

Molly's stubborn streak raised its head. He kept pushing her away, but it was clear he was going through something and he was either too scared or too ashamed to talk about it. Luckily for him she didn't scare easily. It would take more than his rudeness to make her leave.

"I wish I could honor your request," she said carefully, "but I think maybe you could do with a friend. You pushed me away yesterday and then you changed your mind. Whatever's going on with you is your business, but you asked me to come and I'm here. You've been through a traumatic experience. Serious injuries. A long road of healing and rehabilitation ahead. You'll need a friend. I'm volunteering."

He made a sound of protest, but she held up her hand and cut him off. "For some reason, our paths crossed. Right now, you need me, whether you're willing to admit that or not. Once your family arrives, or maybe you could ask Flynn to take some time off... Then I'll leave and you won't have to see me again."

He looked at her, his eyes dark with confusion and pain. "Why? Why would you do that for me?"

Molly regarded him steadily. "Because, as crazy as it sounds, I like you. And you're cute," she added with a cheeky wink. "It's true, we hardly know each other, but why don't we change that? Just accept my offer and we can get on with being friends."

He looked at her intently, as if weighing up what she'd said. "Friends? I'm not sure I make a very good friend."

She forced a smile. "Everyone needs friends. Flynn's obviously your friend and he's a good judge of character."

He was silent a long time. Then finally he sighed. "I kept wondering if I'd dreamed you."

She smiled. "No dream."

"This feels so surreal. The accident. My legs. You. I keep expecting to wake and discover none of it's real." He grimaced. "Except my legs. That pain is way too real."

Sympathy surged through her. The pulleys holding his legs elevated were a stark reminder of the seriousness of his injuries. "Is it hurting now? I can call for the nurse and ask for some pain relief."

He grimaced. "It always hurts. A constant ache. Unfortunately, I have another hour before I'm due for more medication. I'll just have to tough it out."

"Why don't I tell you a story? That might distract you from the pain."

"Like you did at the scene of the accident?"

She looked at him. "You remember that?"

The look he gave her was so intense, she was taken aback. "You were the only thing that kept me from giving up."

She didn't know what to say to that. After an uncomfortable moment, she cleared her throat. "What would you like me to talk about?"

"Tell me something I don't know about you."

She grimaced "We could be here all night."

He smiled and the slow, sexy warmth of it curled her toes. It was so unexpected after his earlier rudeness, and despite her insistence that she wasn't interested in a boyfriend, she had to fight back a blush.

The man was beyond gorgeous. Even battered and bruised, with cuts and scrapes all over his face and both of his legs plastered from hip to ankle and elevated, he was still the most good-looking man she'd ever met. The thick dark blond hair that was messy from lying several days in bed still managed to look sexy. The bright green eyes that flashed with so much emotion. The chiseled jaw, the stubble that shadowed his cheeks. She might not be looking for a boyfriend, but she wasn't blind.

That Flynn knew him, worked with him, *and* had bothered to come and visit and wish him well had put paid to her earlier misgivings. She wasn't going to let any further moodiness frighten her off.

Careful... I'm getting way ahead of myself. Why don't I just start by telling him a bit about myself? Get to know him, too... That's how people usually do this...

Taking a deep breath, she started talking. About her family. Her mom and dad. Her eight brothers and sisters. She reminded him she was a triplet.

"That's right. Who came out first?"

"Not me. In fact, I was pulled out a whole minute after my brother."

"So, he's the oldest of the three?"

"No. That's my sister, Charlotte. She's a cop based in Cronulla."

He grimaced and his expression closed. He didn't comment any further.

Molly forged on. "Of course, on a cop's salary she can't afford to live by the beach, but she's not too far away. I live only a couple of blocks away from her."

"That must be nice," he mumbled.

"Yes. Although we're both on rosters and it's not easy to line up the same day off. I managed to have lunch with her today." Molly's eyes widened as another thought struck her. "You know what? She's just become engaged to a lawyer. He works at Sydney Legal, too. You might know him."

Shane's expression went blank. Molly frowned, sensing an underlying tension she couldn't explain. "Yes, his name's Grayson Thorpe," she said tentatively. "He's an estate lawyer."

A look of relief passed over Shane's face. Molly wondered at it but didn't comment.

Shane shook his head. "Sorry, I don't know him. It's a big firm. Hundreds of lawyers. I tended to spend most of my time on the same floor as the other family law guys. That's how I know Flynn."

"Of course. Anyway, we celebrated their engagement last month at my parents' place. It was so romantic."

Molly peeked at Shane, expecting him to look uncomfortable. Most men she knew turned tail at the slightest hint of a woman talking about long-term commitment, but Shane's face remained impassive.

"That's nice," he said without further comment.

But she heard the wistfulness in his tone. She recalled he'd already told her during those fraught couple of hours at the accident scene that there was no wife or significant other in his life. Did he prefer things that way? She decided to find out.

"You said you had no wife or girlfriend. Is that by fortune or design?"

He shook his head. "Neither. I'm not against relationships, but these past few years have made it impossible to have any kind of relationship."

She wondered briefly at the latter part of his comment but focused on the former. "I'm glad you feel that way. These days it's hard to tell if a man's interested in long term or whether he just wants to have fun."

"What's wrong with having both?" Shane quipped, his seriousness of a moment ago dissipating.

Molly blushed. "Nothing. It's just that... The guys I usually date... They all want the fun, but not so many of them are interested in commitment. Of course, I'm not all that interested in commitment either, so I guess it works out."

She glanced at him. "You said the past few years have been impossible for you to have a relationship. Why?"

Shane brushed off her question with a slight shrug and then immediately grimaced as the movement pulled on his injuries.

"Are you okay?" she asked.

He winced. "Yeah. I'm fine. Sometimes I forget how banged up I am."

She smiled sympathetically.

"So, I take it you're single?" he asked.

She blushed again. "Yes."

"How old are you? Twenty-five? Twenty-six?"

"Twenty-six."

"I see. Over the hill."

She opened her mouth to protest and then saw his teasing grin. It transformed his face into a thing of beauty. *Friends, that's all I want...* She tore her gaze away and tried to remember what they'd been talking about.

"H-how old are you?" she asked, grasping at the first thing that came into her mind.

He frowned. "Didn't you already ask me that at the accident?"

"You're right. I did. I can't believe you remember that. You were out of it with pain."

He compressed his lips. "Yeah."

"I'm sorry, I didn't mean to remind you. Focus on the positive. You survived the accident and at some point, you'll walk out of here."

This time he grimaced. "Right."

His tone was far from positive. Their earlier camaraderie had vanished. She bit her lip in regret. And then his face relaxed. He shot her a strained smile.

"So, do you remember how old I am?"

She shook her head. "No, sorry. I ask the question of every patient I treat. It's hard to keep them all straight."

He gave an exaggerated sigh. "And here I thought I was special. Okay. I'm thirty. Ancient, right?"

She giggled. "Absolutely."

He gave her the rude finger. She dissolved into laughter. "All right. Not over the hill. Not by a long shot."

He moved slightly, no doubt trying to get more comfortable. His breath hissed in protest. She bent over him, immediately concerned.

"You're in pain. Are you sure there's nothing I can do?"

"Not unless you have access to the drug cabinet," he half-joked between gritted teeth.

She sighed and brushed back the hair that had fallen over his forehead. It was such a spontaneous act of tenderness, she froze.

"I-I'm sorry. I had no right to do that."

He stared at her through pain-glazed eyes, looking almost as surprised as she was. When he spoke, his voice was rough with emotion. "It's fine. It felt good. Like you care." He closed his eyes and whispered raggedly, "I can't remember the last time someone cared."

She frowned. "But what about your family?"

"They're ten thousand miles away. They might as well be on the moon."

She compressed her lips and nodded. "You're right." And then she brightened. "Well, friend. For now, you've got me! If you'd like, I can pop in whenever I can to give you a hard time. Deal?"

He sighed exaggeratedly. "Okay. Deal."

She smiled, feeling elated. "Great."

"I'm wondering if you can do me a favor."

"Of course."

"I have a cat. Garfield. He's not particularly friendly. He's a rescue cat. But I've gotten used to having him around. I live on my own in Sutherland. I don't have anyone else to feed him. I always make sure he has plenty of water, but he'll be out of food by now."

"Poor cat! Of course I'll feed him! Garfield. How original," she quipped, rolling her eyes as she reached into her handbag and pulled out a notebook and a pen. "Give me your address."

He did and she took it down, still smiling. As she looked back at him, his expression grew somber. "Thank you, Molly. I really appreciate this."

"No problem. Is your place alarmed?"

"No. And there's a spare key underneath the big blue ceramic pot outside the front door."

She gave him a droll look. "Really? The pot outside your front door?"

He smiled and went to shrug, but then pulled himself up in time. "Why not? Everyone will think it's way too predictable, so they won't bother to look, right?"

She grinned. "Okay. I guess that makes a weird kind of sense." She paused and then added, "Is there anything you need? I'll write a list."

"Maybe some toiletries. A few changes of clothes. Fresh underwear."

She blushed at the thought of going through his drawers, but hastily set her embarrassment aside. She took it as a show of trust. Afterall, he probably could have asked Flynn.

As if he could read her thoughts, he said, "I could always ask Flynn, but he lives in the city. It would be more than an hour round trip for him to come out here again."

"It's okay," she said hurriedly. "I don't mind doing it."

And she realized that was true. She wanted to help him. *That's what friends did, right?*

She added the items to her list and then looked up. She caught him staring at her. There was something like wonder on his face before he quickly concealed it.

"W-what is it?" she stammered as heat crept up her neck.

His gaze remained fixed on hers. "I was right the first time," he finally said.

His voice was husky with emotion. She steeled herself against its impact and cleared her throat. "About what?" she asked as casually as she could manage.

He continued to hold her gaze. "You're an angel."

Chapter Seven

A few minutes later, Shane pleaded fatigue and Molly took her leave. Though he did it with a bit more grace than he had the last time, she still looked confused and a little embarrassed and he felt like a heel, but after calling her an angel, he was in panic mode. As soon as she pulled the door closed behind her, he stared at the ceiling and cursed.

What the fuck am I doing? Now she'll get the wrong impression. She'll think I have something for her...

He could already tell she liked him. Hadn't she said as much? Oh, she'd couched it as a "just friends" thing, but he'd seen the shy glances she'd given him from under her lashes, the willingness to stop by and check on him, the blushes. He wished he wasn't so damaged. That he hadn't so royally screwed up his life. One wrong decision and he'd live with it for the rest of his life and anyone who came into close contact with him would also be tainted by it.

She's too good for you.

He'd already been over all that. He'd already decided to hold her at arm's length. Asking her to visit was about thanking her again for the part she'd played in getting him to the hospital and leaving things at that. But then she'd arrived looking so fresh and beautiful, so sweet and kind and he'd found himself encouraging her.

He was a selfish bastard. He wasn't fit to tie her bootlaces, let alone anything else. Even worse, she was related to his best mate. *Shit. Tricky.* Not that Flynn seemed bothered by her visit.

Flynn had stuck by him when the going had gotten rough and Shane's world had been turned upside down, but mate or not, he was pretty sure Flynn would kill him if he broke Molly's heart. And that's exactly what would happen if he kept encouraging her like that and didn't tell her the truth about his past. She had stars in her eyes.

And now I've smiled at her, called her an angel, given her hope... And as if that's not enough, I've given her a key to my house, free rein to my underwear drawer and asked her to feed my cat. Stupid! Stupid! Stupid!

He needed to stop this madness now. Cut her off. It would be harsh after the way he'd just been with her, but better to do it now than later, when her heart might be truly engaged. Maybe he could send her a message via nurse Belinda again. Take the coward's way out. Then he remembered he wasn't in nurse Belinda's ICU ward anymore.

Fuck!

He sighed. He'd have to see her again anyway because he'd asked her to bring him some clothes. He was such a heel.

As soon as Molly cleared the hospital building, she pulled out her phone and called Flynn. Though they were only loosely related through her half-brother, Christopher, she'd been in Flynn's company on several occasions at family functions and felt able to call him now and grill him about Shane. Of course, she'd have to come clean about her interest in the guy and that would be a bit embarrassing, but she was willing to put up with a little discomfort if it meant getting the lowdown.

To her relief, Flynn answered her call.

"Molly, what's up?"

A rush of nerves clogged her throat, but she pushed through. "What can you tell me about Shane Lucas?" she asked without preamble.

If Flynn was surprised by her question, it didn't show in his voice. "He's a work colleague and a good mate. Why do you ask?"

Her face flamed. Though she'd known Flynn would be curious about her call, now that the moment was upon her, she stumbled. And then she decided on the truth. After all, she'd done nothing wrong.

"I like him. And I think he likes me too. We... We kind of bonded at the accident scene."

"You *bonded?* While he was trapped in a vehicle, bruised and battered and bleeding?"

Flynn's dry tone and obvious skepticism only increased her embarrassment, but she'd come this far. She was determined to see it through to the end.

"I understand the circumstances might not have been ideal. But the truth is, we seemed to connect and after all he's been through, I think he could do with another friend."

"So, is that all this is? You only see him as a friend?"

The skepticism in Flynn's tone heated her face all over again. "Of course," she replied in a firm voice. "I'm not looking for a boyfriend. As far as I'm concerned, love and all that goes with it is highly overrated."

"Oh, Molly," Flynn said.

She hated the edge of pity in his tone. So what if Flynn had recently married the love of his life? Jayde Hassad was a cop who'd worked for years undercover. She was a kickass DEA operative who'd been instrumental in a sting that uncovered the illegal drug trade carried on by Flynn's late uncle. At one point, Jayde had even suspected Flynn of involvement in his uncle's business operations. But the fact he was apparently head-over-heels in love didn't give him the right to judge her or feel sorry for her.

"What else can you tell me about Shane?" she persisted, ignoring his comment.

Flynn sighed. "What else do you want to know?"

"How long have you known him?"

"Four years."

"How did you meet?"

"At work."

"Do you like him?"

"What kind of question is that? We're mates. Of course I like him."

"What about Jayde? Does she like him?"

"She adores him. She treats him like a brother. They've grown even closer since her real brother's death."

Molly hadn't heard about that. She sympathized with Jayde. Molly thought about her six brothers. She'd be devastated if she lost one of them.

"Is he married?"

"No."

"In a relationship?"

"Not as far as I know." Flynn's tone became tinged with impatience. "Are we nearly done? You really should be asking him this stuff. And what do you care anyway? You just said you weren't looking for a boyfriend."

Molly flushed. Fynn was right. And she *had* asked. It was just that she wanted to cross-check Shane's answers. Then she was filled with guilt. They weren't teenagers passing notes between their friends in the school yard.

"Look, Shane's had some tough times lately, but he's come out on top. He's a good bloke. I'm proud to call him friend. But Molly...take it easy on him."

Molly opened her mouth to question Flynn further, but then decided against it. He was right. She should pull on her big girl panties and ask Shane himself. It wasn't fair to ask questions behind his back. She should give him the chance to share. Or not.

As she thanked Flynn for his time and ended the call, she thought about what he'd meant by "tough times." No doubt it had something to do with the way Shane blew hot and cold and the way he'd warned her off. She also hadn't forgotten his comment about relationships having been impossible the last few years and the way he'd brushed off her question about it.

She set the thought aside, focusing instead on the "good bloke" bit. The fact Flynn called him a friend was another tick in the box.

He called me an angel...

She was anything but an angel, but his words had filled her with warmth just the same. And that might just become a problem. Every time she thought of Shane her body flushed with heat. He was so darned attractive. His secrets only made him more desirable. How ridiculous was that? Especially when she was determined to keep him at arm's length.

Friends. That's all I'm looking for. Friends.

The word was starting to sound hollow, but the feeling of panic she got whenever she thought about taking the leap and entrusting her heart to someone was still there. Attractive or not, being friends was definitely the safest option.

Unlocking her car, she climbed in behind the wheel and pulled on her seatbelt. Before she could start the ignition, her phone rang. She checked the screen and frowned. It was her boss.

"Hi, Raoul. What's up?"

"Oh, Molly. I know you're on a day off, but I was wondering if you could possibly work tonight. Benson's called in sick and so has Willa. We're already short-staffed. I've been ringing people to see if they can fill in, but so far, I haven't had any luck."

Molly's shoulders slumped. She blew out her breath on a sigh. She knew how difficult it was to get staff at short notice.

She also knew how tough it was on the other paramedics when they didn't have the full complement of staff on shift.

"Sure, Raoul. Count me in."

He sighed with relief. "Thank you, Molly! I owe you big time."

"Yeah, yeah, yeah. It's fine," Molly replied, brushing away the thanks.

"You're an angel, Molly Barrington."

Molly smiled. Twice in one day, albeit in different contexts. How about that.

"Who else is on?" she asked.

"You'll be partnered with Tessa. Is that okay?"

"Of course. I love working with Tessa. She has the coolest head I know in a crisis."

"You've got that right," Raoul agreed and ended the call.

Switching on the ignition, she checked the address of Shane's apartment and entered the details into her GPS. She still had time to feed his cat and collect a few of his things and drop them off to him before she was required at work. With that in mind, she pulled out of the hospital carpark and joined the stream of traffic heading south.

Less than ten minutes later, she arrived at a modern apartment complex in an upmarket part of Sutherland. The street was lined with mature trees that lent it a shady, tranquil air. Traffic was minimal. From somewhere in the distance, she heard children laughing and playing and figured there must be a school nearby. Either that or a daycare center.

Climbing out, she checked the apartment number on the piece of paper and made her way over to Shane's door. As instructed, she found a key under a blue ceramic pot that housed a small palm tree and couldn't help rolling her eyes at his lax security, particularly given he lived in a ground floor apartment. At least the location would come in handy when he returned home.

The cement-rendered building was painted in a modern shade of gray. The tiled roof was a contrasting charcoal color and the window treatments were white. The complex was small, housing no more than six or eight apartments. Each had its own lock up garage.

Mindful of the time getting away from her, she fitted the key into the lock and let herself in. The inside was surprisingly spacious with an open plan kitchen and living room that went out onto a paved outdoor area, complete with garden furniture and a barbeque. She could imagine balmy summer evenings eating out there with friends.

The kitchen was all shiny white cabinetry, stainless steel appliances and granite countertops. A bowl of slowly withering oranges and green apples provided a splash of color on an otherwise bare work surface. She looked around her. The place was as neat as a pin. Not even a dirty dish in the sink.

Late afternoon sunlight poured through double French doors that led to the outdoor area, filling the living room with light. The leather couch, side tables, and rugs were expensive-looking and tasteful and had been chosen with an eye for both design and practicality. This was no throw-together bachelor pad.

A doggy door had been cut into one of the lower windowpanes. She assumed it was for Shane's cat. Right on cue she heard meowing. She watched as a big ginger tomcat pushed his way through the doggy door from the rear courtyard. Upon spying her, he came to a halt and gave her a disdainful look.

"You must be Garfield," she said, trying on a smile.

The cat continued to regard her with wide, suspicious eyes, no doubt wondering what she was doing there and where his owner was. She stepped closer and held out her hand toward him, but he moved out of the way and sat on the other side of the kitchen.

"Okay, well I guess we can work on being friends. Let's find you something to eat. You must be hungry, right? It's been a few days."

She hadn't asked Shane for instructions about where to find the cat food, but after opening several doors and then finally the pantry, she found a bag of dry cat food on the bottom shelf, along with several tins of wet food. Looking around, she saw a food and water bowl near the garbage bin.

She spooned the contents of the tin into one bowl and filled the adjoining one with dry food. Then she topped up the water dish. Garfield continued to eye her distrustfully from his position across the room.

"It's all right. I'm not going to hurt you. Come on. Time to eat."

She looked around for a tray of kitty litter and then saw it outside in a corner of the courtyard. Pulling open the French doors, she stepped outside. A gentle breeze lifted her hair and brought with it the scent of wattle.

There must be a tree in flower close by...

It sure smelled better than the kitty litter. Holding her breath, she emptied the pungent-smelling contents of the tray into a garbage bag and after tying off the ends, dropped it into the large bin that stood outside the apartment. Then she refilled it with fresh kitty litter she found under the kitchen sink and returned the tray to where she'd found it. Garfield remained where he was, still looking decidedly unfriendly. He hadn't yet come forward to eat, even though he had to be hungry.

"Well, I guess you'll eat when you're ready," she said to him.

Leaving him to it, she wandered down the hall, opening doors and stopping to peek inside. A spare bedroom that had been converted into an office. A bathroom, a compact laundry room with washer and dryer. A linen closet built into the hallway and then the main bedroom. The king-size bed was neatly made. Like the rest of the house, the room was scrupulously neat and tidy with not even a towel out of place in the master bath.

She returned to the bedroom and pulled open a door to the wardrobe. There was a large duffel bag on the top shelf, along with an impressive collection of baseball caps. Rows of business shirts, suits and casual jackets filled the generous hanging space. Drawers were filled with underwear and socks, neatly folded jeans and T-shirts and an assortment of pajamas. Shoes were lined up neatly in a row on the bottom shelf. She compressed her lips.

I guess he won't be needing them anytime soon...

The thought momentarily gave her pause. Even though Shane had asked her to go over to his place, it felt weird being in the house of someone she barely knew, especially when the house owner was absent.

Taking note of the time, she focused on what she'd come there for. Reaching up for the duffel bag, she opened the chest of drawers and pulled out several pairs of underwear, T-shirts, shorts, socks, and pajamas. In one part of her mind, she took note that he wore silk boxers and not briefs. She found herself rubbing the silky fabric between her fingers before she realized what she was doing and with her cheeks burning, hurriedly stuffed them farther into the bag.

Stepping into the adjoining master bathroom, she opened more drawers and found his toothbrush, toothpaste, and razor, shaving cream and deodorant and tossed them all into a toiletry bag she found under the sink. There was a bottle of expensive cologne on a shelf. She pulled off the lid and brought it up to her nose. The sweet and spicy smell immediately reminded her of Shane. She quickly dropped it into the toiletry bag and then added it to the duffel.

Returning to the bedroom, she looked around for anything else he might need. She spied a new release paperback of a popular thriller writer on the bedside table and added that to the bag. She zipped it up, hoisted it off the bed and then headed back down the hall toward the kitchen.

As she approached, she saw that Garfield was now eating from the bowl. He looked up when she entered and gave her a baleful glare. He didn't look away until she stepped toward the

French doors that led to the outdoor courtyard. She'd noticed earlier there were several potted plants, including an Aram lily with its glossy, green leaves, two purple-and-gold African violets and a large maiden-hair fern. All three were protected from the elements by a balcony above the courtyard.

Setting down the duffel, she looked around for a watering can and found one at one end of the outdoor area, right beside a garden hose. She filled the watering can and then went about watering Shane's plants. She cast a glance over toward Garfield. He was still by the food bowl. As if aware of her scrutiny, he shot her another distrustful look, but went on eating.

Definitely not ready to make friends...

Returning the watering can to where she found it, she pulled the French doors closed behind her and locked them. She bid Garfield goodbye and then left. As she went to return the key to where she found it, she realized there was a mail key hanging off the keyring.

On her way into the complex, she'd noticed a row of locked metal mailboxes all fixed together on a brick wall in the front yard. She walked over to them and saw that Shane's was so full there were letters half-hanging out of the slot. Inserting the key, she opened the mailbox and reached in and retrieved his mail. She'd drop it off to him along with his other things.

Setting the duffel bag down on the ground, she unzipped it and stuffed the mail inside. One letter fell out. She picked it up and turned it over. The words "NSW Community Corrections Office" were stenciled in dark blue lettering on the top right-hand corner of the envelope. She frowned and studied it more closely. Sure enough, the letter was addressed to Shane Lucas at this address.

She knew from Charlotte and her cop brothers that the Community Corrections Office was another name for probation and parole. They dealt with convicted felons after they were released from jail. An offender had to attend upon his parole officer as often as his parole conditions provided for, usually once a week. The parole officer's job was to make sure the parolee was complying with the terms of his parole.

Why is Shane receiving a letter from probation and parole? Is he an ex-con? Is that what he meant about relationships having been impossible over the past few years?

With her heart beating fast and adrenaline surging through her veins, Molly stuffed the letter into the duffel bag with the others and then quickly zipped it closed. Hurrying now, she returned to the front door of Shane's apartment and put the key back where she'd found it. All the time, her head kept hammering with questions.

I need to ask him straight out. Give him a chance to explain. That's what I need to do. That's fair. No. That's not fair. It's none of my business. I'll simply hand over the mail and let him tell me when he's ready...

All the way to the hospital, she kept imagining how long it might take before Shane chose to tell her and whether she could wait for him to do so. Now that she knew about the letter, it was impossible to forget about it. But the simple fact was, they were almost strangers. She had no right to delve into his private life and no right to expect any kind of explanation from him.

Then another thought occurred to her. Flynn had said Shane worked with him, that he was a lawyer. How did that work? How could Shane be a lawyer with a criminal record? Then she remembered Shane saying he hadn't practiced for a while.

Is that because he was doing time? Sitting on his butt in jail? Is that what Flynn meant when he talked about Shane facing tough times? And what had he been convicted of? Rape? Murder? Drugs?

Okay, she was being ridiculous. Letting her imagination run away from her. Flynn thought Shane was a great guy. It couldn't be anything like that. It might not even be anything serious. Except no one spent time in jail if it weren't serious. And what other explanation was there for him to have a letter addressed to him from probation and parole in his mailbox?

As she pulled into the hospital visitor parking lot once again, her stomach churned with nerves. She vacillated between telling herself it was none of her business, to wanting desperately to know the truth. With a sigh, she collected the duffel off the back seat and crossed the carpark. She entered the main building on the ground floor and caught the lift to the orthopedic ward. As she approached the open doorway of Shane's room, she came to a sudden halt.

Two uniformed police officers were inside, talking to him. One held a notebook and pen. The other one was asking questions. She turned away, wanting to give them privacy. From her position a little farther down the corridor, she could only make out the low murmur of conversation. It was impossible to hear what was being said.

A few minutes later, the officers left. One nodded toward her in silent greeting as they passed. With her heart thumping, she strode into Shane's room and plastered a smile on her face.

"Hi! How are you doing? I see the police were here. That's good. What did they say? Have they found the person who hit you?"

Shane shook his head, his expression grim. "Hi, Molly. No. They just wanted to touch base, introduce themselves. Let me know they're investigating the accident. Apparently, there's been conflicting reports from eyewitnesses. Some say it was a silver SUV. Others say white. One person thought it was a truck." He rolled his eyes. "Seriously. I told them what I could remember. I don't know how much weight they gave it."

"Why wouldn't they believe you? You were the one who was hit."

He averted his gaze and then cleared his throat. "Yeah. Whatever. They've put in a request for the CCTV footage. Hopefully they'll know more then."

"I hope they catch whoever did this. You could have been killed!"

His expression remained grim. Molly guessed he didn't want to be reminded of how close he'd come to death. She lightened her tone and changed the subject.

"I stopped by your place as you asked. Are you always so neat and tidy?"

She meant it as a joke, but his expression grew darker. "Yes. I like order. Is that a crime?"

She was taken aback by his abruptness. Embarrassment heated her face. "O-of course not," she stammered. "It was merely an observation. I didn't mean to offend."

Shane let out a weary sigh. "Fuck. I've done it again. I'm sorry, Molly. I didn't mean to snap at you."

She gave him a tentative smile. "That's okay. No doubt you're still in a lot of pain. I understand. I just wanted to drop off these things for you. I need to get going anyway. I was meant to be on a day off, but I've been called into work tonight."

With that, she sat the duffle on his bed, mindful not to accidentally bump any part of him. "Do you want me to unpack your things?"

He glanced at the bag and then looked away. "Sure. Yeah. That'd be great."

In silence, she pulled out his mail and set it on the table in front of him. "I noticed your mailbox was overflowing. I brought it in for you."

He barely looked at the pile of letters. She continued to unpack his bag, folding the T-shirts, pajamas, and underwear into the drawers beside his bed. The toiletries she sat on top of the bedside table, within easy reach. She still itched to ask him about the letter from the parole office, but she resisted the urge and instead, asked him if she could get him a coffee from the café she'd passed on her way into the hospital.

"I'm not sure what the hospital food's like, but I can't imagine it beats a cappuccino and a fresh piece of banana bread." She winked. To her relief, he smiled, albeit grudgingly.

"I'm nothing but an asshole, Molly. Why are you being so nice?"

Chapter Eight

S hane's question hung in the air between them. Molly's cheeks had turned crimson and her gaze was now fixed to the floor. Guilt surged through him. He was in a bad mood and he'd taken it out on Molly—again. And after she'd gone out of her way to do him a favor.

What a prick.

The arrival of the cops had filled him with a mixture of hope and dread. He hoped they had something to tell him about who'd T-boned him, but after spending a couple of years behind bars, he had an instinctive dislike of cops. When they discovered he was an ex-con, as they invariably did, their attitude toward him changed. He'd seen it time and time again. These two were no different.

It was obvious they'd arrived at the hospital already aware of his status. The first thing they'd asked him was how long it had been since he'd last checked in with his parole officer. Shane had been meticulous in his attendance at the parole office. He'd made every single one of his appointments. In fact, only a week earlier, he and his PO had met for the final time.

Bert Heller had spent all forty-two years of his career as a parole officer. He'd lost count of the number of parolees he'd met with and counseled over those years. His vast experience with ex-cons had honed his skills to the point where he only had to look at a parolee fresh out of jail to know whether they had what it took to survive on the outside.

Shane had told him straight out about the circumstances of his arrest and that he'd taken full responsibility. Bert had expressed surprise and told him most of the ex-cons he met were bitter against the system that had stolen their freedom and years of their life they'd never get back. They blamed anyone from the cops to their victims for their sad circumstances. All too often, they also blamed a drug addiction. That Shane was willing to take responsibility earned him some respect from Heller.

Shane blamed no one but himself. No one had forced him to drink too much. No one had told him to get behind the wheel. It was no one's fault but his that he'd hit someone and ended up behind bars. The two years he'd been incarcerated were the worst years of his life, but they'd also given him time to contemplate the importance of the little things—being able to go for a walk whenever he wanted; watching a movie; eating out. They were things he'd taken for granted. He'd vowed to appreciate every minute of his life and was determined never to go back.

Now I'm the one in a hospital bed...

The irony wasn't lost on him. Right now, he didn't know if he'd walk again. Though the doctors were confident there was no nerve damage and his spinal cord remained intact, they wouldn't know for certain until the swelling had completely subsided and the bones had been given a chance to mend. But at least he was alive. Not everyone got that lucky.

It was a sobering reminder and one he hadn't fully appreciated until now. He'd been so busy feeling sorry for himself, he'd lost sight of the fact that not everyone survived a car accident. Not everyone had the chance to start anew. Not everyone had a Molly Barrington wanting to help in any way she could. Now he'd gone and ruined it by giving the one person who thought him worthy a hard time

He wasn't sure if the two uniformed officers had really believed he was being dishonest in his account of what had happened or whether they were merely giving him a difficult time just for kicks. It was impossible to know for sure and he'd learned the hard way not to question those in authority. Fortunately, they no longer had any power over him. He'd done his time and had finished his period of parole. He was now a free man.

Still, it wasn't fair to take out his bad mood on Molly. She was good and decent. She saved lives for a living... It didn't get much more decent than that. He still wasn't sure why she'd want to hang out with someone like him, but then again, she knew nothing about his past. And that was another reason he felt so out of sorts.

His past was none of her business and yet, he was filled with guilt every time he thought about encouraging their burgeoning friendship. He didn't know if him having done time would make a difference to the way she saw him, but he suspected it would. Most people were wary of an ex-con.

She looked up at him, her eyes narrowed in a glare. It appeared she wasn't going to be as tolerant of his rudeness as she'd been the last time.

"I thought we cleared this up already. Stop being such a jerk. I'm your friend. I want to be here. I want to help you out. Quit being such an idiot about it and just accept my offer. Now, do you need something for the pain? Do you want me to call the nurse?"

"No, I don't want the nurse."

Embarrassment at the dressing down heated his cheeks. Even after everything, she was worried about him. What she'd said was true. He was being a jerk.

The worst of it was, he was happy to see her. She was the only bright spot in his day. The thought of not seeing her again filled him with a panic of another kind. He was such a mess. He didn't begin to understand how someone he barely knew had become so important to him. He enjoyed her company. He wanted to get to know her better and that meant telling her about his past.

He needed to come clean, to tell her what he'd done. Though he hated the thought of having to explain himself, unless he was prepared to be brutal and lie about not wanting to see her ever again, he had no choice.

He tamped down a wave of nervousness and cast around for some courage.

Just tell her, damn it! Tell her before she finds out from someone else. Someone like Flynn, or one of the cops in her family…

If things ever got more serious between them, he was certain at least one of her cop siblings would enter his name into a database. They weren't supposed to do that kind of thing, to check up on a private citizen, but only a fool would believe that didn't happen.

He hated thinking of himself as an ex-con, but the news would be better coming from him than anyone else. At least he could answer her questions. If she had any. If she hung around long enough to ask them.

Her brow was now furrowed. "Shane...?"

Drawing in as deep a breath as his battered body would allow, he dived in.

"There's something I need to tell you."

Her expression didn't change. "Okay. What is it?" And then she gave a nervous kind of laugh. "Should I be worried?"

He shrugged and then grimaced as the pain in his chest reminded him of his recent trauma. "I don't know. Maybe."

Her eyes filled with shadows. She continued to look uncertain. "Okay. Well, that's not exactly reassuring."

I need to rip off the Band-Aid... Pull it off in one fell swoop... Get it over with...and then deal with the fallout... If that means saying goodbye to her, then so be it. I've dealt with worse disappointments...

Bringing his chin up, he stared at her. "I've been to jail."

There. He'd said it. He watched closely for her response. The widening of her eyes was the only indication she'd heard. After a few moments, she simply nodded.

"Okay."

He frowned. "*Okay?* Is that all you have to say?"

She looked away. "The thing is," she continued. "I kind of guessed."

It was his turn to be surprised. "You *guessed?* How could you guess something like that? It's not like I have a number tattooed on my forehead."

She flushed and kept her gaze averted "The thing is, in that pile of mail there's a letter addressed to you from the probation and parole office. I wasn't snooping," she added a little defensively. "I just happened to see it. I know enough about how the justice system works to know there's probably only one explanation for that kind of letter."

Her gaze remained fixed on the bedspread. Her color was high. He couldn't believe she'd already had an inkling that he might be an ex-con and yet she'd still come to visit him, had brought him his things, had stayed.

"Why didn't you say anything?" he asked quietly.

She slowly met his gaze. "I wanted to." She shot him a hesitant grin. "The truth is, I was dying to ask you. I'm a naturally curious person. But it's none of my business. I still feel that way."

Admiration for the depth of character of the woman beside him grew. "Most people wouldn't have acted with such restraint," he said.

She nodded. "I agree. I didn't say it was easy for me to keep my mouth shut."

She smiled. It transformed her face from pretty to unbelievably beautiful. Her blue eyes appeared to be lit from within, twinkling with good humor. The sight of her took his breath away. He found himself smiling back and feeling better than he had in a long time. And then his smile faded.

She might not have asked for any details, but he wanted to tell her everything. To put his whole life on the table and let her decide if he was worthy of her time. Better to know now, before he got in too deep. As tension took hold of him once again, he began to tell her about the worst time of his life.

"Three years ago, I hit a cyclist and killed him. I was two times over the minimum legal alcohol limit. I'd been at a work Christmas party, surrounded by a roomful of judges and lawyers." His lips twisted into a grimace. "You don't have to point out the irony of that."

She merely nodded, her expression somber, her gaze intent on him.

Steeling himself, he continued. "It was late. Around half-past two in the morning. I should have called a cab, but there were none around. I tried to call for an uber, but they were also busy. It was a week before Christmas. Sydney Legal wasn't the only one holding a Christmas party."

He drew in a breath. "I could have stayed in the city, booked into a hotel, but I wanted to get home. Feed Garfield. Wake up in my own bed. It was stupid and selfish and I've called myself all kinds of fool every day since, but at the time, I thought I was okay to drive."

Molly regarded him somberly. She opened her mouth as if to say something, but then closed it again. He went on.

"I was nearly back to my apartment when it happened. It was now going on for three. I was tired, a little lightheaded. I still remember thinking about how good it would feel to take a hot shower and climb into bed."

He shook his head and compressed his lips at the memory. "The cyclist came from nowhere. A dark blur, nothing else. At least, that's how it seemed to me. The next thing I knew, I heard a loud sound and felt a bump and knew I'd hit something. I climbed out, thinking it might be a dog or a cat. That would have been bad enough. I was shocked beyond belief when I realized I'd run over someone."

"What did you do?" Molly asked quietly.

"I panicked. I didn't know what to do. The street was deathly quiet. There was no one around to help. For a split second, I thought about climbing back into my car and getting the hell away from there..." He forced himself to make eye contact. "I'm not proud of that."

"So, what happened?"

"I did the only thing I could. I called an ambulance. Then I went over to the guy to see if there was anything I could do to help him. He was in pretty bad shape. Conscious, but only just. I waited with him until the ambulance arrived. When the police came to talk to me, I told them exactly what happened. I submitted to a roadside breath test and was arrested there and then and taken back to the station. It was there I discovered the cyclist I'd hit had died. I was charged with negligent driving occasioning death. I pleaded guilty and was sentenced to three years."

He saw surprise flash in her eyes and understood where it came from. Three years didn't seem like enough for taking someone's life, no matter how unintentional.

"The cyclist had no light on his bike, nor any high visibility clothing," Shane explained. "The police agreed it would have been almost impossible to see him. If I hadn't been over the limit, they might not have charged me at all. But I was and they did. I served two years of my sentence behind bars and the last year on parole. I had my final visit with my parole officer a week ago." He smiled humorlessly. "That letter you saw is confirmation I'm done with the parole office once and for all."

Molly stared at Shane, her heart pounding. Though she'd already accepted the letter she'd found could only mean one thing, it wasn't easy to sit there and listen to him recount what must have been a devastating time in his life. She felt sympathy for what had happened to him, but she didn't excuse his actions, and it seemed he wasn't looking for an excuse. He'd pleaded guilty and served his punishment. Now he was getting on with his life. She admired him for having the courage to remain at the crime scene, knowing that decision would irrevocably change his life. It had been a brave thing to do and spoke volumes about his character.

Nor would she judge him for climbing behind the wheel when he'd had too much to drink. Though she couldn't imagine ever doing something like that, it happened. No one was perfect. That included her. He'd owned up to his mistake. He'd killed a man. It didn't matter that he hadn't intended for that to happen. His actions had resulted in a man's death. He'd carry that around for the rest of his life. As far as she was concerned, that was punishment enough.

"Does Flynn know?"

"Yes. We worked together. We're mates."

Molly nodded. No doubt that's what Flynn had meant when he'd told her about Shane having gone through some tough times. The fact the two of them were still friends told her a lot about what Flynn thought about Shane, despite his brush with the law.

More than a brush... He'd killed someone.

Yes, but he'd paid his dues and was obviously remorseful. If she were honest, she felt a little in awe of his decency and his courage. He'd done the right thing, even though he must have known that by staying at the scene, it would almost certainly mean going to jail. He was a lawyer. There was no way he hadn't comprehended the consequences and how it would affect his life forever. And yet he'd done it. Now he was trying to get on with his life.

Except now he's the victim of an accident and this time the driver didn't stop...

The irony.

"Are you sure the police don't have any clue who did this to you?" she asked.

Shane searched her face for a moment, as if wondering if there wasn't more she wanted to ask him about what he'd just revealed. After a little while, he shook his head.

"No. Like I said, there are conflicting eyewitness statements. They're still waiting for the CCTV footage."

She drew in a deep breath and eased it out on a smile. "I'm sure they'll find them. It's amazing what they can do these days and if it was all captured on camera... Surely, it's only a matter of time before they identify the other driver."

Shane nodded. "Yeah. Let's hope so."

On impulse, she reached out and squeezed his hand. "Thank you for telling me about your past."

He compressed his lips and nodded again. She could tell he was finding it difficult to formulate a reply. She squeezed his hand again. "It's okay. I understand. I..." Embarrassment heated her cheeks.

He frowned. "What is it, Molly?"

She stared at the bedspread and gathered her courage. "I really like you, Shane, and I still want to be your friend. What do you think?"

The words came out in a rush. She forced her gaze upward and met his eyes. To her surprise and relief, they shone with happiness.

"Even after everything I've told you?"

She nodded.

He sighed. "I'd really like that."

Her breath rushed out in a *whoosh*. And then she was grinning like an idiot. A moment later, she caught sight of the time and gasped. If she didn't hurry, she'd be late for work. With that, she stood and leaned over and pecked him on the cheek.

"That's from Garfield. He wants you to get well, pronto. I need to get to work. See you soon."

Still grinning madly and with her cheeks on fire, she gave him a cheery wave and fled the room.

Shane sank down against the pillows and sighed again. He felt like he'd just finished a marathon—physically and emotionally drained, but strangely euphoric. His cheek still tingled from the brief touch of her lips. The smile was still on his face. He was so glad his secret was out in the open and Molly appeared to have taken it well. The warning she'd had with the letter she'd found might have helped with tempering her reaction.

But best of all, she wanted to see him again and he was done with trying to deter her. Not so long ago he'd prayed for God to take his life. Now he couldn't imagine not wanting to be alive and having the opportunity to explore whatever this crazy thing was between him and Molly. Except she'd said she wanted to be friends.

Friends, not lovers. Of course, why would she want to get romantically entangled with an ex-con? The goodness inside her didn't allow for her to judge someone for that, but neither was she willing to get close. Friends.

But what was with that kiss? Okay, so he could hardly call it a kiss, but no one had forced her to touch her lips to his cheek. Would a new friend do that? Maybe she wanted to take things slowly. Maybe she was just being cautious. After all, they'd only met four days earlier. Of course, he'd been aware of her as a man from the moment they'd first set eyes on each other, despite the desperate circumstances, but maybe things were different for her? Maybe she was still trying to get her head around the fact she was attracted to her patient? *Former patient*, he corrected.

There was an air of innocence about her that led him to think she wasn't very experienced in the ways of love and she'd admitted she'd never been in love. Maybe she didn't recognize the signs of physical and emotional attraction and that whatever this was between them could become so much more if only she'd let it?

He closed his eyes on another quiet sigh as the questions swirled in his head. She'd told him she really liked him. That was enough for now. Though he still hurt all over, somehow the pain didn't matter so much now that Molly was going to hang around and he was going to do everything he could to convince her what they had between them went far beyond platonic.

Friends, be damned.

Chapter Nine

M olly arrived at work for her nightshift with barely a minute to spare. Hurriedly hanging up her coat, she tossed her handbag in her locker and headed outside to the plant room where she saw her colleague, Tessa Barone, carrying ventilation equipment to one of the ambulance vehicles.

Molly smiled. "Hey, Tessa. How were your days off?"

Tessa was a senior paramedic and had been stationed with Molly at the Sutherland Hospital for the past four years. Though Tessa was almost a decade older, they'd become firm friends and worked well together. Tessa had a cool head in a crisis and generously shared her knowledge and expertise, which Molly appreciated. Staying on top of developments in emergency healthcare was vital and Tessa had been doing it a lot longer than Molly.

Tessa placed the equipment into the ambulance and shrugged. "Yeah, you know. It was good not to have to get out of bed at the crack of dawn every day, but I still had to drag the kids out of bed and get them ready for school. Then refereeing the inevitable squabbles at the end of the day. Sometimes I think it's easier to come to work."

Molly shot her a sympathetic smile. "I can't imagine how tough it is to raise three kids on your own."

Tessa grimaced. "You bet."

"Do you ever hear from Martin?" Molly asked, referring to Tessa's ex.

"Nope and I guess that's a good thing. Though I feel for the kids. It's hard to explain to them why their father doesn't want to have anything to do with them. Now he's got a new wife and baby, it's like they don't exist. He thinks that as long as he keeps paying child support, he's done his bit. The asshole."

Molly's sympathy rose. A messy divorce and being left to raise three children alone would be hard on anyone. Tessa had the most amazing kids—ten-year-old Baxter, twelve-year-old Sonia, and fifteen-year-old Nell—but having seen them in action, Molly knew that meeting their needs was often as challenging as a full-time job and Tessa had no one to share the load.

Molly inwardly grimaced. Tessa's situation was another reason Molly spent too much time thinking about what would happen if things didn't work out in a long-term relationship. Okay, so she'd grown up sheltered and secure in a loving home, but her mother's life hadn't always been so blessed. Molly found herself thinking way too often about how she'd cope if a marriage she'd made didn't last. Especially if there were children involved.

The growing divorce rate was a good indicator of how difficult staying married was. Another reason to steer well clear of love and everything that came with it. Tessa's daily struggle to hold it all together as a single mom wasn't something Molly wanted to endure. It only served to reinforce her belief that it was better to stay single, no matter how tempted she might be.

Shane's image filled her mind. She felt embarrassed all over again at the fact she'd given him a parting kiss. And after making it clear she only wanted to be friends! She'd been taken by surprise at how nice it had felt. His skin had been firm and warm beneath her lips, a touch scratchy from his five o'clock shadow. But nice. *Too nice.*

What must he think of me? Probably that he was right the first time. That I'm a crazy woman... I tell him I want to be his friend and then I go and kiss him!

"What are you doing here anyway? I thought you were on days off?" Tessa asked, interrupting Molly's thoughts.

"Yeah. I am. I was. The boss called me in. Benson and Willa are out sick. That's left us short-staffed."

Tessa grimaced. "Aren't we always?"

Molly nodded. Tessa was right. They were always short-staffed.

"Hey, you couldn't give me a ride home from work in the morning, could you?" Tessa asked, interrupting Molly's thoughts.

"Sure."

"Thanks. I put my car in for a service the other day and it's still not ready. They keep finding stuff they need to fix. They're telling me it's a matter of safety." She shrugged. "I don't know if they're telling me the truth or if they just see a gullible female who doesn't know the difference, but what am I supposed to do?"

"I guess you could take it to someone else. Get a second opinion."

Tessa shook her head. "I don't have time. And quite frankly, there's no guarantee the next mechanic won't be the same. I mean, when you don't have a clue about the difference between a spark plug and an alternator, what choice do you have? No, I'm going to have to just bite the bullet and get them to fix what they want. I wouldn't want to be driving a car that's unsafe."

"No, that's for sure. Did you hear about the car accident Benson and I attended on Monday?"

"No. Was it a bad one?"

"Two cars involved. The one at fault fled the scene."

Tessa busied herself sorting supplies in the back of the ambulance. "A hit and run? That's terrible," she said. "How many people were hurt?"

"Only one, thank goodness."

"How bad was it?"

"Pretty bad. Multiple leg fractures, lacerations, some internal injuries. The other car T-boned him on the driver's side. His car flipped and then got wrapped around a power pole. Not good."

Tessa shook her head. "He's lucky he survived. Where did it happen?"

"Caringbah. According to the victim, the other car ran a red light. I just hope the police find who's responsible. I understand some people might panic in that situation and take off, but it's been four days. They've had plenty of time to get their head on straight and come forward. It's appalling cowardice, that's what it is. I bet they haven't even tried to find out whether the other driver survived."

"Ouch." Tessa held a reddening fingertip up and then popped it in her mouth.

"What did you do?"

"I just shut the storage locker door on it."

"Are you all right?"

Tessa grimaced. "I've probably blackened my fingernail, but I'll be fine."

"Okay. Well, if you're sure. Let's run through the checklist of supplies and make sure we're all stocked up."

"No worries." Tessa reached for the clipboard that hung inside the back of the truck. "Ready?"

Molly started organizing the ambulance. Quiet times like this provided an excellent opportunity to do the all-important inventory. Officers re-stocked after an emergency, but it was always done on the run.

"Did the mechanic give you any idea how long before they're going to finish with your car?"

Tessa sighed. "Nope. But hopefully not too much longer. Life's darn difficult without it."

Molly chuckled. "You have that right. Too bad you can't take one of these home. Plenty of room for groceries." She winked.

Tessa laughed and Molly was pleased to hear it. Her friend had been down for so long, it wasn't often that she laughed. No doubt the daily struggles she faced made laughter seem impossible some days.

"Hey, if you ever need a night to yourself, let me know. I'm more than happy to take the kids for the night."

Tessa sent her a grateful look. "Thanks, Molly. You're a true friend."

"I mean it."

"I know and that's why I love you. I might just take you up on it."

"I wouldn't have offered if I didn't want to do it. Your kids are angels."

Tessa rolled her eyes and gave her a wry grin. "You wouldn't say that if you had to live with them."

Molly laughed. There wasn't a more devoted mother than Tessa. Her life revolved around her kids. They were her world. It was too bad she'd been left to raise them on her own. Her ex-husband might have been providing financial support, but everyone knew it took much more than money to raise strong, independent, happy kids.

It was weird. Even though she was reluctant to risk her heart on the love stakes, she'd always thought she'd have a family. A desire completely at odds with how she felt about relationships, but that's the way things were. She wasn't sure what kind of man could overcome her instinctive aversion for love, but she'd have to take the leap someday if she wanted children.

Or maybe I could just adopt?

Except, adoption wasn't as easy as it used to be. Too much demand and not enough babies to go around. Besides, didn't she want the experience of carrying a baby and giving birth? Yes, she did. That meant overcoming her fear of getting her heart broken and taking a chance. But first she had to find the right man.

Could Shane be that man?

Maybe. She smiled at the memory of how pleased he'd looked when she'd told him she'd like to keep visiting and get to know him better. Physically, he ticked all her boxes. Nice eyes, nice hair, good skin. Tall, broad-shouldered, good looking. But there was a deeper appeal.

He'd shown honesty, courage, and integrity in sharing with her the horrible mistake he'd made—a mistake for which he'd taken responsibility and paid the price. They might have met in unusual circumstances, and he was carrying a load of baggage, but the butterflies in her stomach and the fast pace of her heart whenever she thought of him had her wanting to know more.

And then she remembered all the reasons why she'd remained single and unattached all these years. Love hurt. Love was painful. Tessa was a harsh reminder of how awful love could get.

Do I really want to take that risk?

Right now, she couldn't answer that.

Shane pressed the buzzer and waited for the nurse to arrive to remove the bed pan. While he was grateful to have survived the accident, it was humiliating not to be able to go independently to the bathroom. With his legs still in pulleys, he was forced to call for the nurse and have her hand him a bottle or a pan. He thought he'd hit rock bottom when he'd been forced to use the toilet in front of his cellmate. At least he'd been able to tend to his own needs in prison. Now he'd sunk to a whole new level of humiliation.

Thank God it didn't appear to faze the nurses. They'd slide the pan underneath him, pulling the curtains around his bed to give him privacy. They were just as efficient when he'd finished. He had a whole new appreciation for the hospital staff.

The door to his room opened and then he heard the curtains around his bed parting. He looked up, expecting to see the nurse, but it was Molly. He flushed with embarrassment.

"Oh, um it's you. I... I'm sorry. I'm just... Could you give me a minute?"

She frowned and then seemed to realize he was on the pan. His embarrassment deepened. Of course, she was used to dealing with people at their worst, including probably seeing bodily functions and all kinds of messes, but that didn't mean he was comfortable having her see him in such a situation.

"Oh, sorry." She looked momentarily flustered, then gathered herself. "Do you need any help?"

Her tone was casual, conversational. They could have been discussing the weather. He flushed again and looked away, feeling awkward and uncomfortable. This was far too much information to be sharing with a tentatively potential girlfriend.

"No. Please, do you mind stepping outside? I'm waiting for the nurse."

To his relief, she turned and left, closing the curtains behind her. A moment later the nurse appeared and with quiet efficiency, got him cleaned up and settled once again. She pulled back the curtains from around his bed and left.

Molly reentered the room. "All done?"

He heard the laughter in her voice and barely suppressed a groan. "Sure. Come in."

She walked up to the bed and briefly touched him on the arm as if it were the most natural thing in the world to do. His embarrassment dissolved. Her fingers were soft. She smelled so good. His injuries notwithstanding, he wished he could snag her around the waist and pull her against him, but he resisted the urge.

Whatever this was between them, it was still early days. Neither of them knew the rules of engagement or where it all might lead. In fact, as far as he knew, Molly was still in the friend zone. Still, she was with him and the bed pan incident hadn't scared her off. He guessed that was progress. It was barely half-past seven in the morning. She was dressed in her uniform. The royal blue material brought out the color of her eyes. She must have come there straight after the end of her shift.

No doubt she'd had a busy night, but she looked bright as a button. He was still trying to figure out why she'd be spending time with him at such an early hour, or at any hour for that matter. The thought filled him with warmth and confusion and a quiet kind of comfort he refused to analyze.

She set her handbag on the table. She must have had it with her before, but he hadn't noticed it. Then he started in surprise. He recognized the iconic Chanel logo. The handbag cost more than what most people made in a month. He frowned momentarily in confusion. He didn't know many paramedics who could afford such an expensive accessory. It filled him with disquiet. Then she smiled.

"Shall we start again? Good morning."

Setting aside his musings, he smiled back. "Good morning."

"How was your night?"

"Not too bad. Managed to sleep on and off. How about you?"

"Nope. No sleeping for me. It started out a bit slow, but we ended up having a busy night."

"I'm sorry."

She shrugged. "Don't be. Without the busy I'd be out of a job." She winked.

"You love it, don't you?"

She nodded and smiled. "Yep. I really do. There's nothing like the rush of adrenaline when you're on your way to a callout, particularly a serious accident. All sorts of things are running through your head. Mostly you're just hoping you can help the people in trouble."

"Is that how you felt about me?"

"Well, I didn't know it was you at the time, but yes. I got the same feeling when I was heading toward your accident."

He looked at her, hoping to convey the depth of his gratitude through his gaze. "I got lucky that afternoon."

She chuckled. "Well, I'm glad I was on duty when that call came in and I was able to help. Besides, if I hadn't been, our paths would never have crossed."

He thought about that for a moment. He wasn't necessarily a believer in fate. Shit happened and you dealt with it. But she did have a point about paths crossing.

"That's true," he said softly.

She stepped closer and squeezed his hand. His heart skipped a beat at her touch. It was clear she was a tactile person and it had been so long since he'd felt the touch of a person who cared. The nurses cared, but it was their job to do so. For the two years he'd spent in prison, he hadn't let another person come anywhere near him and had always been on his guard. Upon his release, he'd made up for his enforced celibacy, but that had been with a series of brief encounters with the sole goal being mindless pleasure. He'd been looking for nothing more than physical release, not connection.

But with Molly it felt different. Maybe opening up about his life-altering mistake had changed things. He hadn't been able to resist her caring and concern. *She* was different. He'd felt that the first time she'd spoken to him.

As if privy to his thoughts, she squeezed his hand again and then released it.

"Thank you for coming," he said, his voice husky with emotion.

She shifted slightly away, as if needing to put some distance between them. "That's okay. I wanted to see how you're doing."

A stab of disappointment filled his veins, but he kept his smile in place. "I'm doing okay."

"Have the physios been by yet?"

He groaned. "Oh, yes. They've been working on the bits of me that aren't too badly injured. Mainly getting me sitting upright and doing some deep breathing exercises."

"That will help to prevent pneumonia. It's really important to avoid that. While you're still immobile, they also need to keep the circulation going. The more blood flow into those injured areas, the better."

He grinned. "Yes, Doctor Barrington."

She poked her tongue out at him and he laughed. It felt good. And then his smile faded.

She frowned. "What is it?"

She was way too perceptive. Then again, she was a paramedic. They were paid to notice things. He grimaced and indicated his legs which were still in traction. "What if they never work again like they should?"

The admission left him feeling raw and vulnerable. The doctors had assured him the damage his legs had sustained wasn't permanent and there was an excellent chance he'd recover most if not all of his pre-injury capabilities, but what if they were wrong?

Molly's face filled with compassion. "Let's concentrate on getting them to work first. Then we'll focus on getting you back to full strength. And, so what if you're left with a limp? Some women think a limp is very sexy."

She'd lowered her voice and filled it with innuendo. He couldn't help the way his heart leaped at the look in her eyes. His pulse pounded.

"Does that include you?"

The look of alarm that flashed through her eyes filled him with disappointment. *Okay, so maybe she does really mean the friend thing...*

But then she offered him a gentle smile and stepped close enough to touch his arm again. "Hang in there, Shane. You're a fighter. I am too. We've got this."

The confidence in her voice and having her touch him again lifted his spirits and gave him the strength to banish the demons that haunted him in the dark of the night when the beeping of machines and the uncertainty facing him kept him sleepless. At least for now.

He gave her a shaky smile. "Thank you."

She merely inclined her head.

"You should go home," he said quietly. As much as he enjoyed her company, it was selfish of him to keep her there.

She looked at him in mock outrage. "Tired of me already?"

"Not likely. But... I feel guilty that you're here when you should be home in bed. Sleeping. You must be exhausted."

She nodded. "I am, but that's okay. Besides, I'm off for the next four days, remember?"

"But what if you get called in again?"

"It might happen, but I doubt it. The boss tries hard to give us our rostered days off."

"Well, anyway, I don't want you falling asleep behind the wheel."

She smiled. "That's not going to happen. I only live a few miles from here."

"Still…"

"Hey! I'm starting to feel like you don't want me here."

He smiled and shook his head. "I look forward to your visits. You help the time pass quicker. But I'm trying to be selfless; do the right thing."

"You're lying flat on your back in a hospital bed with two broken legs in pulleys. You're allowed to be selfish. I'll head home soon. Promise. Right after I feed Garfield and check on your plants." She winked.

"Molly!" he protested.

"Hey! It's no trouble. I haven't been there since yesterday. The poor little kitty must be starving!"

"Ha! Hardly little. He's a big boy and no doubt can take care of himself for a while. I'm sure he's fine."

Molly merely shrugged. She collected her handbag and slipped it over her shoulder. Then she surprised him by leaning across the bed and briefly cupping his cheek. "Be good. I'll see you later. Maybe this afternoon."

The feel of her touch lingered long after she'd left. A part of him wished it had been her lips, but that was ridiculous. Early days, he reminded himself. He had a long way to go to convince her they could be more than friends. Still, he couldn't resist lifting his hand and pressing his fingers against the spot, sure he could still feel the warmth of her touch. And then he cursed.

Such feelings were dangerous. What happened if he managed to convince her they'd make a good couple and then she got bored with the novelty of dating an ex-con and moved on? He had a hard road ahead and he needed to focus on getting back on his feet—literally. He couldn't afford to have his heart broken along with his body, no matter how much he wanted her.

The kind of women who carried Chanel handbags didn't go out with ex-criminals. No, they dated doctors and lawyers and wealthy businessmen. He didn't know much about her family, but the handbag had been a wakeup call. It had confirmed his earlier impressions—her poise, her confidence, the way she carried herself... All of that screamed she was more than simply a paramedic. She was out of his league.

Since the time he'd been incarcerated, he hadn't received a single paycheck. He'd managed to keep up his mortgage payments by using his savings and had been living on his fast-dwindling bank balance since he'd gotten out. But it was obvious Molly was used to the best and right now, there was no way he could manage that; he might never manage that again. It was lucky his extended stay in hospital wasn't costing him anything. Thank God for a public health system that supported free medical care for everyone.

He should be dissuading Molly from visiting rather than encouraging her with his pathetic situation, but bastard that he was, he couldn't bring himself to do it. She was a balm to his pain and brought sunshine to his world of gray. He wanted to bask in her goodness and warmth just a little longer.

No harm in that, right?

Chapter Ten

M olly let herself into Shane's apartment and was greeted by the sight of Garfield seated on the floor on the other side of the kitchen near his empty food and water bowls, watching her.

"Are you hungry, mate?"

The cat didn't respond, but neither did he move away as she walked farther into the kitchen. She poured cat food into his bowl and refilled his water bowl. He rumbled at her and she left him to it, stepping outside to refresh his kitty litter. The sun was bright and warm on her face as she turned and looked up at the sky. A perfect blue with only a scattering of puffy white clouds to add interest to its serenity. She checked the plants, but the soil was still moist, so she left their watering for another time. After all, it had hardly been twenty-four hours since her last visit.

She enjoyed the feeling of helping Shane like this. It selfishly made her feel closer to him, more important. He needed someone to do it. He could have asked Flynn, but he hadn't. Though he'd given the excuse that Flynn lived in the city, she preferred to think he wanted to ask her.

She was well aware she'd forced herself into his life. She needed to tread carefully and not push too hard. He was going through an incredibly tough time. Besides, she was only interested in being his friend. She needed to remember that.

So why did she keep touching him? Flirting, even. That comment about a limp being sexy... Her face flamed at the memory. She was giving him mixed signals and that wasn't fair. Still, the way he'd looked at her when she'd made that comment...

She brought her hands up to her face in an effort to cool her cheeks down. She had no business getting hot and bothered over him. Over any man. Had she forgotten already her fear of commitment? Of risking a broken heart? No. So, no more flirting with Shane Lucas. Period.

With a sigh, she reentered the apartment and locked the French doors behind her. With a murmured farewell to Garfield, whose eyes cut sideways in her direction momentarily before returning to his food, she left and headed for home. Arriving at her apartment less than ten minutes later, she pulled into her allotted parking space. She climbed out of her car and strode through to the stairwell.

Two floors up, she unlocked her front door and made her way down the short corridor and into her open plan kitchen and living room. Dropping her keys and handbag on the kitchen counter, she unlaced her boots and toed them off. She was half undressed by the time she reached her bedroom. The effects of her long and busy night were catching up with her. Suddenly, the thought of a hot shower followed by a sleep in her comfortable bed was too much to resist.

Molly woke up hours later feeling rested and refreshed. She reached for her phone and checked the screen.

Four-fifteen.

She'd slept for more than seven hours. No wonder she felt great. She stretched her arms above her head and immediately thought of Shane. Such a simple, automatic movement that was currently beyond him. How hard and frustrating it must be for him! The size of his chest indicated he was used to physical exercise. Now he was confined to a bed, attached to pulleys and in constant pain. He couldn't even go to the bathroom in the usual way and without assistance.

She hadn't meant to embarrass him by walking in on him in the middle of doing his business. She hadn't given the closed curtains too much thought. She probably should have, but she was used to opening closed hospital curtains. It went hand in hand with her job. She thought it endearing that he'd been self-conscious. That was a good thing. It meant he hadn't lost touch with his humanity—a real risk for those who'd been incarcerated where privacy was non-existent and hard shells of indifference developed quickly in order to survive.

She was curious about how he'd coped in jail and whether he still had flashbacks. It had been twelve months since his release, but memories were enduring. He might have lost two years of his life in prison, but from her interactions with him, she knew the circumstances that had put him there would be a life sentence in his mind. An incredible weight even for the strongest of men. She wondered if encouraging him to talk about it might lessen his burden. Of course, chances were, he'd tell her to back off, and probably not in a nice way, but it was worth a try.

She climbed out of bed, took a quick shower and dressed. After heading into the kitchen, she made herself a ham and cheese sandwich and a cup of coffee. While she munched on her late lunch, she flicked through yesterday's newspaper which she had delivered daily.

On the fifth page, she found a small story on Shane's accident. According to the journalist, the police were still making inquiries and were urging people who might have witnessed the accident or have dash-cam footage to come forward. At least they were still working to track down the perpetrator.

After cleaning up her lunch things, she freshened her makeup, ran a brush through her hair and then collected her keys and handbag. On her way out the door, she spied a pile of board games she had stacked on a shelf near the television. She'd had some of them for years. She loved board games. She had many a fond memory of nights spent with her family and friends playing board games.

On impulse, she pulled out her favorite and tucked it under her arm. She smiled. There was nothing like a boisterous game of Monopoly to bring out someone's true character. She couldn't think of a more excellent way for her and Shane to get to know each other better. How he handled winning and losing would be a good measure of his character. Whether he had the ability to have fun was another. She just hoped she didn't scare him off with her competitive streak.

Shane was bored and irritable. His daily session with the hospital physio had left him feeling weak and exhausted and they'd barely done more than a few simple upper body exercises and some deep breathing tasks. He'd always been athletic, fit, strong, and able to take on any physical challenge he set his mind to. It was frustrating to see his strength depleted to almost embarrassing levels and in such a short time.

Of course, the pain in his legs and chest meant that doing anything too exuberant was out of the question. His enforced immobility meant that the medical staff were still concerned about blood clots. None of that made it any easier to accept. He chafed at the limitations the accident had placed on his ability to do the most basic of things. Like going to the toilet.

Hell. That had been so embarrassing, having Molly walk in on him like that. It was only one of many embarrassments he was learning to accept. There was no such thing as modesty being in hospital. Being so reliant on others to carry out the smallest of tasks, including attending to basic bodily functions, was going to be his lot for some time to come if today was any indication. It was going to be a long, hard journey back to good health.

He supposed he ought to be thankful he was still alive. From what the police and the doctors had told him, he could have easily been killed. If it hadn't been for his seatbelt and the airbag...

Knowing that the person who'd hit him was still out there—might even get away with it—filled him with anger. He might have wished he were dead when it had first happened, but now he wanted his life back. He couldn't help but remember how he'd once been in that position too. He could have driven away from the scene of the crime and no one would have been the wiser.

But he'd manned up—done the right thing and taken responsibility. He'd had his life put on hold for two years and had done his time in jail. The memories of that time would haunt him forever. Now the fact someone found themselves in similar circumstances and was unwilling to come forward and take responsibility—might even walk away scot-free—seemed grossly unfair.

The door to his room swung inward and Molly filled the opening. His heart skipped a beat and then rapped out a staccato rhythm against his chest, which was both welcome and irritating. He couldn't help the goofy grin that spread across his face.

I'm such an idiot. We're just friends, remember? What happened to my earlier pep talk?

She was dressed casually in jeans and a tight T-shirt that clung to her high breasts. Her figure was so much more on display than in her unisex uniform. This Molly was incredibly appealing. She smiled when she saw he was awake

"Hi, you."

He lifted a hand and gave her a weak wave. "Hi." He continued to grin like an idiot.

"You're looking better. How are you feeling?" she asked, moving toward the bed.

"Not too bad." He looked down at her hands. "What have you got there?"

She set a board game down on the table beside his bed. He glanced at it and his eyes widened. "Monopoly?"

She eyed him challengingly. "Scared?"

He chuckled. It felt good to laugh. "It might have been the drugs making me remember things incorrectly, but didn't you tell me you only play to win?"

Her brow furrowed as if in thought, but there was a twinkle in her blue eyes. "I think I told you I'm competitive. Is that the same thing?"

"Absolutely."

She laughed. "You're probably right. In fact, my brothers and sisters would agree. They've had the good fortune (or not) to play with me many times over the years."

He grinned, enjoying their banter. "And do you always win?"

Her eyes gleamed. "Always."

He held her gaze. "Challenge accepted."

With his pain momentarily forgotten, he felt an unexpected surge of anticipation. This was going to be fun. He looked forward to spending time with this beautiful woman and doing his best to beat her at Monopoly. He might even be able to sneak under her defenses and make her see they could have fun together.

"Shall I set up a game?" she asked.

He indicated the table in front of him. "By all means. Let's get it on." He gave her a deliberate look, but she was too intent on setting up the board.

The cardboard box was battered and worn and looked like it had been handled many times. The paper money, though clean and in order, wasn't as crisp as it had once been. It was obvious the game had been played more than once and he was starting to relish the opportunity to test her mettle. Had he mentioned he was competitive too?

The first time she'd talked about playing Monopoly, he'd been wracked with pain and begging God to let him die. Less than a week after his accident and he was ready to take her on at a game she obviously loved and hoping to impress her in the meantime. Dying was the farthest thing from his mind. Life could be so strange.

"I'll be the banker," she announced, shooting him a look that dared him to disagree.

He merely shrugged. He wasn't up to being banker. In fact, he wasn't sure how long he'd last playing the game before his small reserves of energy would fade and he'd be forced to rest. Not that he'd admit such weakness to Molly. He wanted her to think of him as a formidable opponent in the game about to unfold.

I'm an idiot. She's a paramedic. She knows how badly I was injured. She must know I feel as weak as a day-old kitten, no matter how much bravado I exude. In fact, she probably expects me to doze off halfway through...

The thought made him sit up a little straighter. He was going for the ultimate bluff. He didn't want her to know that already he was tiring. The earlier session with the physio had really taken it out of him. But if Molly had even an inkling of how he felt, she'd pack up the board game and leave, taking all the fun and sunshine with her.

"If you're going to be the banker, then I get the race car token," he said with a grin.

"Oh, you do play rough!" she teased. "The car it is."

She reached for the playing piece and placed it on "Go". He noticed she chose the thimble for herself.

"So, you like the thimble?"

She pulled a face. "Actually, I usually go for the race car, but...you know. I can't have things all my own way. At least, not yet. I'm trying to play nice."

She followed through with a wry grin that lit up her eyes. He was once again reminded how beautiful she was. He had to forcibly drag his gaze away when she handed him the dice and suggested they toss for who would go first.

And so, the game progressed with much teasing and laughter. Shane had a run of luck, managing to land on some of the more lucrative pieces of real estate, all of which he promptly bought. When Molly landed on one of his properties and was forced to hand over three hundred dollars, she poked her tongue out at him before grudgingly handing over the cash.

"It's not fair that you own the most expensive lots on the board," she grumbled.

Shane merely laughed. "Who says?"

She grinned. "*I* say."

He gave her a knowing grin. "I think Molly Barrington isn't used to losing."

She rolled her eyes and chuckled. "Who said I was losing? The game isn't over yet, buddy. You'd better watch yourself."

"*Oooh*, I'm so scared!" he joked.

She narrowed her eyes at him, but as she turned her attention back to the board, he caught the smile on her lips.

Shane shook the dice and moved his token the allotted number of spaces. As he counted, he realized with a sick kind of feeling he was going to land in jail. Even though it was only a board game, the dread in his gut was real. Dragging in a deep breath, he counted the last stop and placed his race car on the space.

"Ha! I told you so! Now you're stuck in jail!"

Molly looked at him with a gleeful expression that slowly died when she noticed the look on his face.

"Oh, Shane! I'm sorry. I was joking. I didn't mean to upset you."

He brushed away her apology, embarrassed by his reaction. Hell, he'd been out of jail for a year. He ought to have gotten over it by now. The truth was, he probably wouldn't ever get over it. It had been the worst two years of his life. The ever-present threat of physical violence and the constant noise had been enough, but the feeling of being locked in had been suffocating.

He'd felt caged. Like a dangerous animal. Panic had taken hold the moment he'd entered the prison and he probably would have broken down right there and then in the processing area if it hadn't been for a guard who'd recognized what he was going through.

"First time, right?" the guard had said not unsympathetically.

Shane had been breathing hard, disbelieving of his circumstances, and praying for the nightmare to be over. The guard had talked him through what would happen next. It had helped, but only a little. He'd spent most of his time in jail on edge. That kind of constant hypervigilance took it out of a man. Twelve months out and he still had trouble sleeping through the night.

As if from a distance, he heard a groan of distress and realized belatedly it was coming from him.

"Shane? Are you okay? Shane?"

Molly's concerned features swam back into focus as he struggled to push the memories aside. He blinked and swallowed and unclenched his fists and did his best to force a smile.

"Molly. I'm fine. Sorry. I…" He shrugged helplessly. "Bad memories. Maybe you should go."

"Do you want to talk about it?" she asked gently, ignoring his last comment.

He opened his mouth to tell her no and reiterate that she should go, but found himself instead lost in the concern and compassion on her sweet face. Then he realized he *did* want to talk about it. To unburden himself. To rid himself of the constant weight on his chest. He hadn't talked about his incarceration with anyone, not even Flynn, who'd been there to collect him from the jail on the day of his release.

"I... I..."

"It's okay, Shane. I'm on your side. I already admire you for having the courage to take responsibility for your actions. If talking about it will help, I'm here to listen. No judgment. Talk or don't. Your call."

As he lay there looking at her, it wasn't so much her quiet words chipping away at the wall he'd built around himself over the years since that fateful night, but more the sincerity he heard in her voice that had those walls crumbling. He had a terrible urge to cry, but instead he began to speak.

Haltingly and battling with his emotions, he told her about that first night in the lock up.

"I was scared out of my wits. I'd just killed somebody, albeit accidentally. I'd confessed everything to the police. I was a lawyer and I should have known better. I should have refused to do an interview. I should have kept my mouth shut and had my lawyer do the talking. But I couldn't help it. I had to take responsibility for what I'd done."

"Did you ask to see a lawyer before you talked to the police?"

"No. I waived my right to legal counsel. I knew if I involved lawyers, they'd try to talk to me out of giving an interview to the police. I didn't want to refuse to answer questions and have the lawyers intervene. The feeling of guilt was all-consuming. I wanted to come clean. I needed to unburden." He looked up at her. "Does that make sense?"

She regarded him with a somber expression, her eyes filled with compassion. "Of course. You wanted to do the right thing because you're a good man."

"If I had more energy, I'd dispute the "good man" bit, but yes. I wanted to do the right thing."

He drew in a ragged breath and continued. "That first night in the jail was a nightmare. The noise was deafening and never-ending. The clanging of the gates sliding shut, the shouts and cries of the inmates. The banging on the cell doors, the foul language. It went on for what seemed like hours and hours and the whole time I quaked with fear. But I also knew I had to keep my wits about me, particularly because I was a lawyer, and never let my feelings show. I learned quickly that everyone inside was fair game.

"An inmate can sense weakness, like a lion its prey. They smell your fear before they see it. I knew if I was to survive inside, I needed to dig deep, find my courage, and meet the challenge head-on."

"That must have been incredibly hard," Molly murmured.

Shane's answering smile felt more like a grimace. "You bet. The hardest thing I'd ever done. When those gates closed for the first time behind me, I felt trapped. Endlessly falling into a black hole. I wasn't sure if I'd ever make my way back. There was a moment when sanity met insanity. I knew the only way to make it was to be strong and project an image of not giving a fuck, if you'll excuse the language."

"I can't imagine how that must have felt," Molly whispered.

"No. And I'm glad you can't. I wouldn't wish that feeling on my worst enemy."

His bark of laughter sounded harsh in the silence. "Until that moment, I'd never thought about what it was like to be free; never appreciated my liberty. To be able to come and go as I pleased. To have the right to make all my own decisions, to make a hundred different choices a day, to walk wherever I wanted, when I wanted. Even my mealtimes and meals were dictated. I was helpless, scared, angry, but mostly terrified that first night. All I wanted was to curl up in a ball and pretend I was somewhere else."

Molly reached out and covered his hand with hers. He took comfort from the small gesture and tried to ignore the ache of longing. What he wouldn't have given to have someone care about him while he was doing time. A visitor like Molly would have given him strength. But then, he wouldn't have wanted to taint her with such an experience.

"How did you cope?" she asked quietly.

He drew in a shuddering breath. Though it was difficult to revisit the traumatic memories, a strange compulsion kept him going. He was now determined to tell her all and let the chips fall where they may.

He shot her a wry smile. "This is going to sound like a trite cliché, but it's the truth. I found God."

Her eyes widened in surprise. He could tell it was the last thing she'd expected him to say.

"Wow. Seriously?" she murmured.

"Well, not God exactly. I found Father Damian. He was the prison chaplain. He helped me through the darkness. Kept me focused on the rightness of the decision I'd made. Somehow, he always knew what to say to help me get through another day, another week, another month."

He saw her expression and offered her a rueful grin. "Don't worry. I'm not so enamored with the whole thing that I'm headed for the priesthood, but faith really helped me do my time."

"Were you religious before the accident?"

"I wouldn't say religious. I was baptized a Catholic, but I'd drifted away from the church as I entered my teenage years. My parents were regular church-goers and insisted I join them every Sunday for Mass, but after I left home, I stopped going. I hadn't stepped foot inside a church for years before prison."

"Thank God for Father Damian. I'm glad you found someone to help you," Molly said.

Shane nodded. "Yeah. Though I came out still feeling pretty dark about the world."

"What about your family? Your parents? Your sister? Did they know?"

"Yes. They wanted to come out and support me through the trial, but I told them there was no need. I was pleading guilty. There would be no trial."

"What about while you were in jail? Did they visit you at all?"

"No. I didn't want them to. I didn't want them to see me in that place. They were upset about my decision, but it was mine to make and they couldn't budge me."

Molly looked like she wanted to say more but remained silent. Then she asked, "How does having been in jail still affect you?"

He thought for a moment. "It makes me appreciate the little things. The sky, the stars, the ocean breeze. The peace and quiet of a balmy summer evening. The majesty and power of a storm. All these things I never noticed before. And to borrow another cliché, you really don't know what you have until it's gone.

"It also made me want to do more with my life. To give back. I know that sounds corny and trite, but it's a feeling that has since driven me. Though I was born and grew up in the UK, Australia's now my home. After my release, with the help of Flynn, I enlisted as a volunteer at a soup kitchen in the city. It's run by Callum Craigdon. He's Flynn's cousin. You probably know him."

Molly nodded and smiled. "Yes, I know Callum. And his wife, Grace. They're both beautiful people doing so much good for the less fortunate. Did you know Callum was on his way to becoming a priest before he met Grace?"

Shane smiled with delight. "Really? I didn't know that. Wow. That's... Wow."

"Yes. I don't know all the details, but Callum spent several years in the seminary before he changed the direction of his life. From what I hear, it's a decision he's never regretted."

"Again, wow. Sounds like we've both been given the opportunity to change direction and have a second chance at life. Now it's up to me to make the most of that and not blow it."

She nodded. "It's all about living our best lives. Living fearlessly. Or at least, trying to. Some days I'm not sure that I'm succeeding, but I still try."

Shane looked at her with disbelief. "Are you kidding? You save people's lives! How can that not be living your best life?"

She merely smiled and shrugged. "Do you still attend church?"

"Sometimes. I found a little church not far from where I live. It reminds me a bit of the chapel in the prison. Cool, dark, quiet. Lots of beautiful stained glass. And the priest is a champion. He's not Father Damian, but he's easy to talk to and a good listener. He's helped me a good deal in my efforts to put the trauma of everything that happened behind me. I know it'll never completely leave, but it continues to lessen each time I make a conscious effort to work through it."

Molly smiled with understanding and then came alert. "Does your local priest know you're here?"

"No. I lost my phone somewhere in my car. I haven't been able to call anyone."

"I'm happy to make some calls for you, or even get you another phone. Now that you're feeling better, I'm sure there are plenty of people you want to talk to."

Shane shook his head. "I couldn't ask you to do that."

"You didn't ask. I offered. No more arguments. I'll swing by the shops and pick you up a phone tomorrow and you can download your contacts from the cloud, assuming you saved them. If you're anything like me, you won't remember anyone's number. How's that sound?"

Emotion threatened to overwhelm him. "That sounds great," he choked. "Keep the receipt. I'll cover the cost."

Molly winked. "Of course, but it's not like you can do a runner. After all, I know where to find you."

Chapter Eleven

Molly's heart fluttered with anticipation as she parked her car in the hospital's visitor's carpark and headed for the orthopedic ward. It had been more than a week since she and Shane had played Monopoly and he'd told her about his time in jail. His willingness to share something so personal had initially taken her by surprise, but she was pleased that he had. It was a moment of shared trust and it made her feel special.

Oh, dear. I'm doing it again. Forgetting that I have no interest in pursuing love. I have even less interest in a broken heart. Besides, Shane's been through a lot of trauma. Trusting will be hard for him... And that's if he's even interested in being more than friends...

The truth was, he'd started to chip away at her defenses. Spending time with him before or after each shift, and then on her days' off, getting to know him better, seeing him at his best when he was enjoying the challenge of her board games and at his most vulnerable when memories of his jail time raised their ugly head... It had been hard to remain unmoved. The more time she spent with him, the more she liked him. She was terrified she might be falling for him.

Oh, God. How did I get here?

She ought to take a step back for her own protection, but somehow that intention went right out the window whenever she was with him. All he had to do was give her that smile that lit up his green eyes and she was gone, gone, gone. *So gone.*

Almost as bad was her growing affection for his surly cat. She and Garfield weren't exactly besties, but the cat had begun looking out for her, meowing a greeting when he spied her in the doorway from where he sat by his bowls.

He'd patiently wait for her to fill them and when he was done eating and drinking, he'd find her out in the courtyard watering Shane's plants and rub himself against her legs. He hadn't yet allowed her to pick him up and stroke him, but she was sure they'd get to that point before too long. She wasn't normally a cat person, but strangely found herself looking forward to her encounters with the taciturn and wary Garfield.

Feeding his cat, watering his plants, collecting his mail, and doing his laundry also made her feel closer to Shane. The earlier "stalkerish" feeling was gone. She was doing her bit to help, with his blessing. If only she could help with his physical recovery.

There was no doubt it was slow going. Though the physio was helping, she could tell how frustrated Shane was at not being able to do all the things he used to before the accident. He'd told her how he'd enjoyed so many sports and had led an athletic life. He'd worked out to maintain his fitness and enjoyed working up a sweat in the gym.

Secretly, she found it hard to believe anyone could enjoy working out. She forced herself to the gym three times a week out of a need to stay fit and healthy for work, but she couldn't say she enjoyed it. It was a means to an end; something she had to do to maintain the level of fitness required for her work. Nothing more. Though she'd heard about people like Shane who looked forward to the dopamine hit they got from a good workout, she'd given up on that ever happening to her.

Still, she understood how difficult it must be for someone who was used to being active to be laid up in a bed. Though the pulleys had been removed, his legs were still encased in plaster and he was unable to walk. The doctors warned him it would be another three or four weeks at least before his bones had healed enough to let him bear weight. She'd need to find him a distraction to help with the waiting time.

She rode the lift to the orthopedic ward. The closer she got to Shane, the more the butterflies swarmed in her stomach. She thought about him all the time. When she was at home, cooking dinner, taking a shower, at work. It was ridiculous and making it that much harder to remember why she only wanted to be friends.

She wished she knew how Shane felt. That might make things easier. Taking a leap of faith with her heart wouldn't be so terrifying if she had a soft place to fall. He was focused on getting well, which was how it should be, and he seemed to enjoy her company, but was that all?

The looks, the teasing, the shared laughter. The catch of breath if their hands accidentally touched. She'd seen the way he looked at her when he thought she wasn't aware. With admiration and desire. It was a long way from the man who'd ordered her to leave a couple of weeks earlier. And while she had no crystal ball, she eagerly anticipated the time when he was back on his feet.

Does this mean I'm actually considering him as a potential boyfriend? Am I brave enough to throw caution to the wind and go for it?

The truth was, she wasn't sure, but she had a growing suspicion that if anyone could push her through her fear of commitment, it was Shane. That revelation filled her with equal parts terror and anticipation.

Shane lay on his hospital bed and tried to ignore the dull ache in his legs. The nurse had been by only a short time ago to administer some pain relief, but it only ever took the edge off. He couldn't help but wonder if he'd be in pain for the rest of his life. And then he was immediately disappointed in himself for thinking like that.

He was alive, wasn't he? The doctors had assured him that with hard work and a lot of physical therapy, he'd walk again. As soon as his bones had mended enough for him to weight bear, they could start the therapy with a vengeance.

Great. More pain.

No, pain was good. Pain meant he was putting his injured limbs to work and forcing them to perform and each day he did that was a day closer to when he'd walk again. At least, that was the plan.

As much as he wanted to get back on his feet again and return to the life he had before the accident, he also wanted to walk for Molly. She'd been so wonderful, visiting him whenever she could, feeding Garfield, watering his plants, washing his clothes, and returning them to him fresh and clean and smelling faintly of flowers. He needed to ask her what she'd done with his washing powder!

Between her work and all the other stuff she did, she must have hardly any time to herself.

She was always spending time with him. Not that he was complaining. Her visits were the only bright spot in his otherwise long and difficult days. But he kept waiting for the other shoe to drop. As much as he harbored a secret desire for her to see him as a man, he didn't understand what she saw in an ex-con. A good part of him still didn't feel worthy of her care and attention and though he longed for her to feel attracted to him, he was equally terrified she'd wake up one day and feel exactly that way.

Shit. I'm so gone...

The door to his room swung inward. He looked up with anticipation, expecting to see Molly filling the opening. Instead, it was two men wearing somber suits and expressions to match. Shane immediately guessed they were detectives. They had that look about them. His gut clenched reflexively, like it always did when he was around the police. He forced himself to relax.

"Can I help you?" he asked, hitting the button to raise the top part of his bed to an upright position.

They walked farther into the room. One looked to be in his fifties—drawn face, tired, world-weary eyes. The other was younger and more enthusiastic. He nodded hello to Shane.

"We're Detectives Brown and Sabattini. We've been investigating the hit and run you were involved in a couple of weeks ago."

Shane acknowledged Brown's greeting with a nod. "So, how's it going? Any leads?"

From their somber demeanor, he guessed it wasn't going so well. The younger detective confirmed that with his next words.

"We've managed to capture CCTV footage of the vehicle that collided with yours. It's a late model silver Toyota Landcruiser, but unfortunately, the footage isn't good enough to get a picture of the registration plate."

"So, you don't have shit. Is that what you're trying to tell me?"

The older detective merely grunted. Brown tried a bit harder. "I wouldn't say that. We've sent the footage to our forensic department. They have specialist technicians and equipment which can magnify detail we can't see on a standard computer screen. We're reasonably hopeful they might come up with a plate."

Shane gave them an unimpressed look. "I see. And if you don't get a plate?"

The young cop compressed his lips. "Then I guess we'll have to hope someone comes forward. The car that hit you would have sustained substantial damage. We've put out a call to all the smash repairers and garages in the immediate vicinity, asking for them to contact us if they get a car that fits the description of the one involved in the crash. Of course, there's no guarantee the driver was from around these parts. They could have been traveling through."

"In which case we'll never know who hit me," Shane muttered.

A movement at the open doorway caught his attention. He looked up and saw Molly. Pleasure and relief poured through him. He relaxed against the sheets and looked pointedly at the detectives.

"Are we done? My girlfriend's here for a visit. I'd appreciate it if you would leave."

Their faces expressed surprise. They turned and briefly eyed Molly before murmuring their goodbyes. Brown promised they'd keep him informed of any developments. After they left the room, Molly drew closer. He couldn't read her expression. She looked nervous. Then she quickly leaned closer and pressed a kiss against his cheek.

He tensed in momentary surprise and was then flooded with hope. When she pulled back, her cheeks were rosy and she wouldn't meet his gaze.

"So, I'm your girlfriend, am I?"

He blushed and averted his gaze. His comment had been entirely presumptuous and said mainly to get the detectives out of his room. He'd also wanted to make clear to them that, despite the fact he'd done time, there was a beautiful girl in his life.

But now he might have ruined everything. Though Molly didn't appear annoyed, neither was she brimming with happiness. They'd been growing closer over the past couple of weeks, but they hadn't had any discussions about their growing relationship, or whether they'd progressed out of the friend zone. Nothing like a bit of drama to speed up the process. Nerves bounced around his stomach.

Aware that she waited for his answer, he forced himself to look at her. "Sorry about that. I didn't mean to put you on the spot. It was unfair. But I was pissed at them. The detectives. They came in here all rude and condescending. It wasn't so much what they said, but their attitude. Like the screws were in prison. It still gets to me."

She nodded. "Sure. I understand. So, it was only for their sake then. Is that what you're saying?"

Something in her tone made him frown. He looked at her, searching her gaze for some indication of how she really felt. He cursed under his breath. He'd never been good at reading women. Better to just ask her straight out.

"I like you, Molly. I like you a lot. You said you only wanted to be friends, but I want more than that. Does that change things between us?"

When she remained silent, he cursed again, louder this time. "I'm sorry, Molly. I had no right to ask you that. I'm an ex-con. I have nothing to offer you. You wanted to be my friend and you have. The best friend I could want. Now I've gone and ruined everything by wanting more. I'm sorry," he said again, at a loss.

Her cheeks turned an adorable pink. She worried at her bottom lip. She pulled at a loose thread on his bedspread. She looked even more nervous. He looked away, unable to bear witness to her rejection.

Just get it over with... Tell me we're done. It was fun for a while, but now you're moving on... Getting on with your life, without me...

It was all that he expected, all that he deserved. He wanted to rail against the injustice of it.

Why couldn't I have met her before? When I still had something to offer her? Before one stupid decision turned my life upside down and changed it forever...

When she finally spoke, her gaze was fixed on her hands, her voice rough with emotion.

"All of my life, I've been afraid of falling in love. My mother had a bad experience when she was young. What she told me about it weighed on my mind. My fear of having a similar experience has prevented me from having relationships. It's interfered in so many ways. I've been terrified of commitment. Terrified of getting a broken heart. So, I've kept my distance from men. I've never let myself get close enough to anyone to risk falling in love.

"But from the moment I met you, something changed. We had an indefinable connection. I didn't know if it was because of the traumatic circumstances, or something else. I didn't even know if it was real. And it frightened me. All my life, I steered clear of emotional entanglements, but here you were, hurt, alone, and in need of a friend. I told myself I could do friendship. Friends are good. Friends are safe."

She dragged her gaze up to his. Her eyes were dark with turmoil. "But there was nothing safe about you. About the way you make me feel. I've been fighting it every moment we've been together, telling myself there's nothing between us, nothing but friendship... But that's a lie and it scares the hell out of me."

She shook her head, looking panicked. "I don't know what to do with these feelings. I don't know if you feel the same way. It's been driving me crazy, all the questions... Not knowing if I have the courage to take the next step...."

He hadn't realized he'd stopped breathing until his body forced him to take another breath. He filled his lungs on a gasp.

"You want to know how I feel?" he rasped. "I feel so many things. I couldn't believe someone as good and kind and beautiful as you could come into my life. Me. A poor sinner. An ex-con. I had nothing to offer you, but my stupid brain refused to give up hope. And that's what I feel for you, Molly. When I look at you, my heart's filled with hope."

He swallowed against a lump of emotion. "I want to be a better man for you. I want to be the man you deserve. I want more than friendship from you, Molly. That scares me too. I'm scared I won't live up to your expectations, that I'll fall short of the man you want. That one day you'll realize this was all a mistake."

His bark of laughter was harsh. "See how far I was getting away from myself? I'd let myself hope that someday you'd want to be with me, but worried that eventually you'd work out the truth. You could do so much better than me."

She reached out and cupped his cheek. The tenderness in her eyes stole his breath.

"Stop," she said. "Don't say anything else. You're talking nonsense. I like you, Shane. I like you a lot. Warts and all. Being an ex-con doesn't scare me off. Hearing you say you don't deserve me pisses me off. Let me be the judge of that. If I'm prepared to hold on to my courage and take that leap of faith, do you think I'd do it with a man who didn't deserve me?"

He stared at her. Something very close to happiness surged through him. After the dark years of prison, he didn't think he'd ever feel close to happy again. But this kind, compassionate and beautiful woman kept coming back to see him and bringing her special brand of sunshine. More than that, she wanted more than friendship. He needed to trust that she knew what she was doing in wanting to be with someone like him.

He patted the bed beside him and she perched on the edge of the mattress. Their gazes locked and held. Once again, she looked nervous. She averted her gaze and licked her lips and for once, didn't appear to have anything to say.

His heart pounded. His mouth went dry. He stared at her, drinking in every beautiful inch of her. He couldn't find any words either. And then her eyes widened and her lips parted on a sigh. The tension in her body eased. It was as if she'd come to a decision. That was more than enough for him. He reached up and tangled his hand in her loose hair. The brown waves felt soft and silky against his skin. She tilted her head toward him and he took the opportunity to slowly lean forward and press a soft kiss against her lips.

Though passion simmered just below the surface, he took care to keep it under tight control. She kissed like a novice, slow and uncertain and slightly awkward. Of course, his position in the bed didn't help matters. He didn't know anything about her previous sexual experience, but he was betting it wasn't much. The thought brought out his protective instincts. He fought against the urge to wrap her in his arms and kiss her senseless.

Instead, he pulled back slowly. Though it had been a relatively chaste kiss, she looked as dazed as he felt. She touched her fingers to her lips and smiled. "Wow."

He smiled tenderly. "Yes. Wow."

"That was…"

"Amazing? Wonderful? The best kiss I've ever had?"

She blushed and laughed. "All of the above, at least for me."

He drew her closer again and this time gave some of his passion free rein. This time he kissed her slow and deep. When they finally pulled apart, both were breathing hard.

"Now that was definitely the best kiss I've ever had," she sighed. "Why have I resisted this for so long? Can we do it again?"

He laughed and squeezed her shoulders, wishing he could pull her close. "Soon, but I need to get my breath back. You've worn me out!" he teased.

She smiled widely and then shifted to sit in the chair beside him. "So, why were the police here?"

"They were giving me an update on the investigation."

She brightened. "Any news? Have they found the culprit yet?"

"They have CCTV footage of the vehicle, but that's it. Unfortunately, it's a popular make and model—a Toyota

Landcruiser—and the footage isn't clear enough for them to get a registration plate."

"Oh, how frustrating," Molly said, looking disappointed.

"Yeah. They said they have some specialist department looking at the footage to see if they can't enhance it enough to decipher the number plate. If that doesn't work, they're pinning their hopes on a witness with dash-cam footage or the perpetrator coming forward."

"I still can't believe there's someone out there who hit you and hasn't gone to the police. What kind of person does that? I mean, look at you! You hit that cyclist in the middle of the night. A quiet suburban street like that was unlikely to be guarded by security cameras. There was nobody else around. You could have easily snuck away from the scene, and nobody would have been the wiser. And yet you didn't. You did the right thing, the courageous thing, and turned yourself in."

She reached out and threaded her fingers through his, looking him squarely in the face with eyes that were wide and clear.

"When you first told me about that, I learned everything I needed to know about you. You're an innately honest man with a clear sense of right and wrong and an understanding of the importance of justice. Most people would struggle with that if their own liberty was on the line."

She paused and then released his hand. She leaned forward and framed his face with her hands. "I'm so proud of you."

Chapter Twelve

Molly floated through another day shift and could hardly keep the smile off her face.

Pinch me! I'm Shane's girlfriend! We kissed! And it was soooo good!

It was fortunate she'd been partnered with a paramedic with as much experience as Tessa, because Molly could hardly keep her mind on the job. It was also lucky they hadn't been called out to anything more serious than a couple of heart attacks (although they were always serious), a fall from a roof, a child who'd come off his bike and was concussed, and an elderly man who'd pulled a muscle in his back and gotten stuck on the toilet. She and Tessa had managed the various callouts without any additional drama and were now restocking the ambulance in anticipation of the next emergency. The good thing was, their shift was almost over.

At the thought of seeing Shane again soon, Molly was filled with anticipation. She planned to stop by his apartment and feed Garfield and water the plants and then she'd drive over to the hospital and spend as much time as she could with him before she had to leave for a family dinner. Normally she'd always be up for a get together with her family, but now it was cutting into Shane-time.

Her mother had called a few nights earlier and requested her presence. Unfortunately, Molly had already confirmed her shift would finish at six on the nominated evening. She was disappointed she'd have to cut her visit with Shane short. The thought brought a wry smile to her lips.

"What are you smiling about?" Tessa asked as she handed Molly a cup of coffee.

Embarrassment exploded across Molly's face. She took the cup gratefully and buried her nose in the steam. At the same time, she murmured her thanks and hoped like crazy Tessa wouldn't pursue an answer to her question. To her relief, Tessa dropped into an armchair with her own cup of coffee and sighed.

"Another hour and we're out of here," Tessa said.

"Here's cheers to that," Molly chuckled and briefly raised her cup.

Tessa sipped from her drink. "What are you doing after work? Got any plans?"

Molly's face heated again, but then she paused. She wasn't quite sure why she hadn't yet shared with Tessa her burgeoning relationship with Shane. They spent a lot of time together. The woman was one of her closest friends.

In fact, apart from the rant she'd had with Charlotte, she hadn't shared the details of her new relationship with anyone. The only person who was aware she even knew Shane was Flynn Craigdon and he wasn't about to say anything. He didn't know they'd grown closer. Which was fine. Their relationship was still so new. She wasn't sure she was ready to share with even her nearest and dearest her crush on a man who used to be her patient.

"Molly?" Tessa urged.

Taking another sip from her coffee, Molly responded. "As a matter of fact, I'm driving to Broken for a family dinner." She paused and came to a decision. "Before that, I'm heading over to the hospital to visit a friend. I've been helping him out while he's recovering from an accident. Feeding his cat, watering his plants. Collecting mail. Doing laundry. His family all live overseas."

"Wow." Tessa's eyes twinkled with mischief. "He must be a good friend. Does he have a name?"

Molly fought back another blush. "Shane. Shane Lucas."

Tessa's brow wrinkled in thought. "Funny, I've worked with you for years. I don't think I've ever heard you mention anyone by that name."

Molly's embarrassment deepened. "Well, that's because he's a new friend. We only a couple of weeks ago."

Tessa's grin widened. "This is getting more and more intriguing. Tell me, is he hot?"

Molly burst out laughing. Although she hadn't set out to reveal her growing feelings for Shane, she wasn't upset that the conversation had taken a decided turn in that direction. It would feel good to talk about him, to talk about how she felt. The excitement, the butterflies she felt whenever she was near him. The way she could talk to him for hours. How when the bell signaled the end of visiting hours, she always struggled to leave.

"Come on, Molly! Spill! I can tell he's someone special. It's written all over your face. Oh, my goodness! I can't believe you've kept quiet for so long! You know I have no love life. In fact, aside from my gorgeous, demanding kids, I have no life, period. I'm forced to live vicariously through my friends. Now, tell me everything! I want all the juicy details!"

Molly laughed. "Okay, okay!" She drew in a deep breath. "So, do you remember how I told you about that car accident Benson and I attended a couple of weeks ago?"

Tessa frowned. "The hit and run?"

"Yes. Well, you see, Shane was the one who was hit. He was trapped in his car for two hours while we waited for the jaws of life. I kept an eye on his vitals and shared stories to take his mind off the pain and distract him from what was happening, but once we started talking, we formed a connection and things just went from there."

Tessa's frown deepened. "What do you mean? Are you dating one of your *patients?*"

Molly's blush intensified at her friend's incredulous tone. "Not exactly *dating*. He's still in hospital, for goodness' sake. And he ceased being my patient once I'd delivered him to the ED. We're just...getting to know each other. He told me he had no family in Australia, so I checked in on him that first night. He was in pretty bad shape. He spent the first few days in the ICU in an induced coma. It was awful to see him lying in that bed looking so close to death and knowing he had no one around who cared for him. So, I started visiting him. One thing led to another, and I now visit him every day. We're taking things slow, but... It's nice."

Tessa looked at her in disbelief. "I can't believe you visited a complete stranger. It's...weird."

Molly looked at her. "Do you think so? I don't know. I thought so at first, but we spent some pretty intense hours together waiting to free him from the wreckage. He was in so much pain and struggling to breathe. I wanted to distract him, get him thinking about something positive. I started talking to him about all kinds of stuff. You know how I am and what it's like as a paramedic trying to keep the patient focused on survival." She shrugged. "Somehow, we kind of connected. I'd never felt that way before. He confessed to me later that he felt the same way. That I'd helped him stay focused on wanting to be alive."

Tessa continued to look unconvinced. In fact, she almost looked angry. "I don't think you should have done it, Molly. He was your patient. You crossed a line."

Molly shook her head. "I disagree. Yes, he was my patient while I was tending to him at the scene of the accident, but from the time I handed him over to the ED staff, that relationship came to an end. I haven't done anything wrong."

Tessa continued to look upset. "Okay, maybe not technically. But do you really think you should be seeing him now, with a view to getting into a relationship with him?"

Molly eyed her steadily. "Yes. I do. I don't think there's anything improper about it at all. I'm not sure I understand why you do."

Tessa held her stare for a long moment and then eventually looked away. "I'm sorry, Molly. You're right. I overreacted. I'm tired and stressed and I have a lot going on at the moment." She paused and managed a strained grin. "You know what, forget I said anything. I wish you all the best with the hot patient. Lucky you. It must be nice to look forward to sharing with someone who cares at the end of each shift."

Molly's heart flooded with sympathy. The past four years since her friend's messy divorce had been tough. On top of that, Tessa had told her she still didn't have her car back and had asked for another ride home from work. While Molly was happy to help her friend, the length of time it was taking for the mechanics to fix Tessa's car was becoming ridiculous. No wonder she was stressed. Cutting her some slack, Molly relented.

"Hey, don't sweat it. I get it. I really do. And while I'm at it, I just have to say, I think it's time you started dating again. You're only in your mid-thirties and you're a gorgeous woman. There are plenty of potential Mr Rights out there just waiting to spend time with you. You've already taken the first step, setting up an account on that dating app. Now all you have to do is swipe left or right and let the fun begin." Molly winked. "Got it?"

Tessa laughed. "You make it sound so simple."

"It *is* simple," Molly insisted.

Tessa raised her hands in a sign of surrender. "Okay, okay. Enough already! I've got it."

Molly couldn't keep the smile off her face when she walked into the grand entryway of her parents' house ninety minutes south of Sydney. She was late by nearly twenty minutes, but she'd rung ahead to let them know and knew from experience the only thing she would have missed was pre-dinner drinks. Her mother greeted her with a hug and a brief peck on the cheek.

"Molly! I'm so glad you made it! Everyone but Vaughan is here. Eight of my nine children all under the one roof for a change. It's going to be a great night." She winked and Molly was left with the distinct feeling there was something her mother knew that Molly didn't. Even so, she hadn't missed the brief tightening around her mother's mouth at her mention of Vaughan.

What are you doing in Bali, Vaughan? You need to come home...

At sixty-one, her mother was still an attractive woman. With graying dark hair, sparkling blue eyes and an enviably trim figure, she looked much younger than her years in her chic, knee-length, black Chanel dress and four-inch stilettos.

"You look well, Mom," Molly said.

Evelyn flashed her a smile. "Thank you, honey. You look well, too. A little tired, maybe. No doubt you've been working too hard as usual."

Molly shrugged. "No more than any other paramedic on the payroll."

Evelyn gave her an indulgent smile. "I'm so proud of you, Molly. Saving peoples' lives. And often in very difficult, high-pressure circumstances. Your patients don't know how lucky they are when you arrive on the scene."

Warmth spread through Molly at her mother's words, but she brushed off the praise.

"Just doing my job, Mom."

"Yes. But you do it so well. And you didn't have to take on such a high-pressure job. Any job, for that matter. Your father and I would have seen to your needs."

"I know, Mom. But that was never an option. I want to make my own way in the world, just like the rest of my siblings."

Molly followed her mother down the long corridor lined with family portraits. The hallway opened into a spacious dining room where a table that seated eighteen filled most of the room. Every seat was occupied with Molly's siblings and extended family members, including her oldest brother, Christopher, his fiancée, Lexi, and their eight adopted and foster children. Extra chairs had been brought in to accommodate everyone.

There was a chorus of greetings from those gathered around the table as Molly entered the room. Her brother, Zac, stood and brought yet another chair to the table so Molly could sit down.

"There you go, sis."

Molly grinned up at him. "Thanks, Zac. Boy, it's sure getting crowded in here."

"Just wait until you and Hannah bring significant others home. The folks will have to get a bigger table."

Molly laughed. She looked around the room with fondness. Christopher and Lexi, and their children. Molly's sister, Charlotte was seated beside her fiancé, Grayson. Her father, Frank, sat at the head of the table. Her mother sat on his left.

On the other side were Trace and his fiancée, Cassie Webster, and next to them were Lincoln and his girlfriend,

Zoe Parker. Three tours in Afghanistan took their toll on those who'd served over there. Lincoln had suffered, along with many of the officers in his battalion. Lucky for him, Zoe was a psychologist and had done wonders helping him recover from his PTSD. Molly couldn't remember seeing him looking happier or more relaxed.

Her brother, Wade, was also there, laughing with his new girlfriend, Alice Nelson. Alice's two children, Jack and Luke, sat beside them, playing a game with the cutlery. Zac returned to his seat beside his high school sweetheart, Emily Wilson. Though the two had only recently reunited, it was plain for everyone to see how happy they were.

Molly squeezed in beside Hannah, her youngest sister and the only other Barrington sibling present who was still single. Hannah had always been strong-willed and spirited and the family often joked it would take one hell of a man to tame her. She was currently employed as a mine manager at one of the Barrington coal mines in the Hunter Valley. By all accounts, she was holding her own and better in the traditionally male-dominated field. Molly felt nothing but admiration for her younger sister and was proud of all she'd achieved.

Being surrounded by her large, noisy, and ever-expanding family made Molly think of Shane. He had parents and a sister, but being so far from them in Australia, he might as well be all alone in the world. She couldn't imagine not being able to call or visit her mom and dad and siblings whenever she desired. It had been hard enough with Vaughan overseas for almost six months, unable to contact him and not knowing when he might return home. It was beyond her imagination to conceive living on her own overseas, thousands of miles from anyone.

I guess I'm just a homebody... I hope Shane's okay with that...

Just thinking about Shane brought a smile to her face. The thought of him was enough to make her happy. Risky, yes, but though it was early days, she had a good feeling about the two of them. Their connection had only grown stronger over the past weeks as they'd gotten to know each other. She very much liked what she'd discovered.

She was gripped with an urge to share him with her family. She was sure they'd be happy for her. They'd ask a million questions, but that was okay. She wanted to tell them everything about him. The smile broadened on her face. She opened her mouth to speak. Before she could get the words out, Zac tapped his wine glass with the back of his fork and noisily cleared his throat.

"If I could just have everyone's attention for a minute," he said.

All eyes turned toward him. Molly saw him swallow nervously. He darted a glance toward Emily. She reached for his hand and smiled up at him. Molly looked from one to another. A moment before Zac spoke again, comprehension dawned.

They're engaged...

Zac cleared his throat again. "Mom. Dad. Everyone. Emily and I have an announcement to make. We're getting married."

Amid the loud cheers and congratulations, Molly forced a smile. She was truly happy for her brother and his new fiancée, but she'd just determined to tell the family her good news and now the moment was gone. She didn't want to take away from the excitement of Zac and Emily's announcement, nor did she want her own news overshadowed. So, she kept quiet and offered her own congratulations to the happy couple. Probably just as well. As excited as she was about her growing relationship with Shane, her news could wait.

"Oh, and one more thing," Zac added. "We're getting married in three months. We want a Christmas wedding."

"Why the rush?" Evelyn exclaimed. "That's only a month after Christopher and Lexi's wedding."

Zac and Emily shared a tender look and then Zac looked over to Christopher. "You don't mind, do you, big brother?"

"Of course not. Go for it. Lexi and I wish you both all the best."

Zac turned back to Emily and kissed her briefly on the lips before turning back to his mother. "We're making up for lost time, Mom. Six years in the wilderness... It felt like a lifetime. We don't want to waste another minute apart."

"Where will you live?" Frank asked.

Zac was a cop in Broken. Emily worked as a pediatric oncology nurse in the city. The two of them had been commuting back and forth between each other's places since they'd gotten back together, but that wasn't ideal long term. Molly waited with interest for Zac's response.

"I got a job in Newtown. I can walk there from Emily's apartment. I start next month."

Molly grinned. "Wow. That was quick."

Zac nodded. "Yeah, I got lucky. Another detective from that station was looking for a move to the country. I wanted a job in the city. Things worked out well for both of us."

"And now you have a wedding to plan." Molly smiled.

She was genuinely happy for her brother. He'd pined over Emily for years after she'd broken things off with him right after their high school graduation. It seemed he'd never gotten over his first and only love. The thought of the two of them back together and in love made Molly feel all warm and gooey inside. It was the same way she'd begun to feel when she was with Shane.

Not for the first time, she gave herself a mental warning to slow down. He still had a long way to go before he'd be back to good health. Weeks of rehab, months even. There was no need to rush. Let their relationship develop at a slow pace, give her time to adjust. The fear of getting her heart broken was still there, merely tempered a bit. Slow and steady. Yes, that would be the sensible approach.

Chapter Thirteen

D inner progressed in the usual fashion with several courses followed finally by coffee and liqueurs. When Hannah asked for a private word with their father and the two of them excused themselves and left the room, Molly took the opportunity to escape the noisy dinner table and, with coffee in hand, took refuge out the back.

She shivered slightly in the chilly air. Though it didn't get anywhere near cold enough to snow in Broken, the breeze had a bite to it, despite it being mid-September. She rubbed her cardigan-clad arms to fight off the chill.

"Boy, it's cold out here. I thought we were supposed to be in spring already."

Molly turned to see Charlotte step outside of the house and join her under the covered outdoor area that looked out over acres of manicured gardens and an inground pool.

"Hey," Molly murmured, wrapping her hands around her coffee mug. "What's up?"

Charlotte shot her a sideways look. "I was going to ask you the same thing."

Molly hid a grimace. Charlotte had always been good at reading her. But Molly's earlier determination to tell her family about Shane had faded and she merely shrugged off Charlotte's curious gaze.

"I don't know what you mean."

Charlotte gave her a knowing look. "I think you do."

Molly widened her eyes innocently and shook her head back and forth. "Nope."

Charlotte laughed. "Cut it out, Molly. I've known you all your life and have you forgotten our last lunch conversation? Besides, I'm a hard-nosed detective. I smell bullshit a mile off. You can't pull the innocent act with me."

Molly grinned, giving up. She'd never been able to keep secrets from Charlotte. "Okay. You're right. There *is* something."

"I knew it!" Charlotte chortled triumphantly.

Molly merely rolled her eyes.

Charlotte clutched her arm. "Come on, Molly. Spill. This is about that guy, isn't it? The one you told me about. Give me all the juicy details."

Molly laughed at Charlotte's enthusiasm. "Okay, okay! But I'm not going to give you *all* the details," she teased, her voice thick with innuendo.

"Oh my God!" Charlotte squealed. "You've finally gotten over your fear of commitment and gone for it! I knew it! I saw you smiling like a Cheshire cat over dinner, and I just knew it had to involve a man. Come on, what's his name? Is it the same guy we talked about? The one that didn't want to be friends?"

Molly blushed but couldn't keep the silly grin off her face. Though she wanted to wax lyrical about Shane, she also wanted to play it cool. Charlotte was way too perceptive. She'd be concerned if she thought Molly was rushing into things too fast. Right now, Molly just wanted to share her secret with her sister. She didn't want a lecture.

"Yes. His name's Shane." She deliberately refrained from adding his last name. She wouldn't put it past her cop sister to do a little digging and Molly wasn't yet ready for anyone else to know Shane had served time.

Charlotte grinned. "Please tell me you've skipped over the friendship stage and you're madly going for it?"

Molly laughed. "As a matter of fact, we did become friends. I kind of forced myself on him. I kept showing up at his hospital room. Really, I gave him no choice. But as it turns out, he likes me. Really likes me. It feels nice."

"Oh, Molly! I'm so pleased for you! Your first boyfriend! How wonderful!"

"Yes. He's definitely someone special, but it's too early to tell if it's the real deal."

Charlotte frowned. "Oh, please don't do that, Molly."

Molly looked at her. "Do what?"

"Sabotage things before they've even started. You've always had a problem with commitment. That's the reason you've always steered well clear of relationships."

Molly opened her mouth to protest, but Charlotte cut her off.

"Don't you dare deny it. You think I don't know why you've never had a boyfriend? The very thought of leaving yourself so vulnerable scares you to death." Charlotte's tone softened. "Doesn't it?"

Molly's chest went tight. She managed a jerky nod. "Okay. You're right."

Charlotte's forehead creased. "But, why? Why would you feel like that? We've grown up in a loving, stable home. Why would falling in love be so terrifying? It certainly hasn't held Hannah back. I've lost count of the number of boys she's brought home since she left high school. So, what gives, sis? What are you afraid of?"

Molly closed her eyes briefly against a wave of emotion and sighed. "It's ridiculous when you put it like that, but if you must know... It's because of Mom."

Charlotte looked even more confused. "Mom? What do you mean?"

Molly sighed again. "Don't tell me you've forgotten how it was with her and Henry Craigdon?"

"Of course not. That man was an asshole. I wish he were still alive. I'd like to give him a piece of my mind."

Molly couldn't help but laugh. She could well imagine her feisty sister fronting up to the selfish billionaire who'd broken her mother's heart and abandoned her in her time of need and giving him a severe dressing down.

"And you would have been just the woman to do it," Molly agreed.

"So, what does that have to do with you and your fear of commitment?"

"Don't you see? Mom risked everything for love and it was thrown back in her face. She was left to raise a baby on her own, to live with the shame. You know how it was back in those days. People were far less accepting of single mothers. And Mom was forced to go through that all on her own. All because she'd fallen in love with the wrong man."

Charlotte pounced. "That's right. With the wrong man. It wasn't that Mom had fallen in love, it was that she fell in love with an asshole. Falling in love wasn't her undoing. The only mistake she made was perhaps a lack of judgment. But look how things turned out. If Mom hadn't been left in such dire circumstances, she might never have met Dad. How can you be sorry about that?"

"Of course I'm not sorry she met Dad. Hey, if that hadn't happened, none of us would exist. But the thing with Christopher's father... Imagining what that would have been like scared me. It still scares me. What if I take the same leap of faith and get burned, like Mom did? There's no guarantee it won't happen again. That's why I've been so adamant about keeping my heart intact."

Charlotte's face filled with compassion and understanding. "Oh, my sweet sister. It breaks my heart to hear you speak like that. Now that I know how it feels to be loved and love so deeply in return, I can't imagine going through life and never taking that chance."

"What you and Grayson have... It's wonderful... But how do you know it will be that way for me?"

"Like you said, Molly. There are no guarantees. But you can't live your life guided by fear. That's what's holding you back. You might get your heart broken. It happens. But I don't know anyone who's ever regretted taking that chance. Not even Mom."

Molly stared at her sister. "How do you know?"

"I asked her."

The news that her mother didn't regret anything that had happened gave Molly something to think about. She couldn't deny that even though her mother's heart had once been broken, it hadn't turned her off love forever.

Am I brave enough to take the chance? I told Shane I tried to live my life fearlessly, but that's not really true. I've been letting fear dictate my actions for years. Perhaps it's time to change that.

Deep down, she knew Shane was a man she could spend the rest of her life with. Did she have the courage to set aside her fear and open her heart to him?

Charlotte cleared her throat. "So, Shane. That's a nice name. Tell me more about him. What does he do?"

"He's a lawyer."

Charlotte laughed. "Just like Grayson. What a coincidence! How long have you known him?"

"Not quite three weeks."

"I see. I guess that's long enough to know if you have genuine feelings for him."

"How long did you know Grayson before you realized you were in love?"

Charlotte blushed and ducked her head. "Probably less time than that. So, when do we get to meet him?"

Some of Molly's enthusiasm dimmed. She remembered how Tessa had reacted to the news Molly was seeing a former patient. She didn't want the same judgment from Charlotte. So, she shrugged the question away.

"Let's just see how things go. In fact, do you mind keeping this to yourself for a little bit? I want to give myself some time to really think this through and make sure I'm happy with my decision. I'm not ready to undergo an inquisition from Mom."

"Of course!" Charlotte readily agreed. "But hurry up and get to it. Push that fear aside and go for it. He might just be "the one." I'm not going to be able to sit on news like this forever. And I'm going to want to meet him soon!"

She winked and Molly laughed. The two sisters shared a spontaneous hug.

"I'm so excited for you, Molly!" Charlotte gushed. "You can do this! You're stronger than you know. I hope he's everything you ever dreamed of."

Molly thought of Shane and smiled. "He's all that and more."

Charlotte grinned.

Hannah Barrington sipped from her port glass and set it down within easy reach on top of her father's carved wooden desk. She'd always loved this room. It was furnished in dark wood and heavy damask curtains and the overall feel of the place was bold and masculine. It reminded her of her father, a man who'd created an empire from nothing and who'd put his faith in her and had taught her how to go after her dreams.

Now he sat across from her, contemplating her with a hooded expression.

"What is it you wanted to speak with me about?" he asked.

Hannah grimaced and then bought a few more moments by taking another fortifying sip of port. Though she knew her father trusted her implicitly as manager of one of his largest mines, it wasn't easy to tell him they'd had more trouble. But there was no sense putting it off any longer. She bravely met his gaze.

"We've had more trouble out at the mine."

Her father frowned. "What kind of trouble? Please don't tell me it's another Evan Wilson scenario."

"No, no. Nothing like that, thank God. No one's been killed, but there's been a spate of recent accidents that has me quite concerned."

"How so?"

"It's not just the safety breaches. It's the sheer volume of accidents. There's been an incident almost every other day. Most of them aren't serious, but the downtime's beginning to add up. Then yesterday we had a near-miss between a scraper and a dump truck. Both machines were being driven at speed. It would have been a catastrophe if they'd collided."

Frank's frown was fierce. "How the hell did something like that happen?"

"I don't know. Both operators were certain they'd relayed their presence at the intersection over the mine radio, but that can't be the truth. I haven't yet played the recording back to see which one of them, it not both, failed in their positive communications."

"We can't let that kind of thing happen, Hannah. That's plain incompetence."

She flushed under the weight of his glare. "I agree. I've spoken to the supervisor. He doesn't know how it happened. He hasn't had any trouble with the two operators in the past. This seemed to have come out of nowhere."

"Were they employed directly by the mine?"

"No. Contract labor. I've also spoken to the labor hire firm. They're conducting their own internal investigation."

Frank shook his head, his expression grim. "These safety breaches have been happening way too often. What's going on out there, Hannah? We're going to have the resources regulator all over us again if breaches continue to happen. Not to mention the fallout that'll follow if we have another major incident. They'll likely shut us down."

It took all her courage to hold his steely gaze without flinching. "I don't know, Dad. But I'm sure as hell going to find out."

"Make sure you do. We don't want another fatality on our hands. We managed to keep Evan Wilson's death out of the mainstream media, but we might not be so lucky next time. We have some large contracts coming up for tender. We need to ensure our operations remain safe, not only for our employees and contractors, but for future investment prospects."

"Yes, Dad. I'll get to the bottom of it. I promise."

For Molly, the next few weeks passed in a blur of shift work, tending to Garfield, watering Shane's plants and spending as much time with him as she could. He'd started rehab. Each day, one of the hospital physiotherapists would come and get him and take him to the rehabilitation ward in a wheelchair. Though his progress was slow and often painful, Molly encouraged him in any way she could.

Sometimes she made it to his sessions and took pleasure in seeing him put in additional effort in response to her goading him into doing extra exercises, like now. She'd just demanded he do twenty leg lifts when his previous best was only thirteen. It was unfair, but she was prepared to do whatever it took to get him walking again. As she counted each lift aloud, she watched the strain appear on his face. Sweat popped out on his brow. He grunted with exertion.

"Come on, Shane. Only four more to go," she encouraged.

He shot her a dour look. "Easy for you to say."

She gave him her sweetest smile. "Come on, work it, work it, work it. Lift. Lift. Lift. Again. That's it. Two more to go."

Anger glinted in his green eyes. She could tell he was getting frustrated. He tried to lift his leg again but ended up only managing to get it halfway.

"Just a little farther. Come on, Shane. Lift! Lift! Lift! Don't be a wuss."

He glared at her. His breath came fast. "For fuck's sake! Would you stop it? This is fucking hard. Don't you get it? You and your fucking endless positivity. Just leave me the fuck alone."

Shock held her momentarily immobile. In all the sessions she'd attended, he hadn't once lost his temper like this.

She glanced toward the therapist. Tanya's expression was grim. She made a motion with her head to indicate that Molly should leave. Molly glanced back at Shane. His expression remained cold, his eyes hard.

"I've been nothing but upfront with you from the beginning," she said quietly. "I've never pretended to be something I'm not."

"Yeah, well good for you! Should I give you a medal?"

She closed her eyes briefly against a wave of pain. "I thought you wanted me here. It was your idea."

"Yeah. So, it was. My mistake. I should never have kidded myself into believing you and I could ever work." His voice was icy.

Oh, God. It's happening already... Everything I was afraid of... We were in such a happy place. Now it's come crashing down... I should never have listened to Charlotte... Oh, God...

Feeling deflated and with her stomach churning, Molly turned away. She gathered up her handbag and coat and started across the room toward the exit.

Shane's angry shout reached her from across the room. "Stop right there, Molly Barrington! Don't you dare quit on me! I didn't peg you for a quitter. You want me to do this, you can darn well stand there and watch me do it."

Molly slowly turned. Shane glared at her from where he sat clinging to the bars. As she watched, he raised his legs bit by bit, mostly all the way up, once, twice.

"Twenty!" he gasped.

Panting hard, he dropped his arms and collapsed back into the seat of his wheelchair. His body shook from the strain. With sweat dripping from his brow, he lifted his head to glare at her again.

Molly was devastated. Hurt and rejection pulsed through her. She'd thought by pushing him she'd been helping him. As she took in his trembling body, his fierce determination, and the anger that still lingered in his eyes, tears streamed down her cheeks.

In that moment, he seemed to comprehend the devastation he'd just wreaked. His expression filled with remorse.

"I'm sorry, Molly. Please forgive me. I didn't mean it. Stay. I need you. Please."

His voice was rough with feeling. She closed her eyes on a wave of emotion and tried to stem the tears. She understood his frustration and anger, but his lashing out at her had hurt. She was his girlfriend, his sole outside support and she didn't appreciate being the brunt of his anger when she was only trying to help. They needed to talk about what had just happened because all her fears had just been realized and she was darn sure her heart couldn't cope with being on the end of such a lashing again.

Chapter Fourteen

Shane sat despondently in the wheelchair as Molly pushed him back to the orthopedic ward in silence.

How could I have spoken to her like that? Cursed her out? The one good thing in my life and I treated her so badly…

The door to his room stood open. Molly pushed the chair inside and wordlessly helped him to stand and lower him down on the bed. With gritted teeth, he perched on the edge of the mattress and then shuffled over to one side. He patted the mattress beside him and found the courage to look at her.

"Will you stay with me for a while?"

When she just stood, uncertainty and mutiny warring on her face, his heart clenched. This was his fault. He'd done this to her. He'd put that expression, along with the tear tracks, on her face.

"I'm so sorry, Molly. I was a prick. A complete asshole. Especially knowing how much courage it took for you to shift things out of the friend zone. I should never have lost my temper or spoken to you like that. The fact was, I was frustrated with my weakness and slow progress. It had nothing to do with you and it wasn't fair to take it out on you. You were only trying to help. I know that."

She compressed her lips and nodded. "Thank you for your apology. I understand your frustration, your anger, your pain... But as much as I care about you and want to help, I'm not going to be your whipping girl. And you're right about how hard it was for me to trust you with my heart. It took me a long time to get to the point where I was willing to take a risk on us. Now you've gone and blown it."

His heart clenched. *Fuck.* Him and his stupid temper. Why couldn't he have just shut his mouth? She'd only been trying to help. Her strenuous encouragement was no more than what his therapists said to him every day. Yet he'd blown up at Molly. The thought that he might have done permanent damage to their fragile relationship filled him with panic.

"I'm so sorry, Molly. Please, I never meant to hurt you. I'd do anything to take back what I said. And the thought I might have put our relationship at risk... I couldn't bear that."

Her expression remained closed. His heart sank.

Please, God. Please don't let this be the end. I'll do anything if You get us through this...

But she was slowly shaking her head. "I'm sorry, Shane. I need some time to think about this. I'll see you later."

More devastated than he ever thought possible, he watched on helplessly as she left.

The first person Molly called when she cleared the hospital was Charlotte. The moment her sister answered her phone, Molly started in on her.

"I told you! I told you it wasn't worth the pain!"

"Whoa! Molly! Back up. What's going on?"

With sobs of pain and anger threatening to erupt, Molly told Charlotte what had happened.

"This is all your fault!" she railed. "You were the one who encouraged me to give him a go. And look where it's gotten me! A broken heart!"

"Are you really that upset?" Charlotte asked quietly.

"Yes!"

"Then you must care for this guy more than you're willing to admit."

Charlotte's comment pulled Molly up short. She blinked and then sniffed. "What are you talking about?"

"Think about it, Molly. If you didn't care a great deal for this guy, you wouldn't be this upset. The only reason you're so mad is because you really care about this guy and your relationship. Don't you see?"

Molly took a moment to think about that.

Charlotte's right. I do care about Shane. More than I realized. That's why I'm so mad...

"But he's gone and ruined everything!"

"Has he?"

Charlotte's quietly asked question gave Molly another reason to pause. Before she could contemplate it further, her sister spoke again.

"Nobody's perfect, Molly. People mess up. They say things in the heat of the moment that they don't necessarily mean. We've all done that. It comes down to whether you can forgive him and put it behind you. That depends on how much you care about Shane and how much you want to make this work."

Molly sighed. Her anger eased. "You're right. Again. I like Shane a lot. I might even be falling in love. Oh, God! Did you hear that? There's no hope for me."

Charlotte chuckled. "Welcome to the club."

Molly managed a smile. "Okay, okay. You don't have to rub it in." She paused and then added, "So, how did you get to be so wise?"

"Years of experience," Charlotte joked.

"Funny that, given we're the same age."

Charlotte laughed. "I love you, Molly."

"I love you too. Thanks for being there for me. And for your words of wisdom. You're worth your weight in gold."

"Right back at you, sis. And you're welcome. Anytime."

Shane barely slept that night. It wasn't just that his body was aching from the extra effort he'd put in at the gym, it was how he and Molly had parted and the thought he might have ruined everything between them forever that kept him sleepless. He stared at the dark ceiling and cursed himself for a fool. He'd destroyed the best thing that had ever happened to him and he had no one to blame but himself. By the time the first rays of sunlight filtered in through the gap in the curtains, he felt weighted down with dread.

What if she doesn't come back? I have no way of reaching her. She bought me a phone, but I don't even have her number...

He could track her down through her work. She'd told him she was stationed at Sutherland Hospital, but what if she didn't take his call? He could hardly force her. And right now, he was immobile. It wasn't like he could get all the way down there in his wheelchair.

A nurse came in and saw that he was awake and greeted him with the usual good cheer. Shane barely managed to respond. His world had fallen apart and he didn't know what to do about it.

"How's the pain?" the nurse asked.

"It's okay." He deserved every ache he had. Nothing was going to fix the ache in his heart.

"Well, you let me know if you need something, okay?"

"Okay. Thanks."

"I'll be back soon to help you with your shower."

To his relief, the nurse left the room. He closed his eyes on another sigh of self-pity. With Molly now absent from his life—maybe forever—all the light had gone out of his day. He couldn't imagine how he was going to get through the rest of the long, long weeks of rehab that still stretched out in front of him without her by his side. Tears pricked his eyes.

He didn't even hear her enter, so deeply immersed he was in his depressing thoughts. The first he knew she was there, was when she spoke.

"How are you, Shane?"

His eyes snapped open, and he turned his head to look at her with disbelief. "Molly! You came back! Fuck!" And then he apologized profusely. "I'm sorry! I didn't mean to curse. I'm just so glad to see you. I didn't know if you were ever coming back."

She stepped closer until she stood right beside his bed. Then she frowned. "You look awful. How's the pain?"

A barrage of emotions threatened to overwhelm him. He managed a wobbly smile. "What pain? Now that you're here, I feel great."

"If it's any consolation, I had a rough night too."

It comforted him to know he wasn't the only one who'd been distressed over their last conversation. She drew up a chair near the bed and sat. Then she reached for his hand. His heart flooded with hope.

"I'm sorry for running out on you like that. I should have had the courage to stand and fight. Not that I want to fight with you, but it's important that you hear me out."

"Of course. And let me say again how sorry I am about what I said. I never wanted to hurt you like that."

She nodded. "I spoke to my sister. She helped me to see things from a different perspective. She also helped me realize how much you've come to mean to me."

His heart leaped out of his chest, but before he could say anything, she spoke again.

"I'm not so naïve that I don't accept there will be times in the future when we argue and we'll probably say things that hurt. But all I ask is that you listen to what I have to say and that you always treat me with respect. I don't want you to ever curse at me again. Curse if you have to, but don't ever direct it toward me. Are we clear?"

She looked at him, her eyes a vivid blue. He nodded. It was so much more than he deserved or hoped for.

"Like crystal. I was out of line. You're very important to me and although I can't promise not to curse the fates within your hearing in the future, I won't ever lash out at you in blame like that again, no matter how frustrated I am, or how tough it gets."

Her expression softened. "Shane, it's normal to feel frustrated and it's healthy to express that frustration, but it's important to direct it in the right way—not at those who care about you and who are trying to help. I'm sure the therapists have told you that."

"Yes, they have, and the logical part of my brain understands that perfectly. And when I thought I'd chased you away with my bad attitude, I was gutted. I never want to feel like that again. But just so you know, when I get so tired doing the simplest of exercises, when I can't lift my legs how I want… It drives me crazy!

"Did you know I used to play football three times a week? I used to ride a motorbike for hours along the freeway. I used to go mountain climbing, water skiing, even a three-mile jog. All the things that came so easily to me and that I took for granted now seem so impossible and the task to get back to those days insurmountable. I mean, I can't even stand!"

On a soft sigh, Molly perched herself on the side of his bed. "No one's going to pretend you didn't suffer significant injuries. Recovering from something like that is hard, both physically and emotionally, and it's going to take time. But you'll get there. I know you will."

She smiled gently and his heart turned over. *How did I get so lucky?*

"I have complete confidence in you," she continued. "You've shown me that you're the kind of man that when he puts his mind to it, can accomplish anything. Look at everything you've been through already. That would have broken lesser men and yet here you are, taking up the challenge, albeit a little grumpily. You're more than just a survivor. You've taken that potentially life-breaking experience and made it life-changing for not only you, but others less fortunate."

Tears burned behind his eyes. He didn't think of himself as more than just a survivor. In fact, most days he wasn't sure he was doing much more than barely getting by. But Molly saw something special in him. Where had she come from? Surely, he didn't deserve such faith.

"There you go, doing it again," he said. "Boosting my spirits, refusing to let me wallow in self-pity, believing in me. I was right, Molly. You aren't a quitter, despite the bullsh—stuff I throw at you. I'm sorry for treating you like that. It hurt me as much as it hurt you. I disappointed myself. You're the best thing to have come out of that accident. I wouldn't have gotten to this stage without you. You're my Little Miss Sunshine. My Angel. Always remember that."

Their gazes caught and held. Shane's heart pounded from the emotion he'd unleashed. Molly's gaze shifted to his mouth. Her pink tongue stole out and swiped her lips.

Blood rushed to his groin. Within seconds, his cock stood to attention. He swallowed a wry smile.

Halleluiah! At least something still worked... If only my legs would cooperate...

Molly licked her lips again and Shane could no longer hold back a groan. Her eyes flared wide at the sound of it.

"Molly..."

Her only response was to wiggle herself fully onto the bed. She lay on her side, facing him. Her cheeks were flushed. Her mouth was slightly parted. He watched in fascination as her chest rose and fell in rapid breaths. It pleased him to know he wasn't the only one affected by their nearness.

"I want to kiss you," he said, his voice husky with need.

She stared at him, her gaze fixed on his. "I want to kiss you, too."

Her words sent a shaft of hot desire coursing through him. His cock surged almost painfully, throbbing and hard. With the pain in his legs now forgotten, he reached out and cupped his hand around the back of her head and drew her slowly toward him. Their lips met in a fleeting kiss, no more than the touch of a butterfly's wings. Though it made his heart beat faster, it wasn't anywhere near enough.

He kissed her again, the lightest of touches. Then kissed her again and again. Each time he tasted more of her sweetness and captured each sharp intake of her breath.

He pressed his tongue against her lips, seeking entry. He felt a moment's hesitation and then she opened her mouth to him. His tongue stole inside and swept around the warm, sweet recesses of her mouth. He explored at his leisure, loving the little sounds of wonder and pleasure that came from her. It made him think again that perhaps she was inexperienced. And then she confirmed it.

"I-I'm not very good at this. I haven't had as much experience as you might expect for someone my age."

He pulled back to look at her. Her gaze was averted. Her cheeks were fire engine red. He took her chin between his thumb and forefinger and tilted her head up until she had no choice but to look at him.

"Don't ever apologize for being choosy," he said. "There's something so incredibly enticing about that."

Her blush deepened, but the tentative smile she offered him made it all the way to her eyes. Unable to help himself, he leaned in for another kiss. This time, he exerted more pressure and he groaned when she opened her mouth and started to kiss him back. When her tongue stole out to lick the inside of his mouth, it was all he could do not to take her in his arms and plunder her with all the passion he felt inside.

His cock was rock-hard. He was burning up with need. The self-control it took for him to do nothing more than kiss her caused an ache all its own. Of course, his body couldn't cooperate, no matter how much he wished it. She began to kiss him all over his face. His lips, his eyelids, his cheeks. She was getting increasingly more confident, and the sheer joy of her avid exploration filled him with excitement.

He couldn't wait to show her all the ways he knew of loving, but that would have to wait. He was in a hospital bed with two broken legs and sore ribs. Making love to her in the way he wanted to, especially their first time, would prove impossible.

As much as he wanted to bury his cock inside her, it wasn't going to happen. At least, for now.

As he pulled slowly back from her and witnessed the disappointment in her eyes, he clung to the knowledge that one day he'd walk again and the day he left the hospital upright was the day he'd take her home and love her the whole night and beyond.

"As much as I don't want to, we need to stop," he rasped, needing her to understand.

She frowned. "But I was really enjoying kissing you."

He groaned again. "Oh, Molly! You're killing me! I enjoyed kissing you too, but if we don't stop, I'm going to pass the point of no return and I want more for us than that. Do you understand what I'm saying? My cock's so hard I feel like I might explode, but I don't want our first time to be here, in a hospital bed where we could be discovered at any moment. And given my legs aren't working, you'd need to do all the work. When we make love, I want to take my time. I want to kiss every inch of you and I want you to do the same to me. I want to be fully physically able to love you completely."

He looked at her, his gaze intense. She looked a little confused, but he continued. "What we have, this thing between us, it's special. Like nothing I've felt before. Do you understand?"

Molly's cheeks were crimson. She stared down at the bedspread and then bravely met his gaze again.

"Yes, I agree. It's special. I feel the intensity too."

His breath left him in a rush. Until that moment, despite all that had transpired between them, he hadn't been sure if what he felt was all one-sided. To hear her confirm she felt the same way was beyond anything he could have hoped and only served to fuel his determination to do everything he could to heal and walk out of there.

"Shane?"

The uncertainty in Molly's voice gave him pause. "Yes?"

"I'm not sure I understood all you were saying. I... I guess you should know I'm a virgin."

The words came out in a rush. From her expression, he could tell she was deeply embarrassed. He was quick to reassure her.

"Ah, Molly. I must say, I'm surprised, but being choosy isn't something you should be embarrassed about. In fact, I have nothing but admiration for you." He paused. "Is your fear of love and commitment the reason you haven't been with anyone?"

Molly looked at him and nodded. "I can't believe I let fear take over my life like that. I never wanted to be like that. It just kind of happened."

He frowned. In his experience, such a deeply held fear didn't just happen. There was something she wasn't telling him.

"Where did your fear come from?" he asked gently.

She bit her lip and looked away and he wasn't sure if she was going to answer. And then she let out a soft sigh.

"It started with my mother."

Haltingly, she told him the story and how it had impacted on her right up until the time she'd decided to set her fear aside and take a chance on him. When she was finished, he stared at her in wonder. He felt more honored than ever that she'd found the courage to take that leap of faith. He felt like pinching himself just to make sure this wasn't all part of some wonderful dream and at any moment he might wake. She was his sunshine, his angel, his heart.

Unaware of his thoughts, she glanced shyly at him again. "I... I want you to be my first."

Shane stared at her as a tumult of emotions coursed through him. She wasn't only gifting him with her heart, but with her body. Here he was, an ex-con, a man who'd made mistakes, and this beautiful, compassionate, kind, and generous woman had just offered him the world. He felt humbled. And more determined than ever to be worthy of her.

For the first time in a long time, he was also filled with hope. Molly knew the worst of his secrets and yet she'd accepted him and his failings. Without judgment.

Though he'd suspected she was inexperienced, until now he hadn't known for sure. Now that he did, he was even more determined to make her first time special. As much it would kill him, he'd wait until he could walk again and back home in his apartment (or hers) before making love to her. She deserved to be loved for hours without the risk of interruption and she deserved a man who was whole. Right now, he couldn't guarantee either of those things.

Chapter Fifteen

Molly felt like she was walking on air after visiting hours came to an end and she left Shane for the night. They'd spent the rest of their time together lying on the hospital bed watching a movie, Shane's arm around her shoulders. Her head and hand had rested on his chest. Beneath the soft cotton of his pajamas, she'd felt his firm pectorals. It had been all she could do not to let her hand wander lower.

Kissing him had been like nothing she could have imagined. The liquid heat of his mouth, the softness of his lips. The way he looked at her when he kissed her, like he couldn't get enough. She knew how that felt. Her past kissing experience was limited to a boy in high school. They'd been seventeen. They hadn't even been dating. Just a random moment in a dim corner at a school dance. The sloppy, inexperienced kisses of a teenager couldn't compare to the mastery of Shane's mouth. She could go on kissing him forever. And more.

A fresh wave of embarrassment washed over her when she recalled how she'd told him she was a virgin, but she'd wanted him to know. It was obvious he was experienced in the art of kissing and at thirty, that didn't come as a surprise. But most women her age weren't virgins and she wanted to give him some warning not to expect too much—or at the very least, to anticipate a little awkwardness.

She was relieved Shane seemed to take her news well. He'd certainly said all the right things and the way he'd looked—he'd truly appeared to be in awe that she wanted him to be her first. She suspected most men would flee from such responsibility. She had no illusions the first time would be smooth and wonderful. It was likely to be significantly less than that. But she anticipated the emotion of sharing would be enough. And the fun and pleasure would be in the practicing to come.

She didn't know what it felt like to be in love, but she was pretty sure it felt very much like this. She thought about Shane all the time. She wanted to make him laugh. She wanted to distract him from his pain. She wanted him to walk again. Not for her, but because she knew how much it meant to him. He was such a physical person and she knew he felt like he'd lost a part of his identity when he lost his ability to walk. She wanted him to feel whole again.

She also yearned to kiss him all over, to take him in her mouth. Giving a man oral sex was something else she'd never done, but the thought of doing it to Shane left her feeling warm and tingly inside. And then she thought about what it would be like to make love with him.

Just the thought had her belly swarming with butterflies. Nerves and anticipation and a little touch of fear. But dwarfing all of that was longing. She wanted him to touch her and she wanted to touch him.

Whatever this feeling was that had her all churned up inside, she only hoped he felt the same. They'd talked about connection, respect, and admiration, but they hadn't broached the subject of love. She had no experience with matters of the heart, but she wanted to at least gauge more fully the depth of his feelings and share hers before the relationship moved to the next level.

They'd already come through their first rough patch, but there would be others and though she felt quietly confident that they felt similarly about their budding relationship, it was better to know if he was prepared to commit fully before taking things any further. Her heart wasn't built for casual. Broaching the subject with him however filled her with nerves.

Hey, I told him I was a virgin, didn't I? Surely anything after that will be child's play...?

She could only hope.

Shane lay on his back and stared up at the ceiling. The plain white paneling had become depressingly familiar. He'd lost count of the number of hours he'd spent looking at it. Even a brief visit from the detectives to tell him they had nothing new to report hadn't broken the boredom.

He wondered why they'd bothered. No doubt they'd wanted him to think they were still actively investigating the accident, even when all indications suggested they were doing very little. When he'd asked if the specialist technicians had been able to decipher the registration plate of the car that had hit him, they'd replied in the negative.

"Unfortunately, the angle of the CCTV camera cast a flash of light over the plate. It's impossible to read it properly," the younger detective said.

"What about the smash repairers?" Shane asked.

"I'm afraid we haven't had any luck with them either," the same detective replied.

So that was that. The bastard, whoever they were, would more than likely get away with it. Shane tried not to let that thought get him down. He hoped the person responsible was living in hell with their conscience. It was the least they deserved.

It was late. Visiting hours had long since come to an end. The ward was dim and quiet as patients settled down for the night. The television that hung above his bed was on with the sound down low, but he couldn't find any enthusiasm for the *Seinfeld* rerun that filled the screen. Instead, his mind was filled with Molly.

He was still overcome by a sense of wonder that she wanted him to be her first lover. Despite his checkered past, she wanted to be with him. He still couldn't believe his luck. Her goodness and kindness, her generosity of spirit, her determination to see him do well, floored him. The truth was, he'd fallen in love with her and it filled him with wonder to realize she might feel the same way. It made him want to be the best man he could be for her, starting with his mobility.

He felt a renewed surge of determination to get back on his feet. With that thought in mind, he pulled himself up in the bed and swung his legs over the side. Even that had his heart thumping with exertion. He'd been dismayed and a little daunted at how much strength he'd lost since the accident, but it was slowly returning, one stretch, one exercise at a time.

Think positive... That's what's going to get me through... Only positive thoughts... And a few prayers...

Holding onto the bed, he eased his feet to the floor. The linoleum was cold. He shivered, as much from what he was about to do as from the cold. Until now, he'd been transported back and forth to the rehab unit in a wheelchair and though he'd been doing a raft of leg and arm exercises to build up his strength, he had yet to stand.

With gritted teeth and holding onto his courage, he slowly stood and put weight on his damaged legs. The pain was swift and sure and snatched away his breath, but he did it! He forced himself to count to five before he collapsed back on the bed. His heart pounded, both from the effort of standing and from the exhilaration that coursed through his veins.

I did it!

For the first time since the accident, he'd stood on his own two feet. The feeling of utter triumph and satisfaction was indescribable. He wished Molly was there to share in his achievement.

I did it!

And then the pain set in with a vengeance. Grimacing against the stabbing fire that now shot up and down his legs, he swung them back across the mattress and tried to catch his breath. His heart thumped. His chest was tight. He tried to breathe slowly, in through his nose and out through his mouth, like the physios had instructed him.

Slowly, his breathing settled and the pain in his legs began to ease. He sighed with relief. Despite the discomfort and the aches and pains he'd no doubt put up with for the rest of the night, nothing could shift the smile from his face.

Molly drove straight to the hospital after her shift ended. When she reached Shane's room, it was empty. A query at the nurses' station had her heading back downstairs to the rehab unit. As she approached the gymnasium, she could hear someone talking, encouraging whoever they were with to try again. She silently marveled at the patience of the physios and occupational therapists who spent every day helping people regain their mobility and relearn basic life skills after an accident or injury. They did such important work but were often overlooked by the more glamorous roles in the health industry.

A bit like paramedics...

The thought brought a wry smile to her lips. She pushed against the wooden panel that served as a door into the gym. Her heart leaped forward at the thought of seeing Shane again. She hadn't been able to stop thinking about him and their kisses. She still needed to stop by his apartment and feed Garfield, water the plants, and collect the mail. She also needed to do a load of laundry, but she'd put all of that on hold and had come straight to the hospital. She couldn't wait another minute to see him again.

The door to the gym opened beneath the pressure of her shoulder. She crossed the polished wooden floor of the gymnasium and came to a halt not far from where he sat on a bench lifting weights. Her heart thumped with anticipation and nerves. She strolled over to him. When he finished his last set of repetitions and set the weights aside, she dropped a casual kiss on his sweaty brow. His physio, Tanya, stood by, looking almost as worn out as Shane did.

Molly gave him a cheeky grin. "You're looking good there, Lucas. All hot and sweaty and pumped. Just how a girl likes her man. Right, Tanya?"

Molly winked at the young physio who grinned. Molly looked back at Shane. He looked slightly off-balance, as if a kiss from her was the last thing he'd expected. It was the first time she'd kissed him in public, so she understood his surprise, but then a huge grin lit up his face.

"Hey, there. You're a sight for sore eyes," he said.

The intensity of his gaze sent a wave of heat burning across her face. Flustered, she lowered her eyes. Her gaze snagged on the bulging muscles of his biceps, clearly visible beneath a cut-off T-shirt that showed off his broad shoulders to perfection. She longed to learn the shape and size of them, run her fingers over them, touch them with her lips. But that was for later, after he'd been discharged. For now, all she could do was look.

Shane rolled closer in his wheelchair. As if he could read her mind, he shot her a knowing look. She blushed again.

"What about a proper kiss?" he asked.

Her cheeks grew hotter. She glanced toward Tanya. The physio grinned widely. "Go on, Molly. Give him another kiss. He's worked hard today. He deserves it."

Looking back at Shane, she caught the light of challenge in his gaze. Her heart skipped a beat. She'd always found it hard to resist a challenge… Besides, she wanted to kiss him like he wanted, without restraint and to hell with who was watching…

Her cheeks grew warm at the thought. With a nervous laugh, she threw up her arms in surrender. "Are you two ganging up on me?"

Shane grinned. "Not at all. I haven't said a word to Tanya. She's worked out how madly in love we are all on her own."

Molly's heart skipped a beat. She stared at Shane. "Is that what we are? Madly in love?"

His expression immediately sobered. The intensity of his gaze held her spellbound. "I am," he said, his voice husky with emotion. "Are you?"

Adrenaline surged through her. The blood pounded in her heart, in her ears, in her veins. The noise was so loud, she could hardly hear her words when she finally spoke.

"You bet."

Shane's face became wreathed in smiles. He reached up and pulled her down to him. With his hand holding her firmly behind the neck, he brought her mouth down to his. The moment their lips touched, Molly was in heaven. Just like the first time, a fire of need burned through her veins. His lips were full and firm and supple. He kissed with confidence and ease. Slow and sensuous, gentle and sweet. It was like he was imprinting the feel and taste of her on his memory.

The kiss felt like it went on forever and at the same time, it was over in an instant. As they slowly pulled apart, Tanya wolf-whistled and cheered. Molly burned with a mixture of embarrassment and joy. She couldn't believe Shane loved her! Charlotte had been right. Living life in fear was for cowards. If she hadn't found the courage to put her heart on the line, she'd never have known what it felt like to be loved and to love.

The feeling of joy was indescribable. She wanted it to last forever. And the happiness and joy that was reflected in Shane's face made the risk so worthwhile. Seeing him so contented, after all he'd been through... It was the best gift anyone could hope for.

Now that she knew how good love could feel, she understood the joy and happiness she saw on the faces of her siblings. It was a heady feeling. She couldn't believe she'd waited so long to experience it. Then again, perhaps she'd been waiting for Shane all along. He'd made her want to set aside her fear and take that leap of faith and she'd love him for that forever.

Shane's body was on fire, but he forced his mind off what his body urged him to do. Ravishing Molly on the floor of the gymnasium while his physio stood by and watched wasn't on his list of things to do. Besides, he wanted to wait until he could love her properly and that meant being able to walk.

He'd told Tanya about his attempt at standing the previous night. To his surprise, she'd admonished him.

"Your legs aren't up to that yet. The bones need more time to properly heal. If you put weight on them before they're ready, it can set back your recovery."

Suitably chastened, he'd spent the rest of his rehab session doing stretches and other exercises to increase the blood flow to his muscles and build up his strength. He'd only just finished a strenuous weights session when Molly had arrived. She'd looked so flushed and gorgeous; it was all he could do not to stare. He still had to pinch himself that she was there for him. That she cared for *him*.

He'd guessed she was probably a little reluctant to be the first one to give voice to her feelings, so he'd decided to put it out there, just like that. To his delight, she'd recovered from her initial surprise and had agreed with him. And that kiss they'd shared... Whew! What was more important was that she felt the same way.

She loves me!

Never had he imagined when he'd been lying trapped in his car suffering an agony of pain and the fear of not knowing if he'd ever walk again that he would find love with the paramedic who'd helped save his life. It seemed all those prayers he'd sent up during his time in prison for help to live a better life had been answered in the form of Molly, an angel who was prepared to walk beside him. Life couldn't get any better.

Molly was still floating on air when she climbed into her car the following morning. She was rostered on with Tessa and her friend had called the night before to ask if Molly could give her a lift to work. Fortunately, Tessa only lived in the next suburb. She was waiting on the curb outside her house when Molly pulled up.

Her friend looked tired and drawn and pale, but she greeted Molly with a slight smile. "Morning. You look bright and cheery."

Molly grinned. "Well, according to the weather report, it's going to be another beautiful day in Sydney and they just finished playing my favorite song on the radio. What's not to smile about?"

Tessa climbed in and shot her a sly look. "Your good mood wouldn't have anything to do with a certain patient, would it?"

Molly blushed but continued to grin. Checking over her shoulder, she flipped on her indicator and pulled back out into the traffic. She glanced back at Tessa. "Maybe," she said coyly.

"Oh, I knew it! What's his name again?"

"Shane."

"Shane," Tessa repeated with a nod. "So how is lover boy?"

Molly shrugged. "He's okay. The rehab is tortuous, but we all knew it would be. He gets stronger every day, though, so that's a good thing. Hopefully they'll be able to get him up out of the chair soon and try to properly weight bear. We'll see how well those fractures have healed."

Tessa shot her a sideways glance. "Do the police know who hit him yet?"

Molly shook her head. "No. But they've managed to capture an image of the vehicle before it sped away, so they know the make and model. Unfortunately, it's a popular SUV. A Toyota Landcruiser. There are literally thousands of them in Sydney."

"Don't I know it. I own one too," Tessa quipped, "though I've almost forgotten what mine looks like, it's been so long since I've seen it."

Molly grinned. "As I said, they're everywhere. The last I heard, the police were trying some new technique to try and enhance the registration plate. It's not clearly visible in the CCTV footage."

"Do they think they'll be successful?"

Molly checked over her shoulder before switching lanes. "Who knows? I'm always amazed by the technology they're continually developing. For Shane's sake, let's hope so."

Tessa fell silent. Molly concentrated on negotiating her way through the early morning traffic. Another one of her favorite songs came on the radio and she quietly sang along to it. Then Tessa looked at her.

"Thanks so much for the lift, Molly. I've lost count of how many times this is. I know it's a pain in the neck for you and I feel like such a burden, but I want you to know, I really appreciate it."

Molly glanced at her friend. "Hey, I told you already. It's no problem. I'm happy to help. What are friends for?"

Tessa gave her a tight smile. "Thank you."

"Did the mechanic give you any idea how much longer he'll be with your car?"

Tessa's shoulders slumped on a sigh. "No. Now he tells me they're waiting on another part. Apparently, it's coming from overseas. Who knows how long that will take?"

Molly shot her a sympathetic look. "You poor thing. Not having a car must be driving you insane! How are you ferrying all the kids around?"

"Fortunately, they catch a bus to school, but you're right, it's been a struggle. Doing the grocery shopping is the worst. Having to load all the shopping into the back of a taxi and then haul it all out again... It's embarrassing, as well as expensive."

"I wish I had a solution. Unfortunately, I don't have a spare car and I don't know anyone who does."

Tessa gave her another tight smile. "Hey, it's not your problem. Don't worry about it. We'll be fine."

"Well, listen. Next time you need to go to the supermarket, you let me know. If I'm free, I'll swing by and pick you up. We can shop together."

Tessa shot her a grateful smile. Molly was alarmed to see tears glinting in the other woman's eyes.

"Oh, Tessa! I'm sorry! I didn't mean to upset you! I was only trying to help."

Tessa swiped at her eyes and gave Molly a shaky smile. "I'm not upset. I'm just...overwhelmed. Things have been getting on top of me lately. You know how it's been with Martin... Why do men have to be such assholes? I'm sorry, Molly. This has nothing to do with you. It's not fair to burden you with my problems. You're such a good friend. The best. I don't deserve you."

Molly dismissed the suggestion out of hand. "Nonsense. You and I, we have each other's backs, right?"

"Right," Tessa replied in a choked voice.

"So, there'll be no more discussion about being a burden. I'm your friend. Friends help each other out. And that's that."

Chapter Sixteen

Two weeks had passed since Shane had told Molly he was in love with her and she'd agreed she felt the same way. Two weeks feeling like the luckiest guy on the planet. They hadn't talked about the future, but that could wait. First, he needed to get back up on his feet.

His impatience to be with Molly motivated him like nothing else to walk sooner rather than later. Each day, he worked harder than ever in the gym, pushing his body beyond its limits. And each day he grew stronger, regaining a lot of the muscle tone he'd lost while he'd been laid up in bed. Today Tanya had let him stand unassisted on his feet for the first time and he'd managed to walk a few cautious steps.

The feeling of satisfaction had been overwhelming. Okay, so he'd had to use the two steel balance bars for support, but he'd done it. He couldn't wait to tell Molly. She'd told him she'd stop by after work. It was now a little past six. She was due to arrive any minute. Seated in his wheelchair waiting for her to arrive, his belly churned with nerves and excitement. He'd sworn Tanya to secrecy. She'd agreed it would be a marvelous surprise.

Right on cue, Molly entered through the wooden door, still wearing her paramedic uniform. Her long dark hair was loose and flowed around her face. She must have released it from the customary bun she usually wore to work. As she caught sight of him, a smile lit up her face.

His heart turned over with love. She was a ray of sunshine, banishing the darkness that had consumed his spirit for so long. She kissed him softly on the lips and tenderly ruffled his hair. It had grown much longer than he usually wore it, but she didn't seem to mind.

"Hey, you. What did you get up to today?" she asked with a smile. "You're looking fit."

He'd soaked his T-shirt through with sweat halfway through the session and had gotten rid of it. She now ran her hand over his bare shoulders and squeezed his bulging bicep. His taut belly clenched with need. He tried not to think how good it felt to have her touch him. Instead, he shrugged nonchalantly and deliberately avoided looking at Tanya. "Not much. Just another day in the gym with my slave-driver physio."

Molly laughed and looked over at Tanya. "I feel sorry for you, Tanya. Having to put up with this guy all day."

Tanya merely chuckled. "We have our good and bad days, don't we Shane?"

"Too right," he agreed easily.

"So, was today a good day or a bad day?" Molly asked with a teasing glint in her eyes.

Shane shrugged again and waggled his hand back and forth. "So-so."

"Why don't you show her what we've been up to, Shane?" Tanya suggested.

Molly looked mildly interested. Shane hid his excitement. He rolled his wheelchair over to the parallel bars and hoisted himself out of the chair. Molly went still. When he'd managed to stand a whole twenty seconds upright, she clapped her hands together with delight.

"Oh, Shane! That's so wonderful! I *knew* you could do it! How great does it feel to be upright again, after all this time?"

"It feels pretty good," he admitted. "But this feels even better."

Concentrating hard, he picked up one foot and set it down in front of him and then followed it with the other. Hanging tightly to the railing, he walked the full length of the mat. It was the farthest he'd been. By the time he reached the end, he was sweating profusely and his body trembled from the effort. But he'd done it.

He half-turned to see Molly with tears streaming down her face. She ran toward him, throwing her arms around him from behind and almost knocking him off his feet.

"Whoa!" he said, holding tightly to the railing. "Easy does it."

"Oh, Shane! I can't believe it! You're *walking!*" she cried.

He grinned. "You bet I am."

"Of course, I always knew you could do it, but to see you now... It's so wonderful." She turned to Tanya and hugged her, too. "Thank you, Tanya. You've worked almost as hard as Shane on his recovery. I can't thank you enough."

Tanya swiped at the moisture in her eyes and brushed away the praise. "It was all Shane. I've worked with other patients who were far less debilitated, and they didn't achieve anywhere near what he has in the same amount of time. He's amazing. He's fearless. When I asked him what motivated him, he told me it was you. He wanted to walk again for you." Tanya beamed. "How about that?"

That was about the most romantic thing Molly had ever heard. With a renewed rush of happy tears, she hugged Shane again. He felt so warm and solid and alive against her, but she also sensed his strength was fading. She looked around for the chair. As if reading her mind, Tanya hurried over to fetch it and pushed it behind a trembling Shane. Molly guided him into the chair. He sank back with a grateful sigh.

"I think you might have overdone it, you crazy man," Molly murmured, cupping his cheek tenderly and pushing a hank of sweaty hair back off his forehead.

He stared up at her, his green eyes bright with emotion. "I wanted to show you I could do it."

"And you did. I'm so proud of you."

"Thank you," he said huskily. "That means so much."

Molly stared down at him. She opened her mouth as if to speak, but then closed it again. He frowned.

"What is it, Molly?"

She bit her lip and then sighed. "Is it true what Tanya said? Did you do this for me?"

He held her gaze. "I did it for *us*. I'm in love with you, Molly Barrington. And if it's at all possible, you deserve to have me whole. You deserve a man who can at least walk. So, I used you as motivation to work harder than ever. Does that scare you?"

She breathed out and slowly smiled. "No, it doesn't scare me. It makes me feel great. That you wanted to do this for me. That you love me that much." She grinned. "How did I get so lucky?"

He reached out and took her hand. "I ask myself the same thing every day."

It was another three weeks before Shane's doctor agreed he was doing well enough to be discharged from the hospital. His walking had been improving every day since his first attempt and he was now itching to go home. Though he'd still be required to attend the hospital for daily physiotherapy sessions, his doctor was pleased enough with his progress to approve his release with crutches. Right now, he was waiting for Molly to finish her night shift so she could come and take him home.

He'd thought about calling Flynn and asking him to do it. Flynn's workday usually didn't start before nine and he'd called in to see him only the week before, but he really wanted

Molly to be the one who took him home. Walking back into his apartment for the first time since the accident would be a momentous occasion. She was the one he wanted to celebrate that moment with. It would also be the first time they'd been truly alone in all the time they'd known each other. Privately, he was hoping she might even stay the night. His pulse leaped at the possibility, along with his nerves.

As if he'd conjured her up, Molly arrived right then with a huge grin on her face and her eyes alight with excitement. She carried the same duffel bag she'd brought with her the first time. So much had happened since then. It felt like a lifetime ago.

"Hey, you!" she said, greeting him with a soft kiss. "I can't believe this day has finally arrived! You're going home!"

He grinned. "Yeah. I finally got there. I'm walking out of here. You had as much to do with that as me."

She waved away his praise, even though she looked pleased. "That's nonsense and we both know it. You're the one who did all the hard work. I was merely along for the ride. The cheering squad on the sidelines, if you like."

He looked at her and swallowed against the sudden lump in his throat. When he spoke, his voice was husky with emotion. "You can be my cheering squad any time you like."

They shared a tender look and his excitement grew. Life was looking up.

With quiet efficiency, Molly helped him pack up his few things. She'd taken most of his clothes home the last time she'd been there. All that was left were his toiletries, a few paperbacks, a couple of sets of clothes and some pajamas.

"Is that it?" she asked, when the last of his things were in the duffel.

"I think so," he said looking around. He leaned across from the bed and pulled out the drawers of the bedside table. They were empty. "Looks like we're good to go."

"Do you have to wait for the nurse?"

"No. Someone stopped by earlier with the discharge notes and a prescription for painkillers. Let's hope I don't need them as much in the coming weeks."

Molly smiled softly. "You're getting stronger every day. You're going to be fine."

"Yes," he said. For the first time in a long time, he truly believed it.

He grinned at her. She winked. "Are you ready?"

He stood and took a few steps toward the crutches that leaned against the end of the bed. Though he could walk short distances unaided, for now the doctor had urged him to use the crutches whenever he needed and especially when he felt tired.

Molly shot him a look of concern. "Are you sure you don't want me to fetch a wheelchair? I've parked right outside the hospital, but it's still a fair distance to the street."

He shook his head. "No. I want to walk out of here, even if that means using crutches."

"Fair enough."

Drawing in a deep breath, he straightened his shoulders and with head held high, he began walking toward the door. Molly hoisted the duffel bag on her shoulder and followed him. Their farewells to the hospital staff as they passed the nurses' station were met with a chorus of goodbyes and good cheers. Even Tanya was on hand to give him a goodbye hug, congratulate him on his achievement and wish him all the best.

Shane was buoyed by the warmth and encouragement. He'd spent almost three months in hospital. In that time, he'd gotten to know most of the nurses well. They'd kept his spirits up during the dark times and for that he would always be grateful. He was going home. With Molly. And that was huge.

The morning sun was warm on his face. He tilted his head to catch its rays. A tall, lemon-scented gum tree in full flower grew not far away from the hospital entrance. He breathed in deeply of the lemon-scented air. It felt like forever since he'd been outside. Being in hospital felt too much like the time he'd spent in prison. Not for the first time, he silently vowed never take something so simple as his freedom of movement for granted again.

Molly drove to his apartment and parked as close as she could get to his front door. It was fortunate he lived on the ground floor. She climbed out of the car, fetched his bag, then went around to his side and handed him the crutches.

He looked up at her. "Thanks, but I want to try and do this bit on my own."

She merely nodded and he was thankful she didn't try to talk him out of it. This was the first day of his independence. He wanted to give it his best shot.

He swung his legs out of the car and dragged in a fortifying breath. Then he heaved himself to a standing position. Taking a moment to get his balance, he slowly made his way up the concrete path. Though spring was almost over, its presence still showed in the abundant display of flowers that grew in the beds that bordered the path. Petunias, pansies, kangaroo paw. They filled the air with sweetness. The tall Chinese elms that lined the boundary fence now sported fresh green leaves, along with the ornamental cherry trees. He drew in another deep breath and eased it out. It was good to be alive.

"It's a beautiful day, isn't it?" Molly murmured from behind him.

He half-turned to look at her and beamed. "You bet."

She smiled and then walked ahead of him to fetch the spare key from its hiding place. Juggling the bag and the crutches, she fit the key into the lock and opened the door. He stepped inside and was hit by the familiar sounds and smells of the place. It had been so long since he'd been there. As he made his way slowly into the open plan living room and kitchen, he couldn't help but feel that everything appeared bigger than before.

"There's so much more space than I remember," he mused.

Molly chuckled. "That's because you've spent the past three months in a tiny hospital room. You'll get used to the space again in no time."

He nodded. "Yeah, I guess. At least the hospital room was bigger than my room in the prison."

She winked. "And you didn't have to share it with anyone."

He grinned, grateful that her lighthearted comment managed to lift his mood. He loved that about her. His Little Miss Sunshine. Where would he be without her?

She set his bag down on the floor and propped the crutches against the couch, within easy reach. Then she walked into the kitchen and filled the kettle. "Would you like a cup of coffee?"

She appeared so comfortable in his kitchen. Like it was a familiar space. And of course, it was. She'd been going back and forth from his apartment for months.

He smiled. "Sounds good."

The meow of a cat snagged his attention. He looked around and found Garfield sliding in from the courtyard. When the big Tom realized he was there, he stopped momentarily as if in surprise and then trotted over to Shane. His meow grew more strident and he rubbed against Shane's legs.

"Garfield, my man! It's so good to see you!" he said.

He automatically bent forward to give the cat a pat and then thought better of it as he started to lose his balance. Embarrassed, he reached out for the couch to steady himself. Molly took it in her stride. She came out from behind the counter and bent down and swept Garfield into her arms.

Shane blinked in surprise. "Wow. He isn't usually so friendly with other people. I'm surprised he let you pick him up."

Molly scratched Garfield affectionately behind the ears and brought him closer. "Oh, he was a bit standoffish to begin with, but over the months we've come to know each other. I'm not sure that he likes me, but he's learned to tolerate my presence and he's open to a cuddle now and then. A bit like you and me, right?" She winked again.

Shane laughed, overcome with tenderness and love for the woman who stood beside him. Even his taciturn cat was basking in her attention.

With Molly's help, he settled himself awkwardly on the couch. Molly set Garfield in his lap. Shane stroked the soft fur. The pent-up emotions of the past months overwhelmed him. He was home, safe and sound, well on the way to getting better and he had the woman he loved by his side. His prayers had been answered. He felt so blessed.

Tears welled up in his eyes. He tried to swipe them away, but they kept coming. Molly came toward him carrying two steaming cups of coffee. At the sight of him, she set them down on the coffee table and came and sat beside him. Garfield scooted off his lap. Molly laughed. Then she cupped Shane's cheeks between her hands and kissed him softly on the mouth.

"Hey, you. It's okay. It's okay. You're home. You're going to be okay."

She interspersed her quiet words of comfort with soft and tender kisses. All at once, the passion he'd held back for so long engulfed him. He kissed her with fire and heat, his heart pounding a mile to the minute. She kissed him back, matching his passion, slanting her mouth for greater access, burying her hands in his hair. Blood rushed to his groin and he groaned.

"Molly..."

She pulled back and stared at him with eyes that were tumultuous with desire. "I know. I feel it too. I've waited so long for this. I don't want to wait another second."

She helped him remove his shoes and then pulled off her boots. The look she gave him was a mixture of desire, anticipation, and uncertainty. He wanted to reassure her she didn't need to look uncertain. He had this. She was safe with him. He silently vowed to love her so thoroughly she'd feel like she'd exploded into a million pieces.

Chapter Seventeen

olly reached out to Shane and helped him off the couch. Nerves and anticipation flooded through her. Holding hands, she walked with him slowly down the hallway toward his room. She'd been coming regularly over there for months. She knew the place almost as well as she knew her own. But somehow it felt different with Shane there. His presence filled the empty spaces, made the place feel more like a home. It was almost like the apartment had been holding its breath all this time, waiting for its owner to return and now that he had, the rooms could breathe again.

Molly felt the same. Being in Shane's home without him had made her feel a bit like a stalker or a voyeur, even though she'd been there at his invitation to help him out. Now that he was back where he belonged, she felt like she belonged there too. The warm invitation in his eyes as he led her toward his bedroom only strengthened the feeling.

As he reached the open door of his bedroom, his fingers tightened their grip on hers. The look he gave her sizzled her nerve endings. They'd both been waiting for this day for a long time. Now it had finally arrived. Her heart skipped a beat and then her pulse began pounding.

What if I mess it up? What if make a fool of myself? What if he doesn't find me attractive?

The questions bombarded her and it was all she could do not to turn tail and run. Shane must have sensed her inner turmoil. He stopped and turned to her and cupped her cheek. The tenderness in his gaze stole her breath.

"We're not going to do anything you don't want to, Molly. I've waited so long for this moment, and I've dreamed of it every night, but I'm willing to wait until you're absolutely certain you want this as much as me."

She gazed up at him. The confidence and love that shone from his eyes settled her nerves. "I want this, Shane. I truly do. I... I guess I'm just feeling a bit nervous."

"Of course, you're feeling nervous. This is your first time. I'm going to make it the most magical experience of your life." He paused and then added, "Do you trust me? Trust us?"

"Yes," she breathed.

His head descended. She closed her eyes. His lips touched hers in a featherlight kiss, leaving her yearning for more. Instead, he led her into his bedroom and halted a few feet from the bed. Molly looked around her. Though she'd been in the room before, it was like she was seeing it for the first time. Knowing what they were about to do brought everything into sharp focus.

The king-sized bed with its impressive, silver-colored, padded fabric headboard filled a good portion of the room.

The antique dresser that stood on one wall hosted a collection of framed photographs—an elderly couple she presumed were Shane's parents and a twenty-something young woman who looked enough like Shane that Molly had guessed she must be his younger sister. Her gaze skittered past the dresser to the window where the bright morning sunshine poured in, filling the room with light.

Shane limped over to the window and drew the curtains before returning to her side. He reached up and cupped her cheek, sending her thoughts scattering. She tilted her head. The pad of his thumb scraped across her lips and then back again. He stared at her with hooded eyes, his mouth slightly parted, his cheeks flushed.

Her breath caught at the desire in his face and her heart took off at a gallop. His thumb left her lips and traced a path down her neck until he was stopped by the closed buttons on her uniform shirt. She'd come straight from work to the hospital, not wanting to waste time going home to change. This was the day they'd been waiting for. She'd wanted to be there for every single minute of it.

But now she blushed at the thought of the uniform she wore and the plain cotton underwear beneath it. She should have waited until she'd had time to buy some sexy lingerie and prepare for this moment properly. Thank goodness she'd recently shaved her legs.

"You're overthinking this, Molly," Shane chided gently with a soft smile.

Molly blushed again. It was darn inconvenient the way he seemed to be able to read her thoughts.

"I... I was just thinking I should have gone home and showered and changed before coming to the hospital. I've been at work all night and I probably smell like—"

Her rush of words was cut off by Shane's index finger. He pressed it against her lips and smiled.

"Do you want to take a shower?"

"Umm...." She looked at him, undecided.

"I think you smell delicious. And I know you're going to taste even better."

Once again, the bright light of desire in his eyes eased her nerves and all thoughts of a shower disintegrated. Her heart leaped with excitement. Slowly, her arms crept around his neck and when his head lowered, she stood on tiptoes and met him halfway. Their lips touched and it was like tinder to a flame. She was engulfed by heat. Her lips tingled, her skin was on fire, molten warmth flooded her veins and centered in her groin.

The kiss went on and on. Shane's tongue stole inside her mouth and swept the warm recesses. His arms tightened about her, pulling her close. She felt the unmistakable evidence of his desire. As if privy to her thoughts once again, he cupped her ass and pressed her against his erection.

"Can you feel how much I want you?"

His voice was husky with desire. It sent a shiver of need running through her. She also felt a sense of awe at the power she had over him. She wondered how he'd react if she told him she'd changed her mind and then knew with complete certainty that he'd honor her wishes and stop. The knowledge filled her with confidence and gave her a sense of calm. It was like learning to snowplow on the ski slopes. Once she'd conquered the art of stopping, it no longer mattered how fast she catapulted forward through the snow.

Of course, making love with Shane had nothing to do with snow skiing, but there was a similar feeling of inherent danger accompanied by self-preservation instincts. Or maybe that was merely her nerves...

"Less thinking and more doing," Shane murmured as he turned them around and sat on the edge of the bed. He spread his legs wide, pulling her between them. He reached up and slid open the first few buttons on her shirt.

With him sitting, they were almost at eye level. She stood mesmerized as his hands worked their way down. When he was nearly halfway, he tugged at her shirt and pulled it out of her waistband and then attended to the last of the buttons. Then he spread the fabric wide and looked his fill. She blushed as he stared at her plain black bra, but then he reached out and touched the smooth skin above the top of her breasts, his expression almost reverent.

"You're so beautiful."

The simple statement, said with so much feeling and sincerity, touched her deep inside. Coupled with the look in his eyes, she forgot all about her plain underwear. He slowly pushed her shirt off her shoulders until it fell soundlessly to the floor. Then he reached behind her and undid the clasp of her bra.

Every movement, every action was calm and slow, as if he wanted to give her every opportunity to tell him no. It was lucky for both of them that saying "no" was the last thing on her mind. Desire coursed through her veins. Everywhere he touched, he left a trail of fire. Once again, a burning, yearning sensation centered in her core and they weren't even naked yet. She couldn't wait to lie with him, skin to skin.

He cupped her breasts and squeezed them, as if testing their weight. His thumbs stroked over her nipples, eliciting a groan. His eyes glittered with desire. She thought she'd feel embarrassed standing naked to his gaze, but she realized she enjoyed having him watch her, especially while he looked at her with such pleasure and excitement.

On a surge of impatience, she reached out and tugged his T-shirt free from his jeans. She pulled the soft fabric up over his head and tossed it aside. He was perfectly formed, with prominent pectorals and a washboard stomach. As she raked her fingers over his chest, she heard his sharp intake of breath and his muscles quivered beneath her touch.

"Do you like it when I touch you?" she murmured.

"Very much. I've been dreaming of you doing that and more for so long. I can't believe it's finally happening."

Emboldened by his words, she splayed her hands across his chest and massaged his firm muscles. The light scattering of hair only added to his attractiveness. She ran her fingers over its softness and then bent over him and pressed a kiss just above one of his small, puckered nipples.

Once again, she heard him snatch his breath. Her tongue came out and swiped across the hard nub and then she took it into her mouth and suckled.

"Oh, sweet Molly. You're driving me wild."

His words only spurred her on. Never had she felt so powerful. She kissed and suckled first one and then the other nipple, all the time reveling in his hoarse encouragement. And then even that wasn't enough. As need poured through her, she pushed him back and followed him down onto the bed. She reached for the belt around his waist and slid it from the loops. Then she made quick work of the top button on his jeans and eased the zipper past his swollen cock.

He wore silk boxers. They were as soft and silky as they looked. The stark contrast of his hard cock beneath the soft fabric drove her wild. She'd never touched a man like this before. She was curious, expectant, and a little scared. Not of what was to come, but that she might hurt him. Tentatively, she closed her hand around his shaft.

Shane's groan was so heartfelt, she immediately released him. "Did I hurt you?"

"No. Hell, no. Keep touching me. Please. It feels so good."

He lifted his hips so she could tug his jeans down his legs. She pulled off his shoes and then got his jeans off all the way. She moved back between his legs. With a single-minded focus, fascinated, she stroked the full length of him through his boxers. He pressed into her hand. Growing more confident, she ran her hand all the way down and all the way up and then reached down and cupped his balls. They were full and taut. He spread his legs wider on the bed to give her better access.

"Can you feel how much I want you?" he rasped.

His words excited her. She slid her arms back up his chest and bent her head down to his. This time, she met his lips with hers in a passionate kiss, desperate for more. They kissed and kissed until they were both out of breath and burning with need.

Shane was the first to pull away. Breathing hard, he sat up and shucked off his boxers and kicked them away. He levered himself off the bed and stood before her, naked and erect, letting her look her fill.

He's magnificent... Like a proud, muscled stallion...

She took in the length and width of his erection and her eyes grew round. Though she knew how the mechanics of sex worked, she had a moment of doubt about whether he'd fit. Some of that must have shown on her face. Shane frowned slightly.

"What is it, Molly? What are you afraid of?"

She blushed. "Not afraid. Just... I didn't realize men could be that big. Are you sure...?" She blushed again but forced herself to continue. "Are you sure you're going to fit?"

The words came out in a rush. Heat exploded across her face. Shane merely smiled; his eyes filled with tenderness. He reached down and drew her up against him and folded her in his arms.

"We'll fit," he whispered.

Molly melted against him, loving the feel of her breasts against his skin. His soft chest hair teased at her nipples, turning them into hard nubs and driving her wild. She shifted restlessly, eager to feel all of him against her skin. As if reading her mind, his hands went to her uniform pants. He paused at her belt and shot her an inquiring look. She nodded breathlessly.

Shane made short work of her belt. In no time at all, his hands were smoothing her pants down her hips. She shimmied out of them and kicked them away. She stood before him wearing nothing more than a scrap of black cotton underwear. Once again, his hands went to her hips. Slowly, he eased her panties off. Once again, she kicked them away and let him look his fill.

"So beautiful," he breathed.

And then, reaching for her hand, he led her to his bed and once again pulled her down beside him. They came together, chest to chest, legs entwined. He rolled her beneath him and began pressing kisses all over her face. When he reached her lips, she kissed him back with all the passion she felt inside, loving the feel of him against her. His erection pressed insistently against her stomach and she tensed momentarily, reminded of how big he was, but a moment later, she forced herself to let her anxieties go. He'd said they'd fit and she trusted him. Drawing in a deep breath, she relaxed against him.

Shane continued to kiss a path down her neck, her chest, her breasts. He licked and suckled her nipples. He kissed her stomach and across her abdomen, pausing to dip his tongue into the slight indentation of her belly button. Her muscles clenched with anticipation.

And then he was there, between her legs, burying his face against the most private part of her. His tongue stole out and stroked her tender flesh, long, slow, rhythmic strokes destined to drive her wild. She started in surprise and her breath caught at the tumult of emotions rushing through her. She grabbed fistfuls of the sheets. When his tongue delved even deeper, into the depths of her being, she couldn't hold back a cry of ecstasy.

Shane lifted his head. "Do you like that?"

"Yes," she gasped. "It feels incredible."

"Has anyone ever loved you like this?"

She looked away, still slightly embarrassed over her lack of experience. "No."

Shane's expression filled with love and tenderness. He renewed his efforts, loving her with his tongue and fingers until she didn't think she could stand it a moment longer. Desire had her body on fire. Need built like a freight train that had lost control roaring down a mountain, gathering speed at an incredible rate that could only end in disaster.

But this didn't feel like a disaster. It felt like nothing she'd ever felt before. Though she'd learned to bring herself to orgasm, the feeling couldn't compare to this. She had a fleeting moment of wondering how good it would feel when Shane filled her with his huge cock. If the feelings he'd generated inside her right now were any indication, she was in for pleasure so great it would be indescribable.

His delicious torment continued and the need inside her grew. She moved restlessly against him and buried her fingers in his hair. He licked and sucked and stroked and filled her with his fingers. The constant rhythm drove her mad with desire.

"Come for me, Molly. You can do it. You're so close. Let go and ride the wave."

His words of encouragement pushed her over the edge. With a cry, she reached the pinnacle and wave after wave of pleasure washed over her, leaving her breathless and weak. It was a long time later that she felt strong enough to lift her head.

Still in position between her legs, Shane grinned at her, his eyes filled with triumph and pride.

"How do you feel?" he asked.

"Shattered," she admitted. "Boneless. That was...amazing."

He chuckled and moved up to cover her body with his. He pressed a kiss against her lips. "That was just the beginning."

Once again, she felt the hardness of his erection as it pressed insistently against her belly. The feel of it fanned the dormant flames of her desire back to life. She couldn't believe after experiencing the most mind-blowing orgasm of her life she could feel like doing it all over again, but she did.

She wound her arms around Shane's neck and kissed him back. His lips opened under hers and she thrust her tongue into the warm recesses of his mouth, relishing the taste of herself on his tongue. She'd kissed men before, but it had never felt like this. Like she could kiss him forever and it would never be enough.

His lips were firm and supple and soft. Such a contrast to the hardness of his body. Though he'd lamented the loss of muscle tone from months of lying on his back in a hospital bed, he'd worked hard and looked good to her. She could only imagine how fit and strong he must have been prior to the accident.

She ran her hands over his shoulders and then down his sides. They kissed until they were both breathless once again. Shane pulled away and buried his face in the crook of her neck, breathing hard. Then he shifted until he could see her face.

"I ache to be inside you Molly," he said hoarsely.

His eyes were dark and stormy with desire. His chest rose and fell with his breaths. His cock burned a brand against her belly and she was filled with another surge of white-hot need.

"Yes," she breathed.

His eyes flared with emotion and then he reached across her and opened the bedside drawer. He pulled out a condom and sheathed himself and then quickly returned to her side. He positioned himself between her legs. She felt a momentary twinge of alarm as his cock probed her wet entrance, but she forced herself to relax. Her legs fell open.

The look of concentration on Shane's face as he eased his swollen cock inside her filled her with wonder.

"That's it, Molly. So hot, so tight. Lift your legs around me. Open for me, babe."

And as she did, his hips thrust forward and he was buried deep inside her. She cried out in momentary surprise at the sharp sting of pain between her legs. He was large and uncomfortable, but to her relief, the pain quickly receded and she was left with the sexy feeling of being stretched wide and full of his cock.

"Are you okay?" he asked, looking down at her, his voice hoarse.

"Yes."

"You feel so good. I wanted to make this last, but I'm not sure I can stop."

She reached up and clung to his broad shoulders, pulling him closer. "I don't want you to stop."

That was all the encouragement he needed. With a visceral groan, he began moving, plunging inside her over and over again. She urged him on with quiet murmurs, loving the feel of him filling her. His movements became faster and the concentration on his face grew. And then he cried out and started thrusting faster and harder until finally the tension eased and he collapsed against her, breathing hard.

His voice was muffled against her shoulder. "Oh, sweet Molly. That was...amazing."

Chapter Eighteen

Tessa Barone lay back on the couch after refilling her glass of whiskey. She'd lost count of the number of drinks she'd thrown back already, but from the fuzziness in her head and the fact the images on the TV had started to blur, it was more than a few. Not that she cared. Ever since her marriage had broken down, her life had gone to hell. The only good things were her kids: Baxter, Sonia, and Nell. They were spending the night at a friend's house. She was glad. It meant she could get stinking drunk and not have to worry about them discovering her.

Sonia and Nell were definitely old enough to be concerned about her drinking. This wasn't the first time she'd gotten drunk. Over the years since Martin had walked out on their marriage, it had happened more times than she wanted to admit. And who could blame her? Her husband, the man who'd vowed to love and cherish and protect her all the days of her life was a fraud. He'd fallen in love with someone else. Now he'd had a baby with her. They were his family now. Tessa and their kids were on their own.

My kids...

She didn't know what she'd do without them. They were her life. They were her reason for getting out of bed every day. The very thought of losing them sent her into a panic. That was the reason she hadn't gone to the police. It had been nearly three long, tortuous months since the accident and yet she'd remained silent. If she confessed to being involved, she'd go to jail. Her children would be handed back to their father, a father who'd told her he no longer wanted to be part of their lives. They'd be better off in foster homes than living in a household where there was a complete absence of love.

No! Not a foster home! Not any kind of home! Only there, with her, where she could love and cherish them and keep them safe...

But the guilt of staying silent was slowly killing her. She couldn't eat, she couldn't sleep, she could barely get through a shift at work. She was constantly thinking about the accident and the fact she was responsible. On top of all that was the guilt she felt every time she was around her friend.

Molly. Dear, sweet Molly...

Tessa couldn't ask for a better friend. If Molly knew what Tessa had done, it would destroy their friendship. Just another reason why the best thing to do was to keep her mouth shut.

If only it were that easy...

If only her conscience would leave her alone. But the guilt swamped her every time she thought about what she'd done.

If only she didn't have an asshole for an ex-husband who'd told her in no uncertain terms that he'd moved on from her and their kids...

Tipping up the glass of whiskey toward her lips, she downed it in three swallows. The alcohol burned a fiery path down her throat. She welcomed the burn and looked forward to the hours of oblivion that would shortly follow. That was the only respite she got. Inevitably, the sun would rise the next morning and she'd wake with a dry mouth and a thumping headache. The guilt would crash into her again and she'd be right back where she started, a vicious cycle that damned her either way.

How long can I keep going like this?

Shane woke the next morning with a smile on his face. He couldn't remember ever feeling so good. He looked at the woman still asleep beside him and knew he owed everything to her. Molly's dark lashes cast a shadow on her cheeks. She was just as beautiful sleeping as she was awake. He had to pinch himself to check that this was real.

Molly's eyes drifted open. When she saw him watching her, she smiled. It lit up her face and filled him with warmth.

How did I get so lucky?

"Good morning," she said.

He pressed a leisurely kiss against her lips. "Good morning."

"Yesterday...last night... It was incredible."

He drew her close against him. "*You* were incredible."

She snuggled beside him, resting her cheek against his chest. "Is it always like that?"

He heard the wonder and curiosity in her voice and smiled. "Not always. It depends on how much you care for the person."

"Have you been with women you didn't care about?"

He nodded. "Yes."

"One-night stands?"

"A couple."

"So, you know what it feels like."

"Yes. There's no comparison. Such encounters, it's just sex. A physical release. There's no emotional involvement. No connection beyond physical pleasure. But with you…" He paused, wanting to find the right words to express exactly how he felt.

"With you, I was making love. I was connected to you on every level, physical and emotional. It makes all the difference to make love to a woman you're head-over-heels in love with."

Her smile was slow and glorious. "You're head-over-heels in love with me?"

"You bet."

They looked at each other and their smiles of contentment grew wider. It felt so good to finally be with this woman, his woman.

"So, what are you up to today?" Molly asked.

Shane threaded his fingers through hers and pressed a soft kiss on the back of her hand. "I'm happy to stay right here all day. What about you?"

Molly laughed, her eyes full of tenderness. She shifted until she was lying on top of him. "Sounds like a plan."

She dipped her head and kissed him on the mouth, teasing him with her lips. He opened his mouth to her and reveled in the feel of her tongue stroking inside it. She might have been a virgin yesterday, but she was a darn fast learner. Less than twenty-four hours since they'd first made love and she'd picked up the art of kissing so well she could drive him wild with nothing more than her lips.

Desire kindled inside him and sent a surge of blood straight to his cock. It didn't take her long to notice. She laughed softly, confidently, and pressed herself against his burgeoning erection.

"Do you like what you feel?" he teased.

She nipped at his bottom lip. "I like it a lot."

She kissed her way across his chest and took first one and then the other of his puckered nipples in her mouth. She licked and suckled just like he'd done with her the day before.

"A fast learner indeed," he murmured.

She shot him a mischievous look. "Do you want to know what else I want to learn?"

His gut clenched with desire at the intent in her eyes. "Show me."

With her teasing gaze still on his, she moved lower down his body, pressing kisses against his skin as she went. When she got to his cock, she first encircled the thick shaft with her hand before bending her head and sliding it into her mouth. The hot moistness sent shards of desire straight to his groin. His cock twitched. It felt like he was inside her again, his cock surrounded by wet, snug heat. And then she started using her tongue to stroke along his length. At the same time, she sucked him hard into her mouth.

Shane's eyes closed against an involuntary groan of desire. There was no one and nothing but Molly and her magical mouth. She sucked and licked and squeezed and it was all he could do to hold onto his self-control.

"Am I doing it right?" she asked, her expression a mixture of knowing and innocence.

"Oh, yeah. You're doing it right."

His voice was guttural with need. His hands fisted in the sheets. He wanted nothing more than to flip her over and plunge into her warmth, but he resisted. This was about her need to feel in control, to explore his body at her leisure. After all the things she'd let him do to her the previous day and night, giving her this control was the least he could do, even if lying there, tense and still while she drove him insane with desire nearly killed him.

She continued to suck him deep into her mouth, licking and stroking and driving him wild. He was close to exploding, but he didn't want it to end just yet. As if sensing how close he was to the edge, Molly's teasing ministrations eased and she slid back up his body. He opened his eyes and looked at her.

"Did you like that?" she asked, looking a little shy.

He nodded. "I liked that a lot."

"Do you mind if I sit on top? I'm a bit sore."

Once again, she looked adorably shy. A faint tinge of pink colored her cheeks. His heart turned over with love and tenderness.

"You can sit wherever you like. And I'll try to be gentle." He smiled.

She smiled back at him and shifted until she straddled him. His cock pressed urgently against her.

"Do you have a condom?" she asked.

He quickly reached over and pulled one out of his bedside drawer and handed it to her. Her eyes widened with surprise.

"Have a go," he urged.

She smiled again. "Well, okay. Just as long as you know, I've never done this before."

He winked. "You're a smart woman and a fast learner. I have complete faith in your abilities."

She chuckled and tore open the foil packet. With excruciatingly gentle hands, she took his cock and after a couple of attempts, managed to pull it on. When she was done, she gave a happy little sigh of accomplishment. He couldn't help but smile.

God, she's adorable. I'm so much in love with her, it's scary...

And then she eased herself down on his cock and all thoughts but the feeling of her tight warmth encompassing him disappeared. As she seated herself fully upon him, he moved his hips and she sank even deeper. Her mouth parted on a gasp of surprise. Taking hold of her hips, he guided her movements until she was riding him like a wild brumby galloping across the Snowy Mountains.

It was all he could do not to explode inside her, but he wanted her to reach fulfilment before him. Her breasts bounced in time with her movements, further intoxicating him. As she leaned forward, he reached up and dragged one toward his mouth, closing his lips over her erect nipple. She gasped again and ground her hips against him. A flush of pleasure tinged her lips.

She closed her eyes and threw back her head and bounced on his cock like crazy. He loved to see her so abandoned, engrossed in nothing but reaching her climax. And then she was there, crying out and shuddering against him. He felt the contractions of her inner muscles around his cock and he was done for.

With a shout of triumph, he thrust his hips forward and pumped his cock deep inside her with all his might. Within moments he'd reached the precipice and with another cry, toppled over the other side. She collapsed against him and held him close. Her breasts were crushed against his chest. Her breath came as fast as his.

Slowly, they came back down to earth. He opened his eyes and found her grinning down at him.

"Good?" she asked.

He stared up at her with all the love he felt for her in his heart. "Amazing."

The sun was a lot higher in the sky when Molly woke a second time. She discovered Shane was already awake and was watching her. The tender expression in his eyes stole her breath. She couldn't believe how good she felt.

If this is what being in love feels like, no wonder my siblings all look so happy.

The thought brought a smile to her face.

"What are you thinking about?" Shane asked idly.

"Just about how much I love you and how wonderful I feel. I'm the luckiest girl in the world."

"That's exactly how I feel," he said softly. "It scares me a bit."

She nodded. "I feel the same way. For so long, I was too scared to let myself fall in love. I was scared of what might happen if things didn't work out. But what I should have focused on was how wonderful love can feel and how I just have to have faith that you won't break my heart."

"It's perfectly normal for you to have some doubts, especially after all the emotional barriers you've had to overcome to be here. You had that fear for a long time. That's not just going to disappear."

With infinite tenderness, he brushed a lock of hair off her face. "This is all so new and unexpected. It happened so fast. It's like a dream. We'd both be forgiven for wondering what we did to deserve it and how long it can last." His expression sobered. "Just know this: I've never felt this way about anyone and I can't imagine feeling this way again. I promise you this: I won't ever break your heart. I love you, Molly Barrington. Nothing's ever going to change that."

Molly's heart turned over. She reached out and cupped his cheek. When she spoke again, her voice was husky with emotion. "Thank you. I feel exactly the same way."

They shared a slow and tender kiss. When they finally pulled apart, Molly was embarrassed to hear her stomach rumbling.

Shane merely laughed. "Sounds like someone's ready for breakfast."

Molly grinned and looked at her watch. "Probably brunch more like it."

"It's a good thing I got up and fed Garfield earlier. He'd have meowed the place down otherwise."

Molly laughed. "Poor Garfield!"

"When are you due back at work?" Shane asked.

Molly grinned. "Didn't I tell you? I've just started five days off. Plenty of time to eat and drink and…get to know each other better." Her eyes gleamed with intent.

Shane groaned. "You're going to kill me, woman!"

As Molly leaned over him and began kissing him with increasing passion, he took her in his arms once again.

"But what a way to go, right?" she murmured against his lips.

"You bet."

Chapter Nineteen

Molly floated into work after spending the past five days with Shane. They'd filled their days with short walks along the promenade that ran parallel to the beach, going out to eat, attending Shane's daily physio sessions, and making love. It felt like they were on their honeymoon, each day better than the last. Molly never wanted the feeling to end.

She'd never felt so happy. Once or twice over the past five days, she'd reached for her phone to call her family. She had Charlotte on speed dial. But then she'd paused. She wasn't ready yet to share Shane with her family. She wanted him all to herself for just a little while longer.

There would come a time when she'd introduce him to everyone and sit through the onslaught of questions, particularly about his criminal record. She and Shane had discussed it. She respected his privacy. As far as she was concerned, his past was nobody's business.

But Shane was adamant he wanted her family to know. With so many cops in her family, there was always a chance they'd find out anyway and he didn't want them to think he had anything to hide. He wasn't proud of what had happened, but he'd taken full responsibility and paid his dues. Molly agreed.

Her family wasn't judgmental, and she was confident they'd accept Shane despite his flaws, but they'd no doubt have some concerns about the speed with which Molly and Shane had fallen in love.

She could understand that. Every now and then, she had some worries herself, but then she'd look at Shane and see the love in his eyes and her fears would melt away like snowflakes in the sun. She smiled at the analogy. Shane had told her he loved to snow ski, among other things. She'd been going to the snow with her family since she was a child. She couldn't wait to take on the slopes with him. She had no doubt he'd be back to doing everything he'd done and more before the accident. She looked forward to being by his side and sharing in those achievements, cheering him all the way.

She spotted Tessa in the crib room, heating up something in the microwave. Molly walked in and greeted her with a smile.

"Hi, Tessa. How are things?"

Tessa turned and gave her a brief, strained smile and then turned away again without replying. Molly walked over to the coffee machine and filled her cup. As she added milk and sugar, she glanced sideways at her friend.

Tessa's hair was lank and oily and hung like matted string around her face. The full face of makeup she usually wore to work was also non-existent. Nothing more than a slash of red lipstick that only served as a stark contrast against the pallor of her skin.

"Is everything okay?" Molly asked quietly.

Tessa merely shrugged. The microwave beeped and she opened the door and reached in and pulled out her food. It looked like Chinese takeaway leftovers. She took a fork out of the cutlery drawer and took a seat at the dining table. Without a word, she began to eat.

Feeling a little rebuffed, but intent on finding out what was wrong with her friend, Molly took her coffee to the table. Before she could pull out a chair, the station phone rang. Setting down her cup, she turned and answered the call. As the operator relayed the information for their first callout of the morning, Molly's belly filled with dread. She hung up the phone and turned to Tessa.

"MVA, head-on collision. Two cars involved. Multiple victims."

"Where?"

"Cronulla."

Food and coffee forgotten, within moments, Molly and Tessa were in their ambulance and heading to the scene of the accident. Tessa opted to drive and remain in charge of communications, leaving Molly to be responsible for the patients. As usual, they arrived before the police. Already a large crowd had gathered. People surrounded both vehicles, pulling open car doors and shouting. Above it all, Molly could hear screaming.

Tessa found a safe spot to park and relayed their position back to base. Molly climbed out of the ambulance and hurried to the first vehicle. A late model, navy-blue Ford, the sedan had suffered extensive damage. The front of the car was crushed. Molly pushed her way through the crowd.

"Excuse me. Paramedic coming through. Excuse me! I need to get through."

The crowd parted reluctantly. One look at the driver and Molly could see the elderly woman was dead. Blood trickled down her face from a wound higher up on her head. Sightless eyes stared at Molly, opaque in death.

Molly quickly checked for a pulse to confirm her first impressions. Nothing. She turned away. There was nothing she could do for that victim. She hoped the passengers in the other car had fared better. As she strode over to the red Honda, the screaming got louder. Once again, she pushed her way through the crowd until she was beside the second vehicle. The rear passenger doors were open, but three young children remained strapped in their car seats along the back seat. Quickly approaching them, Molly forced a smile.

"Hi, guys. My name's Molly. I'm a paramedic. I'm going to help get you out of there."

The youngest child was a baby, maybe two or three months old and was screaming piteously. The child in the middle, another boy, looked like he was about seven. The little girl nearest to Molly was maybe three or four. The older children were also crying, but on first glance, all appeared to have escaped serious injury.

Thank God for those car seats...

Molly then moved to the driver's side. One look through the broken window and her heart sank. It didn't take a paramedic to realize this woman was also dead. Though quite a bit younger than the other driver, she'd sadly met a similar fate. Molly had no way of knowing the relationship between this driver and the children, but it was difficult not to draw the conclusion that the children might very well have just lost their mother.

With a heavy heart, Molly looked around her. The police had finally arrived. Thankfully uniformed officers were now herding the crowd back and setting up crime scene tape. One officer came up to her. Molly walked a short distance away from the car and lowered her voice.

"Both drivers are dead."

"I'll call the morgue," the officer said, his expression grim. "Is that it?"

"No. There are three kids in the Honda, all alive. I haven't yet properly assessed their condition, but they look like they're going to survive."

Relief flooded the officer's face. "That's something at least."

As the officer left to get on with the work of processing the scene and arranging for the removal of the bodies, Molly returned to the children.

The baby was still screaming. The other two children had quieted to the occasional sob. They both looked so scared and shaken it broke Molly's heart. She looked around for Tessa but couldn't see her through the crowd. Assuring the children she'd be right back, she strode back toward the ambulance. She found Tessa still seated behind the wheel.

"Two fatalities. The morgue guys are going to deal with them. We also have three kids who've survived the impact. I haven't given them a proper examination yet, but they don't look too bad. All three are suffering shock and are understandably upset. I could use your help in getting them onto stretchers."

Tessa was pale. When she raised a hand to push back a hank of hair, Molly could see she was trembling. It was so unlike Tessa. She was usually so cool and calm and collected at an accident scene.

Molly frowned. "Are you okay?"

Tessa nodded quickly. "Of course. I'll call for a counsellor. Do you think that will help?"

"Yes, that sounds like a good idea."

Members of state-funded counseling services were always on call and could be used in circumstances like these. They were particularly utilized when there were children involved in traumatic situations. Having a counselor on site would help to calm the children down and allow Molly do proper assessments on them.

"How old are the kids?" Tessa asked.

"One's a baby. The other two are young kids—the first one's maybe three or four and the other six or seven."

Tessa nodded. As she climbed out of the ambulance and headed to the side, Molly left her and returned to the children. Once again, she tried to reassure them.

"It's going to be okay, guys. What's your little brother's name?" she asked the oldest child.

"M-Matthew," the boy stammered.

"And your sister?"

"S-Summer."

"And how about you?"

"I'm D-Doyle."

"Well, Doyle. You're being very brave. I bet it was scary when you collided with that car."

"Y-yes." His eyes filled with tears. "H-how's Mommy?"

Molly closed her eyes briefly against a surge of pain and avoided answering the question. "How old are you, Doyle?"

"S-seven."

"And your little brother? How old is he?"

"M-Matthew's only a baby. He was born in the middle of September."

That made the infant about nine or ten weeks old. Molly's guess had been right.

"What about Summer? How old is she?"

"I'm four," Summer piped up, swiping at her tears.

"Do you hurt anywhere, Summer?"

The little girl shook her head. "Where's Mommy? I want my mommy!"

She started crying again. Doyle looked like he was on the verge of losing it again too. Molly looked around for Tessa and was relieved when she finally spied her pushing through the crowd.

"Did you get onto a counselor?" Molly asked.

Tessa looked at her blankly. "What counselor?"

Molly frowned. "The trauma counselor. We just talked about it."

Tessa looked away. "I'm sorry. I didn't hear you."

Molly felt a stirring of unease. Something was going on with Tessa. Something weird. "Tessa, what's going on? Are you all right?"

Tessa kept her face averted. "Of course."

The children were now crying in earnest again. Molly returned to their side and did her best to reassure them, but they'd lost it. She suspected the older children could see their mother in the front seat and had realized she wasn't moving. She sighed. There was nothing she could do about that.

"Keep talking to them," she said to Tessa. "I'm going to check the baby over."

Tessa didn't respond. Swallowing her impatience, Molly tried again. "For goodness' sake, Tessa! Can you stay with the older two kids?"

Tessa gave her a blank look but shifted a little closer to the car. Molly didn't know what the hell was going on with her friend, but she didn't have time right now to find out. There were children who needed her help. She walked around the other side of the car where the baby was. She reached in and released the child from his restraints.

He was still crying. Carefully checking for broken bones and other injuries, when she found nothing to cause alarm, she was finally satisfied he was fine. Gently, she eased him out of the car seat and held him in her arms.

"*Shh*, little man. It's okay. You're going to be okay. *Shh*."

Molly looked over the roof of the car to where Tessa continued to stare blankly at the two older children. They were still sobbing. She'd made no attempt to bend down and speak with them or offer them any reassurance.

What the hell is going on with Tessa?

Molly made a note to speak with their supervisor, the duty operations manager, Raoul Kumar. Perhaps he knew something about Tessa's situation that Molly wasn't privy to.

And if he didn't, he might be able to suggest to Tessa that she take some leave. Whatever was going on with her, it was clear she wasn't in the presence of mind to attend callouts and that put everyone's safety at risk.

Shane heard the front door of his apartment open and close and his heart skipped a beat. Anticipation flooded through his veins. He'd spent the day taking it easy, doing some general cleaning and a load of laundry. When his legs started to ache, he took his novel out into the courtyard and spent some time relaxing in the warm sunshine. Now Molly was home and he couldn't be happier.

They hadn't really discussed their living arrangements, but she lived on the second floor of a three-story building that didn't come with a lift. It made more sense for her to stay with him. Besides, she'd looked after the place for nearly three months. She was hardly a stranger to the apartment.

And Garfield had warmed to her. He now preferred to sit on Molly's lap. Shane pretended to be peeved that his cat had ditched him in favor of the newcomer. Secretly, he was pleased Garfield had accepted her into his life as completely as Shane had.

"Hey, you," Molly said, coming into the kitchen. She dropped her designer handbag on the counter and walked around to give him a kiss.

Shane took her in his arms and kissed her properly. "How was your day?" he asked. "You look beat."

She sighed. "Yeah, I am beat. It was a hectic day."

"Can I get you a glass of wine?"

She smiled gratefully. "That would be wonderful."

He reached into the fridge and pulled out a bottle of Chardonnay he'd put in there a few hours ago to chill. Twisting off the top, he poured her a glass and handed it to her.

"Thank you. You're an angel."

"Hey, you've been hard at work all day. I've done nothing but lounge around."

"Well, that's what you're meant to be doing. Not so long ago, you couldn't even walk, remember? The doctors have urged you to take it slowly. You're still not fully recovered."

"Yeah, yeah, yeah." He grinned. "I ordered Thai takeout. It should be here in the next ten minutes. Is that okay?"

"Of course. I love Thai food."

"Good. I would have liked to cook for you, but my legs aren't quite up to standing for that long." He winked. "I'm just following doctors' orders, right?"

"Right."

They both smiled at each other and it felt so natural and good. Every moment he spent with her was that much better than the last. He couldn't wait to spend the rest of his life with her. With glass in hand, she walked over to the couch and sank into its leather luxuriousness. Leaning her head back, she closed her eyes and sighed. Shane moved behind her and started massaging her shoulders.

"Oh, that feels so good."

"You're as knotty as a pine tree. What happened today?"

She sighed again and took another sip of wine. "Tessa and I were called out to a motor vehicle accident. There were two cars involved. A head-on collision."

Shane's belly clenched. "That doesn't sound good."

She grimaced. "No. It wasn't."

"Any fatalities?"

"Yes. Both drivers died at the scene."

"Oh, Molly! I'm so sorry."

She opened her eyes and looked at him. "That wasn't the worst of it."

He remained silent while she told him about the children who would now go through life without their mother.

"That's terrible," he said quietly when she'd finished. "Do the police know what caused the crash?"

"No. It happened on a quiet suburban street. Someone wasn't paying attention. Either that, or one of the drivers might have had a medical episode that caused them to accelerate through the intersection. Whatever happened, nothing's going to bring those women back."

She fell silent. He continued to massage her shoulders, hoping to ease at least some of the tension in her muscles. She sipped her wine and stared off in the distance. At one point, Garfield padded into the room and jumped up onto her lap. She stroked his soft fur distractedly. And then she spoke again.

"There's something going on with Tessa."

"Tessa? Your friend from work?"

"Yes. She's been a paramedic for many years. Much more experienced than me. She's always the cool head in any crisis, someone to rely on getting the job done, no matter what. But today she just lost it. I don't know what was going on. She just zoned out, like she wasn't there. I had my hands full with three hysterical children and she barely did anything to help. It was weird. So unlike her. I'm worried about her."

"Did you talk to her about it?"

"I tried to. When we got back to the station, I asked her what had happened to her back at the scene, but she only got upset and stormed off. I'm thinking about going to our supervisor."

"It sounds like something's going on. Maybe she's not brave enough to ask for help?"

Molly grimaced. "Yes. I think it had something to do with the fact there were children involved in the accident. It hit close to home. She's got three of her own."

"How old are they?"

"Baxter's ten, Sonia's twelve and Nell is fifteen. Tessa's had it so tough since her marriage broke down. It's been four years since her ex walked out on her and the kids. It's been a struggle for her every day, trying to raise them on her own."

Shane frowned. As a lawyer who specialized in family law, anything to do with divorce and custody battles sparked his attention.

"Surely, he's paying child and spousal support?"

"Child support, yes. I don't know about spousal support. I've never asked her about that. I'm not sure if she's under financial pressure, but something's going on with her."

Molly sighed. "I just wish she'd tell me. Maybe I can help her, maybe I can't, but at least I could offer her some emotional support. Then there's the kids. They're old enough to have some inkling that their mom's suffering. That's got to affect them, too."

"Yes, it's always the kids who get overlooked. The adults are so busy hating each other, they forget about them." He compressed his lips. "I've seen that happen too many times."

Molly tilted her head back to look at him. "I guess you have. How do you feel about kids?"

He shrugged. "You mean, kids in general?"

"Yes. Do you want kids of your own some day?"

Though she asked the question casually, he felt the sudden tension in her muscles and realized how important his response was to her. He answered honestly.

"You might think this strange given my occupation, but I still believe in love and marriage. Call me a dreamer, but that's the way it is. I guess I always thought I'd have kids one day. I think spending two years of my life incarcerated taught me just how short life is."

She smiled and relaxed under his hands. He continued to massage her muscles while he waited for her to speak. When she didn't, he couldn't help but prompt her. "What about you?"

She twisted around and gave him a look that was so tender and loving, it stole his breath.

"Absolutely. I'd love to have kids one day. I might have had a hang up about love and relationships, but having kids is something I've always seen myself doing."

He shot her a quizzical look. "How were you planning to do it without a man in your life?"

She grinned. "Hey, there are ways. Haven't you heard of adoption? Then there's IVF and donor sperm…"

"Would you have really gone down that track?" he asked, surprised.

She shrugged. "I don't know. Maybe. I always wanted kids. It was the other I was scared about."

He limped around the couch and sat beside her and took her in his arms. Pressing his lips against hers, he kissed her gently, thoroughly. When they parted, they were slightly out of breath.

He smiled softly, tenderly. "You don't have to be scared about that any longer. I'm here for you. I love you, now and forever."

Chapter Twenty

T essa leaned against the steel railing of her balcony and stared out into the night. The sky was black as charcoal, unbroken by even the tiniest sliver of moonlight. The blanket of utter darkness reflected her mood as she fought against reliving the nightmare of her day.

The accident... The dead mother... The screaming kids...

She'd been drinking steadily since she'd arrived home. Her fifteen-year-old had suggested she might like to take it easy on the whiskey and her younger children had sat across from her at the dinner table and shot her identical worried looks, but they didn't know how hard it was for her to get up every day and go on. No one did. Not even her best friend.

Thank God the kids were now all in bed asleep. She could drink freely and without guilt. Turning to alcohol wasn't a solution to her problems, but there was no denying it numbed the pain.

She was so close to losing everything. Today was only another reminder of how tenuous her grip was on her sanity and how life could turn on a dial. One moment that mother was taking her kids to football practice, to ballet, to whatever.

Now she was dead and those kids were left to battle on without her.

Who knew if there was a father in the picture? And what good were fathers anyway? They inevitably went running for the hills when things got tough. She only had to look at Martin for proof of that.

A keening sound of distress started low in her stomach and escaped out through her mouth. The sound was so filled with pain it was devastating. She was besieged with panic. The walls were closing in. Her chest went tight.

I can't breathe... I can't breathe... I can't breathe...

Tears streamed down her face. Feelings of hopelessness weighed her down. She stared at the glass in her hand and with a cry of fury, smashed it against the iron railing. Glass splintered into a million pieces. One piece lodged in her hand. Sobbing hard now, she pulled it out and threw it away and then scrambled around for a tissue to stem the flow of blood.

There was glass everywhere, but she was beyond caring. As the sobs continued to wrack her body, she slid slowly to the ground.

I can't go on like this...

Flashbacks from the accident that day, along with the crash she'd been trying so hard to forget flooded her mind. She put her hands up to her eyes and pressed hard against them to block the images out. But it was no good. The sound of screeching metal, the screaming children, the tears. It was all too much.

Curling into a ball, oblivious to the shards of glass that embedded themselves into her skin, she cried herself to sleep.

Molly returned to work the next day feeling optimistic about her future with Shane. He'd been so supportive the night before after her rough day at work. He'd listened and offered advice. He'd given her wine and a massage. He'd been there for her. It only made her love him more. Even better, they were on the same page wanting kids. How good was that? The thought made her smile.

"You're looking mighty pleased with yourself."

Tessa's comment startled Molly from her thoughts. She looked around and saw her friend seated alone at the dining table, her hands wrapped around a steaming cup of coffee. Molly immediately recalled what had happened the day before. She hadn't had time yet to talk to Raoul, but she made another note to do so as soon as possible.

The woman looked terrible. Even worse than the day before. Her eyes were puffy and red. Her cheeks were pale. She had a gauntness about her that Molly only just noticed. A strip of white bandage was wrapped around her hand.

"What happened to your hand?"

Tessa held up her right hand. "This? It's nothing. I accidentally broke a glass last night. Don't worry. It's just a scratch."

Molly's heart went out to her friend. It seemed lately Tessa couldn't catch a break. The long, drawn-out divorce and property settlement had taken its toll on her. The formal court process might have been finalized, but it was obvious something was still going on.

"What is it, Tessa? What's going on? Is it the kids? Is Martin still being difficult?"

To Molly's surprise, Tessa burst into tears. Molly's concern ratcheted up another notch. She moved closer and put her arm around her friend's shoulders.

"Oh, Tessa. Please don't cry. What is it? What's wrong?"

Tessa only howled louder. Molly rubbed her friend's arm. "It's okay, Tessa. It's okay."

Tessa lifted a tear-stained face toward Molly. The devastation in her friend's gaze broke her heart.

"It's not okay, Molly. It's never going to be okay again."

Tessa's voice cracked with emotion and she dissolved into a fresh wave of tears. Molly felt helpless against the woman's pain. She kept murmuring words of reassurance, but she'd never felt so useless.

Then Tessa lifted her head again. "It's all my fault, Molly. I'm the one who did it. Now I'm going to jail."

Molly frowned in confusion. "Did what, Tessa? You're not making sense."

"I did it. I hit your boyfriend's car and almost killed him. It was me. Then I fled the scene."

Molly stared at her in shock and disbelief. Her heart thumped. Blood rushed through her ears.

Surely, I didn't hear her right... It can't be true... Tessa would never do something like that...

Her shock and disbelief must have shown on her face. Tessa shook her head slowly from side to side, her voice ragged with emotion.

"I'm so sorry, Molly. I had to tell you. It's been eating me up inside. I can't bear the stress of hiding it anymore. I needed to tell someone. To tell *you*."

Molly heard the words, but still struggled to process them. *It was Tessa? Tessa's the one who nearly killed Shane?*

"I was on days off when it happened," Tessa continued in a monotone, staring into nothingness. "I was driving home from the shops. I wasn't concentrating. I'd just had a nasty phone call from Martin. His words kept reverberating in my head. I ran the red light. I didn't even see the other vehicle until it was too late.

"The sound of the screeching metal as we collided is a sound I'll never forget. My blood ran cold. I'd hit someone. I didn't know what damage I'd caused. Everything happened so quickly, but I was inundated with panic. I reversed out of the way and fled the scene. All I could think of was that if I stayed, I'd go to jail."

She turned tortured eyes toward Molly who was still immobile with shock.

"I can't go to jail, Molly. Who'd look after my kids? Their father doesn't want them. He's made that very clear. He's moved on with his new wife and baby. That was what we'd been fighting about right before the crash. He told me he was relinquishing all rights to visitation with our children. Like they were something he could set aside whenever he felt like, dispose of like unwanted rubbish, ignore when it suited him. I mean, they're his kids!"

Tessa's breath came fast. She threw another tortured look at Molly. "I was furious. It was like I saw everything through a haze of red. I didn't even realize I'd driven through the red light. The next thing I knew I'd collided with another car."

Molly tried to say something, but she couldn't form the words. Tessa continued in a distressed voice.

"I didn't know anything about the man I'd hit until you told me. I didn't *want* to know. I'd deliberately refrained from watching the news or reading the newspaper. Then you told me who it was and I realized he was my ex-husband's divorce lawyer."

Molly gasped. She'd had no idea of that connection. Just another shock to deal with.

"Of course, that wasn't the reason I plowed him down," Tessa continued, "but I was terrified the police would think it was a motive; that I'd hit him out of revenge. It's not true, but how can I prove it?" She sucked in a ragged breath. "It's only another justification not to turn myself in."

In the ensuing silence, Molly finally found her voice. "So that's why your car was out of action for so many weeks. It wasn't in the garage for a service, it was getting fixed by the smash repairers."

"Yes." Tessa hung her head in shame. "I took it all the way over to a garage in Hornsby to make sure they didn't make any connection with the accident. I'm so sorry, Molly. I'm so sorry."

Molly stared at her, a tsunami of emotions coursing through her. She felt disgusted, anguished, torn. This was her friend, a woman who'd already been through so much. Being left by her husband for another woman and then being dragged through a malicious and nasty divorce. And now she was being forced to raise their kids alone. That would be difficult for anyone.

But none of that excused her actions. Shane could have been killed! Tessa had run a red light and collided with another car and then left the scene. She was a paramedic! They were trained to deal with that kind of stuff. To attend the worst of accidents and render assistance. To do all they could to save lives.

She'd failed to render assistance...

With her head pounding with questions and terrible images from the scene of Shane's accident filling her mind, Molly strode away from Tessa without a backward glance.

I have to get out of here... I have to clear my head...

Thank God they had an extra staff member rostered on that day. She grabbed her handbag. On her way out, she stopped briefly to talk to her supervisor, telling him only that she needed to take time out.

"For how long?" Raoul shouted as she stalked out of the ambulance station.

She didn't stop. Her only thought was to put some distance between her and the woman she'd thought was her friend. The urge to talk to someone overwhelmed her.

Who do I go to? Who can I call?

She couldn't go to Shane. Not yet. He'd want to go straight to the police and she didn't blame him for that. But she needed time to think things through before she betrayed Tessa like that, no matter that it was the right thing to do.

Despite her closeness to all her siblings, her go-to person had always been her older brother, Vaughan. He was the one she'd turned to for advice when she was growing up. But Vaughan wasn't there anymore. He'd dropped out of society. Was hiding out on a Balinese beach doing God-knows what. No one knew when he was coming back. If ever. The thought filled her with sadness. She resolutely pushed it aside.

No, I don't believe that. Vaughan will return. We're his family. He can't stay away forever...

As Molly reached her car and unlocked it with the remote, she pulled out her phone. Sliding in behind the steering wheel, she called Charlotte. As the phone dialed out, she prayed silently, desperately that her sister would pick up.

As the kettle started to boil on the stove, Charlotte pushed away from where she was seated on the couch beside Molly and walked into the kitchen to make the tea. Grayson had moved in with Charlotte a couple of months earlier, in anticipation of their wedding which was scheduled to take place early the following year. Molly was grateful he was still at work. It meant she could spill everything to Charlotte without fear of being overheard.

She'd arrived there only a few minutes earlier, babbling incoherently. No wonder Charlotte had looked concerned.

Molly found the wherewithal to reassure her that she was all right, but that wasn't altogether true. Any moment, she felt she'd splinter into a thousand pieces. Tessa's confession had been shocking. Molly still found it hard to believe. Now she needed to gain some perspective from someone not immediately involved. Someone like Charlotte.

Though her sister was a cop and would urge Molly to do the right thing, she was also very wise and sensitive to the nuances of the world. This was complicated. It involved a friend who'd already gone through so much. It helped that Charlotte knew Tessa, too.

Charlotte came back into the living room bearing a tray with two cups and some milk and sugar. There were also homemade chocolate chip cookies.

"You made my favorite," Molly said weakly.

Charlotte smiled. "I must have known you'd be stopping by."

Molly grimaced. "With a crisis, no less."

Charlotte smiled again. "What are sisters for?"

Charlotte added milk and sugar to the teacups and then handed one to Molly. "Thanks," she said, taking a grateful sip. The tea was hot and milky and sweet, just like Molly liked it.

"You're welcome," Charlotte said and offered Molly the plate of cookies. She took one and once again murmured her thanks.

"Now, tell me everything," Charlotte said, taking her cup and making herself comfortable next to Molly on the couch.

Molly sighed and then drew in a deep breath. Her thoughts were still all over the place, along with her emotions. But she'd come here for advice. It was time to come clean.

"Do you remember when I told you about Shane?"

Charlotte frowned. "Of course I do! You two are getting along all right now, aren't you?"

Molly nodded. "Yes. And thank you again for forcing me to see what was right in front of my nose. We… We're blissfully in love."

"Oh, Molly! I'm so happy for you!"

Molly dragged in a breath and eased it out. "Thank you. I probably would never have given him a chance if it weren't for you. It's like nothing I've ever felt before. Shane feels the same. It's…magical."

Tears of happiness glinted in Charlotte's eyes. "Oh, Molly! That's so wonderful. When do we get to meet him?"

Molly blew her breath out on a sigh. "That's the problem."

She told Charlotte about the accident and Tessa's role in it. When she'd finished, Charlotte looked as shocked as Molly had been.

"Poor Tessa. I understand she might have been shocked and disorientated at the time, but that's no excuse. To leave the scene of an accident without rendering assistance… An accident she'd caused… and particularly when she's a paramedic…" Charlotte shook her head. "That's…unbelievable."

"Yeah," Molly agreed. "I spoke to her about Shane's accident not long after it happened. She knew we were seeing each other. I still can't believe she didn't say something back then. I thought we were friends."

"You have a right to feel upset. Have you told Shane?"

"No. I wanted to talk to you first."

"You have to go to the police."

Molly's shoulders slumped on a heavy sigh. "Yes. But..."

"There are no 'buts', Molly. Tessa caused an accident that resulted in serious injuries. Not only that, she also left the scene. That's a crime too. She must be punished."

Molly sipped from her tea. Her sister was right. That didn't make things any easier.

"You also need to tell Shane," Charlotte added quietly. "He deserves to know."

Molly compressed her lips. The thought of telling Shane filled her with dread, but she had no choice. As much as she wanted to protect her friend, she had to do the right thing. Surely Tessa would understand that. And as Charlotte said, Shane had a right to know.

Finishing her tea, Molly set the cup back down on the saucer and swiped another cookie. She stood and collected her handbag from the kitchen table and then turned and gave Charlotte a hug.

"Thanks for being there for me, sis. Again."

Charlotte hugged her back. "Anytime. Despite what happened, I'm so happy for you and Shane. I can't wait to meet him."

"Soon," Molly promised and let herself out.

Shane spent the day puttering around the house, going through mail, paying bills, and answering emails. The sizeable nest egg he'd managed to save during his time at Sydney Legal had dwindled away to almost nothing. He was going to have to do something about getting a job. While he loved volunteering at the soup kitchen, it didn't pay the bills. Besides, he wanted something more to offer Molly. She deserved nothing less.

It seemed like forever since he'd been in his home, going about his normal life. Nothing would ever be the same again. Not the least the fact that he'd found Molly. It had been three months since they'd met. Three months that had changed everything. He barely thought about the dark days he'd spent in prison. Accident notwithstanding, his life these days was more sunshine than rain and much of that was down to Molly.

Before Molly, he'd been going through the motions, only half-heartedly trying to get his life back on track. He'd kept up his friendship with Flynn, but most of his other friends and colleagues had deserted him the moment they discovered what he'd done. Given the poor state of his finances, he needed to give serious consideration to returning to practicing law. Flynn was always encouraging him to come back.

Perhaps now is the time to do more than think about it?

He wanted to offer Molly a future. A future that not only included love, but security and protection from financial pressures. Though she loved him for who he was, he wanted to give her more than that. If he could get his career back on track, that would be really something.

Right now, he was busy making plans to celebrate their three-month anniversary. She had no idea of course. She didn't know him well enough to know he was a hopeless romantic and he couldn't let a day like their three-month anniversary pass without recognition.

He'd already planned for a special dinner that included flowers, champagne, and a four-course meal cooked and served by a private chef. It was ridiculously lavish and would severely deplete his already exhausted bank balance, but his legs were still not up to the task of standing so long in the kitchen and he wanted to relax with Molly and devote every second of his time to her. And of course, he wanted to impress.

She was currently on a morning shift. She usually finished at six, but he didn't want to be caught off guard and ruin the surprise. Better to call and make sure. Pulling out his phone, he dialed her number. The call rang out. Eventually it went to voicemail. He left her a message and then finished by asking her what time she expected to arrive home. He ended the call with a smile on his face. At the thought of his surprise, his heart thumped with anticipation. Life couldn't get any sweeter.

Chapter Twenty-One

M olly returned to work nearly twenty minutes later feeling better for having talked with Charlotte. She still dreaded the upcoming battle with Tessa. She'd decided on her way back to the station that she'd give her friend the option of turning herself in. If she refused, then Molly would go to the police.

The moment she walked back into the station, a call came in requiring their assistance at another accident. This one involved a three-car pileup. Multiple victims with a variety of injuries that all needed attention. Thankfully, this time there were no fatalities. No sooner had they returned to the station and another call came in. Out they went again. As much as Molly wanted to give Tessa her ultimatum, now just wasn't the time.

Finally, late in the afternoon, things quieted down. Molly found herself in the crib room with Tessa. The woman eyed her warily, as if she'd been expecting this confrontation. And maybe she had.

"You know what you have to do, Tessa," Molly said quietly.

Tessa remained silent.

"There's only one thing you can do," Molly continued. "You have to turn yourself in."

"That's easy for you to say," Tessa spat. "They're not your kids who're going to end up in foster homes."

Molly regarded her steadily, refusing to back down. "They have a father, Tessa."

Tessa's lips twisted into an ugly grimace. "You're right. They do have a father. What a gem he is."

"Look, I agree he might not be up for 'Father of the Year' anytime soon, but nothing's going to change the fact they're his kids. If it comes down to a choice between sending them to foster homes and taking them in, I'm sure he'll do the right thing."

Tessa glared at her. "Oh yes. The right thing. All bow down to Saint Molly Barrington. A woman who *always* does the right thing."

Tessa's words stung, but Molly tried not to let her friend see how much she was hurt. No matter that she felt sick to her stomach, she was doing the right thing.

"I hate that it's come to this, Tessa, but you've left me with no choice. Either you turn yourself in, or I'll go to the police. I'll give you twenty-four hours to make up your mind."

With her chest tight and her heart pounding, Molly turned away and quickly left the room. She made it to the bathroom and managed to close the door behind her before her stomach rebelled and she vomited into the toilet bowl. Wiping her face clean with toilet paper, she rinsed her mouth with water from the sink. Giving Tessa that ultimatum had been the hardest thing she'd ever done.

Still, she'd do the same thing again if she had to. She just hoped Tessa would see that too and that maybe one day she'd forgive her for the part she'd played.

Her phone beeped, indicating a voicemail message. She pulled it out and checked the screen. She felt a pang of regret when she realized she'd missed a call from Shane. Putting the phone up to her ear, she listened to his voicemail. His message brought a smile to her face. It was the only hint of brightness in what had been another dark day.

Then and there, she made up her mind to tell him everything. Charlotte was right. He had a right to know. As soon as she finished work, she'd go over to his place and come clean about what Tessa had done. Tapping out a quick text to him, she told him she'd be home by half-past six, barring another emergency.

Tessa shook with fear and fury. Her mind was in a spin. The last hour of her shift had passed in a blur as her thoughts spun increasingly out of control. There was no way she could let Molly go to the police within the next twenty-four hours. That wasn't long enough for Tessa to come to terms with what she had to do; to get her affairs in order; to speak with her kids.

My kids.

She wasn't sure she'd ever be ready to have that conversation. But Molly had left her with no choice. Not unless she managed to convince her friend to hold off on going to the police; to give her more time. That was her only bet.

As they clocked off and headed to the carpark, she watched Molly climb into her car and leave. Coming to a sudden decision, Tessa climbed behind the wheel of her newly repaired Landcruiser and followed Molly out of the carpark. Ten minutes later, she watched as Molly pulled into the driveway of an unfamiliar apartment block in Sutherland.

Maybe she's already moved in with her boyfriend...?

Either that, or she was visiting someone else. Molly lived in Cronulla, not far from the beach. It was a few suburbs across.

Pulling into the curb, Tessa thought fast. It was obvious Molly was on her way to visit someone, which meant she'd be less inclined to want to talk. But the clock was ticking. Tessa was running out of time to convince Molly to wait before going to the police. Whichever way she looked at it, she had no choice: She needed to talk to Molly now. She wasn't above begging her friend not to say anything until she'd had time to think, to make plans, to get her life in order.

As she watched, Molly headed inside the apartment. Tessa sat for a few more minutes in indecision. Then she gathered her courage, climbed out of her car, and went and knocked on the door.

Molly set her handbag on the counter and then turned to where Shane sat on the couch. An enormous bouquet of red roses lay on the coffee table. There were also candles that had been lit and placed around the room, filling the air with the scent of vanilla and spicy caramel.

She walked toward him and smiled with surprise and delight. "What's all this?"

He stood and took her in his arms and kissed her long and thoroughly. "This is to celebrate our three-month anniversary."

She laughed. "It's been three months already?"

"Three months since we met."

"I see." She looked around her and noticed an unfamiliar man in the kitchen. He was dressed like a chef.

"Before you ask, I've engaged Pierre to cook us dinner. Four courses of French cuisine. How does that sound?"

Molly smiled and shook her head in disbelief. Her heart swelled with love. "I can't believe you've gone to so much trouble," she murmured.

"Nothing's too much trouble for you."

His tender words touched her deep inside, but she was also filled with guilt. The information she had about Tessa weighed heavily on her mind. She needed to tell him. It was only fair. He was the victim of the accident. He had a right to know.

But how could she say something right now, when he'd gone to so much trouble to celebrate their anniversary? It was such a romantic gesture. She didn't want to ruin everything by bringing up something that was sure to cause him angst.

A knock on the door spared her from having to decide. She swallowed a sigh of relief and walked down the corridor to answer it. Tessa stood on the other side. Molly blinked in surprise. Tessa was the last person she'd expected to see.

"Tessa. What are you doing here?"

"I need to talk to you."

Aware of Shane in the room behind her, Molly blocked Tessa's entry. "I've said everything I need to say. You need to leave, Tessa."

Tessa went to push past her, but once again, Molly blocked her way. She spoke through gritted teeth. "I said, you need to leave. *Now.*"

Tessa's expression turned frantic. "No! No! Please, Molly. You don't understand! You haven't given me enough time! I have so much to do before I can turn myself in! I give you my word, I'll go to the police. I'll tell them everything about what happened with Shane. But not just yet. Please, Molly. I'm begging you. Think of my children! Please, don't say anything yet."

Shane took a seat on the couch while Molly went to answer the door. Everything was going as planned. The flowers were beautiful. The candles lent a romantic touch, filling the room with scent. The cordon bleu chef had everything set up and had nearly finished cooking the first course.

A commotion at the door snagged Shane's attention. He wondered what was going on. He only caught snatches of the conversation. Then he heard a woman begging Molly not to say anything. His name was mentioned, along with the word "police". Curious, he stood and limped slowly toward the front door.

A woman he'd never seen before stood next to Molly. She was dressed in a paramedic's uniform, although she was disheveled and there was a frantic look in her eyes.

"What's going on?" he asked.

Molly blanched when she saw him. Guilt flooded her face. Then it disappeared. She looked at Shane and drew in a deep breath. "This is Tessa. We work together. The thing is—"

"Please, Molly! No!" the other woman pleaded.

Shane frowned and looked from one woman to the other. His gut stirred with foreboding. He looked at Molly. "What's going on?"

A look of resignation came over Molly's face. She drew in another deep breath. Then she looked him steadily in the face. "This is Tessa Barone. She's the one who ran the red light and hit your car."

Shane stared at Molly in shock and disbelief. He opened his mouth, but no words came out. Then he looked at the other woman. "What the fuck?"

Molly flinched. The other woman's shoulders slumped. She stared at the floor, looking devastated.

Shane shook his head to clear it of his confusion. Something was terribly awry. He turned back to Molly. "What the hell are you talking about?"

"I'm sorry Shane," Molly said. "I should have told you sooner. I wanted to, but there didn't seem to be the right time... I'm so sorry..."

And then the realization struck him. He rounded on her in disbelief. "You *knew!* All this time, you knew who hit me and you never said a word. How *could* you?"

Molly's face lost all color. She looked like she might faint. But Shane could think of nothing but the betrayal that permeated every fiber of his being.

"You don't understand!" Molly cried. "I only just found out! I wanted to give Tessa the opportunity to do the right thing. To turn herself in. That's the only reason I didn't tell you when I first walked in. Please, Shane..."

In some distant part of his mind, Shane was aware of Tessa turning and leaving. Molly continued to implore him to understand but right then he understood nothing. All this time she'd known who'd caused his injuries and she hadn't said a word because the perpetrator was her friend and work colleague.

So where does that leave me? Obviously not as important to her as I thought...

The pain of that realization hit him squarely in the chest. Unable to bear being in her proximity another second, he turned on his heel and limped away as quickly as his damaged legs would let him. He heard Molly cry out in distress behind him. Dismissing the surprised chef with a few curt words and a handful of hundred-dollar bills, he limped down the hallway to his bedroom. He didn't look back.

Sobs of agony and disbelief tore through Molly's body. She raced outside after Tessa. There was no way Molly was going to let her walk away after what she'd done. There was a chance Shane might never forgive her for not telling him earlier. The least she could do was make sure Tessa confessed to the police.

Evening was full upon them. The growing darkness made it difficult to see. Molly looked around her, searching for Tessa. The street was empty. She was still shell-shocked about what had just happened. She couldn't believe Tessa had appeared at Shane's door like that. Worse still, that Shane had found out that way. She'd seen the look of shock and betrayal on his face. It was the worst thing she could have done. Knowing she might not be given the opportunity to explain herself left her feeling sick to her stomach.

If only I'd said something to him the moment I found out... If only Tessa hadn't arrived like that... If only...

There was no point thinking about "if onlys." The damage was done. Shane was devastated. She had a terrible feeling this revelation might have caused an insurmountable rift. She needed to try harder to set the record straight and hope that he'd forgive her. One way to do that was to escort Tessa to the police station. The period of grace was over.

Tessa sat hunched over the wheel, gasping for breath. Her chest was still tight with panic. Any moment, she expected to hear the sound of sirens. Turning up like that on Shane's doorstep probably hadn't been the smartest move she'd ever made, but she had to make Molly see. She had to beg for more time. Putting her in jail wasn't going to solve anything, no matter that she deserved it. Shane was okay. Walking, even. He looked fine to her.

What's the big deal? Okay, so I did the wrong thing, but it was an accident. Surely, Molly can see that. And things have worked out all right. If I go to jail, the lives of my kids will be destroyed forever. Sorry, Molly. I have no choice...

Tessa stared in the direction of Shane's apartment. As she watched, Molly filled the open doorway. Her head turned left and right, as if looking for something. *Or someone. Me.*

A cold ball of dread formed in Tessa's stomach. She had to stop Molly from going to the police. At least until she'd had time to sort things out with her kids.

With her car concealed by the night and mostly obscured behind an overgrown shrub, Tessa switched on the ignition. Flooring the accelerator, she turned the wheel and directed the car toward Molly. Tessa was upon her in an instant. By the time Molly realized what was happening, only a handful of yards separated them. Tessa kept her foot down and her eyes straight ahead as she braced herself for the impact.

Shane stared at the ceiling above his bed and tried to get a handle on his emotions. The faint glow from a streetlight outside his window provided the only illumination in the room. He was still shocked and angry at the discovery that Molly had deliberately withheld vital information, but most of all he was hurt. He couldn't believe she'd keep something so important from him. It wasn't like she was the one responsible for the accident. No, instead, she'd kept quiet to protect her friend. Though a part of him applauded her loyalty, the knowledge that her friend was more important to her than he was, was like twisting a knife in his back all over again.

It brought up all his insecurities. That he didn't deserve her. That he wasn't good enough. That one day she'd wake up and wonder what the hell she was doing with him. An ex-con. He'd thought their first fight had been a big one, but it seemed to pale in comparison to the stakes raised tonight. There was so much more to lose now. So much more of his heart to break. This fight could tear them apart forever.

Is that what I want? Do I want to break up with her? Would that make me feel better?

No! The instinctive protest was sure and swift. He was devastated to think she could do something like this, but loving someone meant forgiving them, no matter what. Hadn't she done that for him the first time?

At the very least, he owed her the chance to explain. She'd told him she'd only just found out. What did that mean? Had she literally only just found out, or was that a figure of speech? He realized he hadn't really listened to her in his immediate shock, but he needed to know.

With a soft sigh, he rolled off the bed and padded down the hallway. The living room and kitchen were empty. He checked the courtyard. It was empty too. Then he noticed the front door was still open.

His heart clenched with pain. He couldn't bear it if she'd left.

What if she doesn't come back?

Molly looked up just in time to see Tessa's Toyota bearing down upon her. The blaze of headlights blinded her. Then there was a split second when she saw the look of determination on Tessa's face and realized her friend had every intention of running her down. With barely enough time to act, Molly screamed and threw herself out of the way of the vehicle. She landed heavily on the ground and rolled, tucking her arms and legs close to her body, frantic to stay clear of the wheels. She heard a screech of brakes and then the car was backing up. She prayed Tessa wasn't making preparations for a second attempt.

The sound of a terrified scream filled Shane's blood with ice. He reached the open doorway in time to see Molly fling herself out of the way of a vehicle headed straight for her. She hit the ground hard and rolled a short distance before she came to a stop. She lay so quiet and still, he froze. At the same time, he stared at the car in shock. Already, the driver had put it in reverse. He stared at the windscreen, but the dark made it impossible to see whoever was behind the wheel. What he did notice was that the vehicle was a silver Toyota Landcruiser. The same kind of car he was sure had T-boned him.

Flashbacks exploded behind his eyes. *It's happening all over again...* The awful realization that he was about to be hit by an oncoming car. The screeching sound of metal-on-metal. The instant, agonizing pain...

But he couldn't think of any of that now. Molly still hadn't stirred. Even from this distance, he could see blood on her face. Fear like he'd never known overwhelmed him. As the car reversed away with a squeal of tires, he forced himself forward, limping as quickly as his injuries would allow, until he stood over her.

"Molly! Oh, God! Molly! Are you okay?" He tried to bend down and then cursed as a stab of pain reminded him he was far from fully healed. He cursed again. He'd never felt so helpless.

And then she stirred, and the breath *whooshed* out his throat. Her eyes opened. His shoulders slumped with relief. He shuffled another step forward, but still couldn't bend to where she lay on the ground. Then she squinted up at him, looking dazed. Her forehead creased with confusion.

Slowly, she rolled over and sat up. There was a nasty graze on her forehead. She reached up and touched the wound. When it came away wet with blood, she pulled a face.

"Oh, God, Molly! Thank God you're still alive! Where does it hurt?" He frantically looked for other signs of injury.

She gave him a shaky smile. "It's okay, Shane. I'm okay. A little bit shaken up and I'm probably going to have a bruise on my hip where I landed on the ground, but I'm okay."

"What about your head?" he asked, still filled with concern.

"It's fine. Just a graze. I hit it on a rock when I went down. But I'm okay. Stop looking so worried."

Bit by bit, the fear that had gripped him from the moment he'd seen the car tearing toward her began to ease. He dragged in a ragged breath. "Are you sure?"

"Yes, I'm sure."

She slowly climbed to her feet. He reached for her and held her close, covering her face with kisses. "I can't believe how close I came to losing you! I saw the car coming toward you and I just froze. I'm so sorry for shouting at you, Molly. I don't care that you didn't tell me about Tessa right away. None of that matters anymore. All that matters is that you're safe."

Tears glinted in Molly's eyes. She dropped her head to his shoulder and he tightened his arms about her. She cried quiet sobs of relief. A delayed reaction to the shock of what had nearly happened. He stroked her back and whispered mindless words of comfort against her hair. When she finally stopped crying and pulled slightly away, her eyes were red. She'd never looked more beautiful.

"Will you let me explain about Tessa?"

"There's no need. I'm just glad you're okay."

She shook her head. "No. I want to talk about it. You deserve an explanation."

"Okay, but I think we should call the police. Whoever that was tried to run you over!"

She drew in a shaky breath, her gaze steady on his. "That's why we need to talk first. The woman in that car was Tessa."

Molly was grateful for Shane's support as they limped back into the house and sat down on the couch. She shot him a wry grin.

"What a pair we are."

"Are you sure you're all right?" he asked, his eyes still filled with concern.

She managed a small smile, wanting to reassure him. "I'm fine." Garfield jumped into her lap. She stroked his soft fur and took comfort from his presence. She still couldn't believe what Tessa had done.

She tried to run me over... She could have killed me! What was she thinking?

She looked at Shane. She was relieved the incident had put their fight into perspective—a life-and-death experience tended to do that—but they still needed to clear the air. She was glad he was giving her the opportunity to do so.

"Let me start by saying, I'm so sorry I didn't tell you about Tessa the moment I found out. The truth is, I was blindsided by her confession. I had no idea she was involved in your accident. For months I've been giving her a lift to work because she told me her car was in the garage. She always had a reasonable explanation as to why it was taking so long. I didn't once question her."

"I wondered why the police didn't get a call from a smash repairer," Shane mused. "They told me they'd contact them all and ask them to be on the lookout for damaged cars that fit the description of the perp."

"Tessa told me she'd taken the car all the way over to Hornsby. That's more than twenty-three miles from the scene of the accident. I guess the police didn't extend their inquires that far."

"No doubt you're right." He paused. "When did you find out the truth?"

Molly drew in a deep breath and blew it out on a long sigh. "This morning. Tessa told me at work."

Shane nodded slowly. "Okay."

"Like I said," she continued, "I was completely shocked when I found out. I didn't know what to think. My thoughts were all over the place. I walked out of the station. I had to get away to clear my head."

"Where did you go?"

"I went over to Charlotte's place. Thank goodness she was on a day off and had time to hear me out."

"What was her take on it?"

"The same as mine. We both knew the only thing to do was to go to the police. Charlotte urged me to call them and tell them what I knew." She paused. "I was in full agreement, but I wanted to give Tessa the opportunity to turn herself in. I returned to work and as soon as we had a private moment between callouts, I gave her an ultimatum. Either she turned herself in or I was going to the police. I gave her twenty-four hours to do it."

"Is that why she arrived on my doorstep? To ask for an extension of time? That's what it sounded like."

Molly compressed her lips and nodded. "Yes."

Shane looked at her. She could tell he still had more questions. "What is it? Ask me whatever you want to know."

Shane was silent a moment. When he looked back at her, his gaze was somber and steady. "When were you going to tell me?"

Knowing how much rested on her response, Molly chose her words with care. "I hope you believe me when I say I wanted to tell you right away, but I also wanted to think things through. Initially, I was in so much shock, my thoughts were all over the place. I wasn't in the right headspace to make any decisions. Then I spoke to Charlotte and I wanted to tell you then, but first I wanted to speak to Tessa again. It wasn't that I didn't think you deserved to know, it's just that... She's my friend... I wanted to give her the chance to come forward."

"So, you were going to tell me after the twenty-four-hour deadline had elapsed?"

"No! I was going to tell you before then. I was going to tell you when I got home, but then you surprised me with our three-month anniversary celebration and I didn't want to ruin that. You'd gone to so much trouble..."

She held her breath and waited to see if he accepted her explanation and whether he forgave her for not putting him first. When he spoke, his voice was quiet and calm and his words were a balm to her heart.

"Thank you for telling me. I should have given you that chance at the outset. I'm sorry for getting so upset at you. I acted emotionally and without knowing all the facts. It was such a shock. I wasn't listening past the roaring in my ears. That's my fault. I'll try hard not to do that again. I should have trusted that you wouldn't let me down or deliberately hurt me like that." He paused. "I'm just so glad you're okay."

Molly gazed at him through her tears as her emotions overwhelmed her. Setting Garfield on the floor, she closed the distance between them. Framing his beloved face with her hands, she kissed him softly on the mouth. Fire ignited between them. Shane's arms came around her and turned her until she lay on her back. He covered her with his body, his lips still joined with hers.

In no time at all they were naked and Shane was filling her with his cock. She lifted her hips and met him thrust for thrust, desperate for this intimacy, the need to connect. Desperate for this act of love, desperate for release. When it was over and they'd caught their breath, they looked at each other in wonder.

"I love you, Molly Barrington," Shane said.

"I love you, too."

Shane's answering smile lit up his face. "Happy anniversary."

Molly grinned. "Um, I'm just putting this out there but... Would you like to go to a wedding?"

Chapter Twenty-Two

"**A** wedding? What are you talking about?" Shane asked, filled with curiosity.

"My oldest brother, Christopher, is getting married next weekend. He's forty-two and never been in love before until he met his beautiful bride-to-be, Lexi. In fact, I can't even remember him ever bringing home a girlfriend. Now he's head-over-heels in love and is the father of eight children."

Shane's eyebrows rose in surprise. "Wow. How did that happen so fast?"

Molly laughed. "Lexi came with a ready-made family."

She explained how Lexi was a foster mom and had cared for nearly thirty children over the years. She now had five adopted children and three foster children, with promises of more to come.

"How did Christopher cope with that?"

"I'm sure it took him awhile to get his head around it, but you'd never know that now. He's a natural father. He loves being with Lexi and their kids. I've never seen him happier."Shane smiled.. "That's a nice story."

"Yes, especially when I tell you Christopher's the last Barrington we ever guessed would marry."

"Why is that?"

"Let's just say he spent a lot of years feeling bitter and twisted at the sorry hand he'd been dealt. I'm not sure if you remember, but he's actually my half-brother. My mother had him before she was married to my dad. Christopher's biological father was the late Henry Craigdon. He was Flynn's uncle."

Shane frowned. "Now I remember Flynn talking about that. Who's Henry Craigdon? Should I know him?"

"I forget you're not from here. The Craigdons are one of the wealthiest families in the country. They even give the Barringtons a run for their money."

Shane blinked in surprise. "What are you saying? That you come from a wealthy family?"

Molly's answering grin was full of mischief. "You could probably say that. My dad's pretty big in the mining industry."

"Ah, that explains the Chanel handbag," he murmured.

Another reason why I need to find a job... Molly's used to the finer things in life...

Oblivious to his thoughts, Molly winked. "If you want to know more, come to the wedding and you'll find out everything about me and my family. Probably too much. On second thought, maybe inviting you to a Barrington wedding isn't such a good idea..."

Shane laughed and shook his head. "Oh no. There's no getting out of it now. You issued the invitation and I'm formally accepting. I'd love to be your date at your brother's wedding and I'm going to talk to every Barrington I can find and get the dirt on their sister."

Molly gasped in mock alarm. "You wouldn't dare!"

Shane merely grinned. "Wouldn't I? I guess you'll just have to wait and see. Now, let's see if we can rescue any of Pierre's cooking!"

Molly woke late the next morning. She'd put in a call to Charlotte the previous night to update her about Tessa. Charlotte expressed shock at what had happened, but assured Molly she'd put out a BOLO—be on the lookout—for Tessa and let Molly know when they'd arrested her. It saddened Molly that things had come to this, but Tessa had made her own choices. There was nothing Molly could do about that.

She looked across at the empty space beside her in Shane's bed. He must have already risen. The smell of frying bacon wafted through the open doorway. Her stomach growled. After making love on the couch, they'd managed to rescue most of what Pierre had prepared and enjoyed the celebratory dinner, albeit without the chef, before progressing to the bed and making love again. They'd fallen asleep wrapped up in each other's arms.

Softly smiling, Molly swung her legs out of bed and padded into the adjoining bathroom. The graze on her forehead had scabbed over and already looked better than it had the night before. She took a quick shower and pulled on yesterday's uniform. She hadn't yet moved any clothes over to Shane's apartment. That discussion hadn't happened yet. Besides, she was content with the current arrangement. There was no need to rush things.

She was rostered on the first of two night shifts and didn't have to be at work until six that evening. Plenty of time to return home and change into fresh clothes and prepare herself for the night ahead. She'd checked the roster yesterday. She and Tessa were both rostered on again tonight.

After what had happened, she couldn't imagine Tessa turning up for work. She must know that time was up, and that Molly would have gone to the police. All Molly could hope for was that Tessa had used the intervening hours to put her affairs in order. It was only a matter of time before the police found her.

Maybe I should try and call her? We used to be good friends... What happened last night... That wasn't the real Tessa... She's been under a lot of strain.

Molly wasn't excusing her friend's behavior, but this wasn't the same Tessa she'd known and cared about all these years. The guilt over the accident had obviously gotten to her. Last night she'd acted like someone unhinged... And maybe she was. Though she deserved to be punished for her crimes, she also deserved understanding and if Molly was any kind of friend, she ought to give that to her.

With a soft sigh, Molly re-made the bed and headed down the corridor toward the kitchen. Thoughts of Tessa filled her belly with dread, but she needed breakfast, starting with a hot cup of coffee. Lucky for her, Shane had just made a fresh pot.

He greeted her with a smile and a lingering kiss. He was dressed in a T-shirt and jeans. His feet were bare and his cheeks were freshly shaved. He looked gorgeous. Despite her inner turmoil, she leaned into him and breathed in his spicy scent.

"*Mm*, you smell good," she murmured.

"Almost as good as the bacon, right?" he teased.

Her stomach growled right on cue. "Right." They both laughed.

It felt so good to wake up like this. Teasing each other, sharing breakfast. Like they were a real couple. And maybe they were. The thought filled Molly with warmth.

If only I didn't have the specter of Tessa hanging over everything...

"Have you heard from Charlotte?" Shane asked.

Molly shook her head. "No. But I was thinking... I want to speak with Tessa. I'm not sure if she'll take my call, but I have to try. Despite everything, she's still my friend."

Shane nodded, his expression now somber. "I understand. Your kindness and compassion are some of the things I love about you. How about you talk to her straight after breakfast? I'm under no illusions how difficult it's going to be for you. Until you've had that conversation, it will play on your mind all day."

"You're right. And thanks for understanding. As much as I'd love to spend the day hanging out with you and doing whatever we feel like, until I've cleared things up with Tessa, I won't be able to relax. And of course, if she's still determined to keep quiet, I'm going to have to go to the police..."

"Hey, if it comes to that you won't have to go alone. I'll go with you."

She shot him a grateful look. The knowledge that he'd do that for her choked her up. "Thank you."

He pulled her into his arms and held her close, pressing a kiss against her hair. "I'm here for you, Molly. I want you to know that. Every step of the way."

They shared another sweet and tender kiss.

"I love you," she whispered.

"I love you too. Let's eat."

Right after breakfast, Molly went out to the courtyard where she was afforded some privacy. Taking hold of her courage, she called Tessa. The phone rang out for a long time. Molly braced herself for it to go through to voicemail.

"Hello?"

Molly blinked in surprise. "Hi, Tessa. It's Molly."

Her greeting was met with silence and then she heard a long and weary sigh. "Before you say anything, please let me speak. I've been driving around all night thinking about what happened and what you said. I'm so sorry, Molly. I don't know what came over me. I could have killed you! My best friend!"

Molly felt a surge of emotion, coupled with relief. Before she could respond, Tessa spoke again.

"You were right about coming forward. I always knew you were, but the consequences of doing what you wanted were so huge, I was desperate not to face it. My life will be ruined. My kids... Their lives will never be the same again. But I have to take responsibility for what I did... Not only to Shane, but to you, too. I'm... I'm going to turn myself in."

Molly's legs went weak with relief. Though she'd fully intended to go through with her threat, it made her feel so much better that Tessa had made the right decision.

"Thank you, Tessa," she managed, swallowing against the lump in her throat.

"I know this is a lot to ask, but... Will you come with me?"

Molly closed her eyes against another rush of emotion. "Of course, I will."

"I want to do it now, before I lose my nerve," Tessa said in a rush. "Before the police come knocking on my door. Is that okay with you?"

"Yes, of course. Where will I meet you?"

"Can you come and pick me up from home? The kids are at school. I want it done before they return."

"Did you talk with them?" Molly asked gently.

Tessa sighed. "Yes. It was the hardest thing I've ever done. I sat all three of them down this morning and explained everything. By the end of it, we were all crying. I told them I was going to the police station today and that they might have to go and stay with their dad for a while."

"Have you spoken to Martin?"

Tessa sighed again. "Yes. And you were right. Again. He's agreed to step up and be their father while I'm...gone. At least I have that to comfort me."

"I'm so proud of you," Molly said softly.

"Thank you for being so understanding. And for being the best friend a girl could hope for. I only wish you could say the same." Tessa's voice hitched. "I wish you and Shane all the best."

The trip to the Cronulla Police Station was made in silence with both women lost in their thoughts. Molly reassured Tessa she'd made the right decision. Tessa merely nodded. Inside the police station, Molly was met by her sister, Charlotte. Until that moment, Molly hadn't realized Charlotte was at work that day, but she couldn't deny she was relieved to see a familiar face and to know Charlotte would conduct the record of interview.

At Tessa's request, Molly sat in on the interview. Charlotte asked Tessa if she wanted to have a lawyer present. Tessa declined. At Charlotte's prompting, Tessa then went through the circumstances of what had happened, including her decision to flee the scene and the incident outside Shane's apartment. Charlotte and another detective listened without interruption, apart from the odd question to clarify something. A couple of hours later, it was over.

Tessa was charged with a string of offenses, including negligent driving occasioning grievous bodily harm, failing to render assistance at the scene of an accident and leaving the scene. When prompted, Molly told the detectives she wouldn't be pressing charges for what had happened the night before. Tessa's eyes filled with tears at her announcement. She was offered the services of a lawyer again and warned that, based on her confession, there was a strong likelihood she'd face jail time.

Molly stayed with her friend while she was fingerprinted and photographed. Tessa looked scared but resigned. She complied with the officers' requests, including submitting to handcuffs without a word. It killed Molly to see her friend like this, but there was nothing to be done. Crimes had to be punished. It had to be that way.

"Will you check in on my kids, Molly?" Tessa asked as she was about to be led away.

"Of course, I will," Molly promised.

"Tell them I love them and I'll see them all soon."

As Charlotte led Tessa toward the cells out the back, Molly turned away. Tears burned behind her eyes. She was still standing in the same spot, staring blindly at the wall, when Charlotte returned. She took one look at Molly and stepped forward and put her arm around Molly's shoulders.

"Oh, Molly. Are you okay?"

Molly swiped at her tears. "Yeah."

"I'll let the two detectives who were on this investigation know about Tessa's confession. They'll be pleased to wrap things up so well."

Molly compressed her lips and nodded. She was still struggling with the fact she was responsible for bringing Tessa there. If she hadn't given her the ultimatum, Tessa might have packed up her life and disappeared. It would have meant she got away without being punished for her crime, but was that really all that important? Shane was okay and so was she. The reality that Tessa would be spending time in prison away from her children was suddenly, horribly real. Molly couldn't help but wonder if she'd made the wrong call. Who would gain from Tessa being jailed? It wasn't going to make any difference to Shane or his recovery...

"Don't think like that, Molly. It isn't fair on you or anyone else. You did the right thing."

"Did I?" Molly rasped.

Charlotte's expression filled with compassion. "I know how difficult this has been for you. She was your friend."

"She's still my friend."

Charlotte nodded somberly. "Of course."

Molly drew in a shaky breath and tried to get herself together. Charlotte was right. Given the circumstances, there was nothing else she could have done. It would just take her a bit longer to get to the place where she could agree with her.

Christopher and Lexi couldn't have asked for a more perfect day for their wedding. They'd opted to have the ceremony among the lush and beautiful grounds of the Sydney Botanical

Gardens with the stunning Pacific Ocean as their backdrop. Ancient Moreton Bay fig trees, surrounded by acres of manicured lawns and exquisitely tended flower beds bursting with bright colors completed the picture-perfect scene. Molly had tears in her eyes watching the loving couple exchange their vows surrounded by their children.

All eight of the kids were in the wedding party. The boys looked smart in their mini tuxedos. The girls sparkled in their shimmering, pale pink gowns. Even the youngest of them, the precocious three-year-old, little Leroy, looked adorable in his tiny suit. He wore a smile that was matched only in its brilliance by the smile on Christopher's face.

Molly couldn't believe how far her brother had come. From a man who for years had been bitter and twisted about how life had treated him, to being a loving husband and father and looking happier than ever. It was a beautiful thing to see his transformation. He was a living affirmation of the power of love.

Her gaze drifted to Shane standing tall and proud beside her, looking sexy in black-on-black Armani. It was a little formal for a garden wedding, but what the heck. He looked gorgeous. She threaded her fingers through his. He squeezed her hand in response. A surge of love shot through her.

To think I was prepared to go through life without love... What a ninny I was!

She'd never been so happy. She hadn't yet introduced him to her family, but if the smiling, sidelong glances from her parents were any indication, she could tell they approved. She looked forward to introducing him to everyone and beginning the next chapter of their lives. Fearless. In love. Together.

The vows had been said and the speeches were over. The wedding party and their guests had retired to the grand ballroom in the Intercontinental Hotel for the reception. An elegant canvas of soft grays, whites and neutral tones complemented the huge urns of fresh, pale pink roses that perfectly matched the bridesmaids' dresses and filled every corner of the room.

Shane had spent most of the evening by Molly's side. She'd introduced him to her parents and to her siblings. Molly had told him she'd already shared with them some of the details of his past, including his incarceration and how he and Molly had met. She assured him they were willing to accept him on his merits and nothing more need be said. Even so, he was still nervous when he came face to face with Frank and Evelyn Barrington.

His anxiety had been for nothing. They treated him with courtesy and respect. Frank even inquired about whether he was interested in learning more about the mining business.

"We're always on the lookout for talented people with grit," Frank said.

Flynn and the rest of the Craigdon clan were also there, including the late Henry Craigdon's wife, Elizabeth. It pleased Shane to know there was no bad blood between Christopher and his other family. From what Molly had told him, that hadn't always been the case. It made him feel good to know he was surrounded by people who believed in forgiveness.

And then there was crazy, funny, feisty Hannah. She was the only Barrington sibling present who was still single. He wasn't sure why. She was just as attractive and confident as her brothers and sisters. When he questioned Molly about it, she just grinned.

"Hannah is her own woman. She's a mine manager up in the Hunter Valley, surrounded mostly by men. Some of whom take offense to having a woman in charge. She's developed a tough exterior and she doesn't put up with anyone's crap. Sometimes that scares men off. That doesn't stop her from dating though. She's had more dates than I've had hot breakfasts." Molly winked.

Shane laughed. He loved the idea that Hannah was tough and confident enough to make it in a world traditionally dominated by men. It told him a lot about her strength of character. He looked forward to getting to know her. It was at times like this, surrounded by the love and warmth of family, that he missed his own.

It had been more than three years since he'd seen his parents. Even longer than that since his sister had flown from New York for a visit. Of course, spending two years in prison hadn't helped. Coupled with his parents' flagging health, the long trip from the UK was almost beyond them. He made a note to talk to Molly about taking a trip overseas in the near future. He wanted them to meet the woman he'd fallen in love with. The woman who made him whole.

The band struck up a slow love song and Shane turned to Molly with a smile on his lips. He reached for her hand. "Would you do the honor of giving me this dance?"

She smiled, her eyes wide and luminous with love. "I'd love to."

He pushed away from his chair and helped her rise from her seat. The regular physio sessions had paid off. He could now walk unaided for longer distances and the limp had all but gone. His legs still ached if he was on them for too long, but a slow dance with the woman he loved wasn't going to stop him.

"How are your legs holding up?" Molly asked, as if reading his thoughts.

"They're holding up just fine. I feel great."

They reached the dance floor and he drew her into his arms. She fit so naturally against him, like she was meant to be there.

"It's been such a beautiful day," Molly said dreamily.

With his hand on the small of her back, Shane pressed her closer against him, overwhelmed with emotion. He tightened his hold on her hand. Being with her felt so right. He never wanted to let her go. For weeks now, he'd been wanting to propose to her, but he hadn't wanted to do it until he had something more to offer her in the way of financial security. Now he did.

"You know how I was talking to Flynn the other day?" he murmured against her hair.

"Yes."

"He's been encouraging me to come back to work."

Molly pulled slightly away from him. "As a lawyer? Is that possible?"

"Yes. I've been in contact with the Law Society. There's a good chance they'll be willing to reinstate my license to practice."

Molly stared up at him in surprise. "Even with your criminal record?"

He smiled faintly. "Yes. Notwithstanding my criminal record, there's plenty of precedent where the courts have determined that someone can still be a "fit and proper" person to hold a law license. The person I spoke to at the Law Society seemed to think my application for reinstatement would be favorably met."

Molly's face broke into a grin. She threw her arms around him, right there on the dance floor.

"That's wonderful Shane! I'm so happy for you! Do you have any idea what you want to do?"

He shrugged and fought back a smile. Her happiness was contagious. "I might return to Sydney Legal or I might open my own practice as a criminal defense lawyer. It's a bit different than family law, but I met some guys in prison who'd been given a rough ride with their state-appointed lawyers. I want to offer my services to the kind of people who might not be able to afford a private lawyer. Being in jail has given me a whole new perspective."

Molly's face glowed with pride and happiness and he basked in her obvious love for him. Not so long ago, he could never have imagined his life turning out like this, with the woman of his dreams beside him, loving him as deeply as he loved her. God worked in mysterious ways.

Tonight, after the wedding celebrations were over and they were on their own in his apartment, he'd dig out the diamond ring he'd bought a couple of weeks earlier and though he'd no doubt pay for it later with aches and pains, he'd get down on one knee. He was certain Molly would say yes. The thought filled him with joy. He couldn't wait to make her his wife.

THE END

Get a free book when you sign up for Chris Taylor's newsletter at: http://www.christaylorauthor.com.au

If you enjoyed Molly and Shane's story don't forget to leave a review at your favorite digital retailer. Evey review is really appreciated and helps with visibility so that other readers can find and enjoy my books.

Broken Dreams is the next book in the Barrington Family Series. Keep reading for a sneak peek at **Broken Dreams**:

CHAPTER ONE

Hannah Barrington hung up the phone and leaned back against her ergonomically approved office chair. She stacked her hands behind her head and smiled. Her sister Molly was engaged! His name was Shane Lucas and Molly had met him during the course of her job as an intensive care paramedic. He wasn't a colleague, but a former patient who'd been involved in a nasty motor vehicle accident. Thank God the other driver had finally come forward to the police.

Hannah was thrilled for her sister. At twenty-six, Molly was well and truly ready to find love. She'd never had a serious boyfriend. Not even at high school. Hannah wasn't quite sure why. Molly was gorgeous, inside and out. She'd been popular enough with the boys. But somehow, she hadn't ever hooked up with anyone. Now she sounded smitten.

Hannah wasn't surprised. She'd seen the way Molly and Shane had been at Christopher and Lexi's wedding. They couldn't take their eyes off each other. Now they were getting married. Hannah was happy for them. She might shudder at the thought of matrimony and the level of commitment that required from herself, but she could be happy about it when it came to her siblings.

Seven of her eight brothers and sisters had recently found love. For all she knew, her adopted brother, Vaughan, might also have found his soul mate. Perhaps that's what had kept him all these months in Bali. Why else had he stayed away so long?

It was enough to make her feel a little anxious that the love bug might be lurking in her vicinity. Look at what had happened to Molly. She was the last person Hannah had expected to fall in love. It was best she steer well clear of such an affliction. Love would only tie her down. It would mean having to take into account someone else's feelings. Her life would be irrevocably changed. No, she was more than happy playing the field. She'd leave the love game to her siblings.

Idly, she picked up a framed picture off her desk of her and Molly. They looked alike, both with dark hair and blue eyes. They took after their mother. But that's where their similarities ended. Molly had always had her heart set on helping people. She'd headed off to university to study paramedics straight out of school. Hannah, on the other hand, had flitted in and out of work, going from one unskilled job to another. She'd tried waitressing, bar work, dog grooming, nannying and had even done a short stint as a pastry chef. She loved to bake and had learned from one of the best. Her mother was an excellent cook.

But though Hannah had enjoyed each job, none of them had held her attention for long. It was the reason why her father, almost despairing his youngest child would ever settle down to a career and make her mark on the world, had offered her a job at one of his mines. Strathwaylin was a coal mine situated in the picturesque Hunter Valley, a couple of hours' drive north of Sydney. It was only one in the string of mines owned by her father. Frank Barrington made his fortune in mining. He now offered his daughter the same opportunity.

Hannah had been intrigued at the thought of managing a mine. Though she had no experience in mining, she'd always been good with people, and she firmly believed managing any kind of business came down to people management. Besides, how hard could it be?

A little over twelve months later and she realized there was a lot more to managing a mine than she'd first thought. The mountain of regulatory compliance, the ever-present need for safety, the massaging of male egos who were put out at having a woman in charge. It had been a battle, but one she found she enjoyed. The need to prove herself in what was a traditionally male-dominated industry was a daily challenge. It was a good thing she liked to be tested.

But for now, she chose to concentrate on her sister's new-found happiness. Hannah closed her eyes on a little sigh of contentment. She was thrilled Molly had found her soul mate. Everyone deserved to find love. Hannah had been in and out of love so many times in her twenty-three years, she didn't know why anyone would choose to avoid it. No, scrap that. She'd never been in love. She'd only been in lust. That's where the real fun was.

Of course, it always sucked when she grew tired of the current object of her affections. It didn't matter that her heart wasn't involved. She always went through a kind of grieving process regardless, whenever a relationship came to an end. Probably because she always threw herself so wholeheartedly into it. She didn't know of any other way. But then she'd find someone else to focus her affections on and the world would be bright again.

Her older siblings rolled their eyes every time she shared with them details of her latest love interest. She understood their dismissive attitude. While she hadn't been into boys in high school, by the time she graduated, things had begun to change. There had been so many boyfriends over the past five years. It was like she was trying to make up for lost time. Like her sexuality had only just awakened and she was determined to explore it to the fullest.

Some relationships, like the one she'd enjoyed with Derek Finnigan late in the twelfth grade, lasted no more than a couple of weeks. They went their separate ways right after graduation. Others were more enduring. The longest relationship she'd had was her last one. She'd had high hopes for her and Chad. He was a marketing manager in a large advertising firm in Sydney. Tall, good looking and with the sexiest laugh, he'd ticked a lot of boxes. They had a lot in common. They both enjoyed outdoor activities, country music and dancing. He also liked to read, something Hannah enjoyed but hardly found the time for.

Unfortunately, after only four months, Chad had gone the way of all her other relationships. She'd realized one day that though she enjoyed his company, and he wasn't too bad in bed, she yearned for something more. She didn't exactly know what the "something more" entailed, but she could tell she didn't have it with Chad.

Another one bites the dust...

The thought of having to seek out a new boyfriend didn't faze her. In fact, the chase was the most exciting part. Navigating the early stages of any new relationship filled her with anticipation. The nerves, the eagerness, the expectation... And the fun! She couldn't forget how much fun it was to start a new relationship.

The fact most of her siblings had found their soul mates and were headed for marital bliss didn't concern her. She loved that they were all so happy and ready to settle down and she knew just as well that she wasn't anywhere near close to that and that was okay. She loved having a boyfriend, someone to talk to, hang out with, but they didn't have to be her soul mate. She wasn't looking for Mr Forever. She was perfectly fine being with a sexy and fun Mr Right Now.

Someone like my new second-in-charge, senior operations manager, Nathan Romano...

Now, he was a sight for sore eyes. Coal-black hair and laughing brown eyes that harked back to his Italian heritage. A smile that made her pulse race. Broad shoulders, narrow hips and a glint in his eyes that hinted at naughty things. The only problem was, he was her colleague and she had a strict rule about dating people she worked with. When the relationship ended, as it inevitably did, things got awkward. She'd always steered clear of that kind of complication.

Still, if anyone could persuade her that he was worth breaking her self-imposed rule it was Nathan. He'd been there almost as long as she had. Right from the start, she could tell he was interested. So far, she hadn't given him any encouragement, but now she and Chad were consigned to the history books, maybe it was time to change that.

As if she'd conjured him up, Nathan filled the open doorway to her office. Despite the fact he could have no way of knowing her thoughts, she blushed. Flustered, she opened the file on her desk and pretended interest in the typed pages.

Nathan interrupted her with a knock on the door. Without waiting for her to respond, he walked in. She forced herself to look up.

"Nathan. What can I do for you?" Belatedly she noticed his grim expression. Her stomach tensed with alarm. "What is it?"

He compressed his lips and strode further into the room. He wore the standard garb for a mine worker, no matter their level of seniority. A fluorescent-yellow, high visibility work shirt and durable navy-blue work pants. He held a mine-issued, white hard hat. "There's been an accident."

Hannah's heart sunk. "Oh, no. Not another one."

"Afraid so."

"How bad?"

Nathan blew out his breath. "Not too bad. It's been reported as a collision between an excavator and a dozer. No one injured, thank God. But a decent amount of damage. It'll have to be reported to the regulator."

Hannah grimaced. "Great. Just what we need."

Nathan's expression remained grim. He knew as well as she did about the spate of accidents the mine had been plagued with over the past twelve months, starting with the death of Evan Wilson. Despite the complete overhaul of all their safety operations since Evan's fatal accident, the incidents continued to happen.

Until the accident involving Evan's death, the Strathwaylin mine had been fortunate to suffer very few serious incidents, and no deaths. That had changed with Evan, and it seemed that the incidents had kept piling up ever since. Hannah was at a loss to explain why, but she was determined to get to the bottom of it.

That was one of the reasons she'd brought Nathan on board. To be her eyes and ears on the ground. He had a background in workplace health and safety. She only hoped his expertise rubbed off on her and together, they managed to put a halt to what felt like a continuous string of safety infringements.

"I'll take you to the site of the accident," Nathan offered.

Hannah nodded and muttered her thanks. She collected her hard hat on her way out of her office and followed Nathan outside. He'd parked a few yards away. Hannah opened the passenger side door of his vehicle and climbed inside. Nathan took a seat behind the wheel.

"Who was it?" she asked as he headed toward the pit.

"Fred Williams was driving the dozer. He's only been with us a few months. Still, he came with years of experience at other mines and has been driving that thing since he got here."

"Who else?"

"Joe Hammond. He was on the excavator."

"Have you spoken to him yet? What's he saying?"

"No. I called you as soon as I heard. I'll talk to him when we get there."

Hannah digested the information. The last thing they needed was another accident. The fact most of them weren't serious wasn't the issue. Safety was the number one priority at any Barrington mine. Strathwaylin was no exception.

Once again, her thoughts turned to Evan Wilson. The tragic accident that had stolen his life had happened during her very first week on the job. Though the ensuing litigation had now been settled and due compensation paid to the man's family, the fear of a fatal accident happening at her mine again kept her awake at night. She might not have earned her position in the mine through sheer hard work, but she was determined to make up for that. Ever since she'd taken on the role of mine manager, she'd been unwavering in her resolve to lift their safety record. Unfortunately, that record had just taken another hit.

Nathan pulled up beside the two machines. Hannah couldn't prevent a gasp of alarm as she surveyed the damage. Most of the windscreen of the dozer had been crushed beneath the force of the excavator bucket. How it had managed to collide with the other machine was anyone's guess. From what she could see, it was an accident that should never have happened.

She climbed out of Nathan's truck and strode to the men gathered nearby. Most had their heads down and their hands jammed in their pockets. As soon as they spied her, they moved farther away, but remained close together, silently closing ranks.

"What happened here?" she demanded in an authoritative voice.

The men shuffled their feet and kept their faces averted. Anger licked at Hannah's belly. She asked the question again. This time, one of the men stepped forward. He had a sly look and a swagger that immediately set Hannah's teeth on edge. She'd seen that kind of attitude before on some of the men in her employ. They resented the fact she'd frog-leaped into the top job merely because she was the mine owner's daughter. They also hated that she was a woman. To some of the men, women had no place on a mine site. Thank goodness her father wasn't one of them.

"Fred here was on the dozer. He called me up and asked for permission to slide on by me. I answered in the affirmative.

I thought he was well out of the way before I picked up my bucket and swung it." The man who spoke turned his head sideways and spat a globule of phlegm on the ground. He smirked at Hannah. "Appears I was wrong."

Hannah glared at him, her anger soaring into fury. With an effort, she held onto her temper and addressed Nathan through gritted teeth.

"I want a full written report on my desk before the end of this shift. Understand?"

He nodded. "Of course."

With that, she turned on her heel and stormed back to their vehicle. She climbed back into the passenger side and sat fuming while she waited for Nathan to join her. Fortunately, she didn't have to wait long.

He threw her a sideways look as he switched on the ignition and put the vehicle into gear. "It could have been worse."

"It's not the accident I'm furious about!" she exploded. "It's the attitude! Did you hear what that man said? And his tone! He couldn't give a damn about the damage he's caused to that dozer, let alone the nightmare of paperwork I'm now going to be buried under. On top of that, I'm going to have to deal with the Resources Regulator." She turned to look at Nathan, her breath coming fast. "This shouldn't have happened."

"You're right," he said calmly. "I'll speak to everyone involved. Don't worry, I'll get to the bottom of it."

"And what about the excavator operator? What did you say his name was?"

"Joe Hammond. He's a good operator. A first-class safety record. I don't know what went wrong."

Joe Hammond...

The name imprinted itself on Hannah's mind. The arrogant swagger, the disrespectful smirk, the challenge in his eyes... He was just the type of employee she despised.

Okay, so she hadn't been born breathing coal dust. She couldn't lay claim to generations of family members who'd made their living in the mines. But that didn't mean she couldn't do the job she'd been appointed to do. She might have been fast-tracked into the top position, but after more than a year at the helm, she'd earned her stripes. Too bad some of the men there still refused to accept that.

Nathan shot her another wry look. This time he followed it with a lopsided grin. "Come on, Hannah. It's not that bad. We could have been dealing with a serious injury, or a death. That would have been far worse."

"Nathan, that's not the point. The thing is, we have safety protocols for a reason. Obviously, someone failed to follow them, or the accident wouldn't have happened."

"You're right and I'll be sure to speak to both men and issue them with warnings. But as far as incidents go, it's not in the most crucial category."

"But—"

Nathan held up his hand, cutting her off. "I'll put a review of safety protocols on the top of the list for tomorrow's start-up meeting. I'll go through every manual with the men. It'll be all right, Hannah. Trust me. I've got this."

She looked at his calm and reassuring demeanor and her shoulders slumped on a sigh. She was grateful to have him as her second-in-charge. He was prepared to get in and work as hard as she did and often stayed back to work extra hours. Better still, his casual and calm manner always managed to cut through her stress. He was a good man to have by her side.

Once again, the notion of dating him entered her mind. She glanced at his hands on the steering wheel. He drove with a lazy self-assurance that instilled her with confidence. She felt safe with him. She was also growing more and more intrigued. His hands were large, his fingers were long and tapered. She wondered what if might feel like if he were to touch her. Her nipples hardened in response.

This is ridiculous! I'm in the middle of a serious incident and I'm fantasizing about my operations manager. For goodness sake, Hannah! Get a grip!

They traveled the rest of the way in silence. Nathan dropped her off outside her office and she thanked him and waved him off. She looked up at the sky. It was as blue and cloudless and beautiful as late spring days in the Hunter Valley got. A good day for mining coal. She only hoped the excavator accident was the only safety breach she had to deal with that week. Now she'd spend the rest of the day filling in the paperwork and reporting the incident to the authorities.

Great. I can't think of anything I'd rather be doing...

Chapter Two

Liam Hennessy flashed his government credentials at the young and attractive woman seated behind the reception desk of the Strathwaylin coal mine and introduced himself.

"Hi, I'm Liam Hennessy. I'm from the Resources Regulator. I'd like to see the SSE," he said, using the acronym for the senior site executive.

He was filled with curiosity at the thought of stepping onto a Barrington Mining mine site. He wondered if any of Frank and Evelyn's nine kids had followed in Frank's footsteps and worked in the mining industry.

He'd gone to school with some of the Barrington offspring. Wade Barrington had been in his class. Zac had been in the year below him. The triplets, Trace, Charlotte and Molly, were a year older than Wade and there were a few more who were older than that. The one that stood out in his mind for all the wrong reasons was Hannah Barrington.

Hannah was the youngest Barrington child and had been a couple of years below him in school. She'd made his every living moment a tortuous hell. Not that she had any clue he existed. That had been the problem. He wondered what had become of her. Not that he cared. The less he thought about Hannah, the better. In fact, he wouldn't care if he spent the rest of his life without seeing her again.

The receptionist gave him a friendly smile. "Do you have an appointment?"

"No," he replied. "But I'm here about an incident that was reported to the Resources Regulator a few days ago. I'm sure your boss will see me"

The woman picked up the phone and spoke quietly into it. Liam turned away and moved over to one wall where various framed pictures of the mine site in action were displayed. They were good quality images and perfectly captured the organized mayhem and hive of activity that was most often present on a mine site.

The sound of boots coming toward him caught his attention. He turned and then froze in shock. Hannah Barrington strode toward him. She wore the same fluorescent yellow, high visibility work shirt and navy-blue pants common to everyone who worked on a mine site. As she drew nearer, his head spun madly with a kaleidoscope of thoughts.

In a distant part of his mind, he acknowledged how good she looked. Tall and curvy, the promising figure she'd had as a teenager had morphed into something luscious and womanly. Even in the masculine clothing, she oozed sex appeal. His belly churned. Despite the fact this was a Barrington mine, she was the last person he'd expected to see there. He couldn't believe it was her. His nemesis. The woman he despised more than anyone else.

And here she was. Manager of the mine site, no less. The big boss. At the ripe old age of twenty-three. Of course, she was. Her daddy owned the mine.

She looked at him without the faintest flicker of recognition, only serving to infuriate him further.

No surprise she doesn't recognize me... What did I expect?

"Mr Hennessy, I'm Hannah Barrington. It's nice to meet you."

He forced himself to shake her outstretched hand. The whole time, anger burned inside him. He'd spent his final years of high school loving her from afar and she didn't even know who he was – not then and certainly not now. It might have been seven years since he'd put his high school days behind him, but the bitter memories were as fresh as if they'd walked those long and noisy corridors only yesterday.

The realization incensed him. He'd worked so hard to eradicate her from his memory and yet with the first glimpse he'd had of her in seven years, she once again saturated his mind. It was beyond infuriating. It was totally and completely unacceptable and it just went to show how weak he was.

Damn Hannah Barrington!

He glared at her. She blinked in surprise, taken aback by his animosity. His predecessor had obviously had a more cordial relationship with her. Well, she'd get no common courtesies from him!

"I'm sure your receptionist informed you I'm from the Resources Regulator. I'm here about the incident you filed earlier in the week."

"Yes. I guessed as much."

She turned on the heel of her boot and strode back in the direction from where she'd come. It incensed him all over again that she expected him to follow her without protest, like an obedient lap dog. She walked into an office at the end of the corridor and took a seat behind an enormous carved oak desk and folded her hands in front of her.

"So, Mr Hennessy. Welcome to Barrington Mining. I didn't realize Mr Warren had left."

Liam sat in the chair that stood opposite the desk. "My predecessor requested a transfer to be closer to his family," he replied by way of explanation, his tone curt. "I've been appointed to take his place."

"I see." She spread her hands open, palms up. "Well, I hope you and I get along just as well as Mr Warren and I did. It certainly helps to have a professional working relationship with each other. I think it makes both of our jobs easier."

She smiled. It was the same brilliant white smile she'd had in high school. It lit up her face and shined from her deep blue eyes. He flinched as if he'd been struck and then took refuge in his briefcase to hide his reaction. Her failure to recognize him had been insulting enough. He wouldn't give her the satisfaction of knowing how much she still affected him.

Pulling out a sheaf of papers, he thrust them across the desk. Once again, she looked taken aback by his aggression.

Good. Let her wonder who the hell I am and why I'm acting so rude. It will serve her right to be embarrassed when she finally works out who I am...

Then again, maybe it was wishful thinking on his part that she'd remember him at all, even later, when she'd had time to think about it. The possibility filled him with a fresh surge of anger.

"You haven't submitted all of the required paperwork," he bit out. "I'm sure you're aware of the penalties for failing to comply with our regulations."

Hannah looked at him in surprise. She frowned and sat forward. "What are you talking about? I submitted everything I was required to do."

"No," he bit out again, "you didn't. A new regulation came out last week requiring you to fill out an additional section specifically addressing the reasons why safety protocols were breached. That section was not received by me."

Hannah's eyebrows rose at his continual display of anger, but she merely drew in a breath and sat back against her chair. She was smart enough to realize she needed to keep him on side. If he was of mind to do it, he could make her life very difficult, to say nothing of halting production of the mine.

"Oh, I see. Well, I apologize for the oversight. It wasn't intentional. I'll get the additional paperwork to you as soon as I can."

Liam continued to glare at her. "You'd better. I need it like...yesterday."

To her credit, Hannah held his gaze, but the anger in her eyes was clear to see. "I've already said I'll get onto it. Now, is there anything else?"

Liam slowly shook his head back and forth, a humorless smile turning up his lips. When he spoke, his voice was filled with scorn. "You Barringtons are really something."

Another flash of anger flickered in Hannah's blue eyes. "Excuse me?"

His gaze narrowed, became steely-eyed. "You heard me."

Hannah stared at the man across from her. There was something perplexingly familiar about him, but for the life of her she couldn't place him. The thick blond hair, the brown eyes, the athletic physique that gave lie to the fact he spent most of his time behind a desk... He had more than his fair share of good looks and physical appeal. That alone should have made him memorable. And though his name rang a faint bell in her memory, it wasn't enough for her to know who he was or what the hell she'd done to upset him. And it was clear he was upset. Furious, even.

She'd gotten used to her fair share of arrogant investigators who were employed by the Resources Regulator. The regulatory body had been established by the New South Wales government in 2016 and had been tasked with the job of dealing with all mine and petroleum sites across the state. Their primary job was to act as the state's work, health and safety regulator. Their jurisdiction extended over open-cut and underground mines, petroleum sites, quarries and extractive operations, tourist mines, opal and other small-scale mines and mining exploration activities. They were also responsible for undertaking compliance and enforcement activities in relation to the Mining Act 1992, with a key focus on mine rehabilitation. In short, they wielded incredible power.

That was the reason she'd gone out of her way to befriend Hennessy's predecessor. Michael Warren was in his fifties and had spent most of his career enforcing work, health and safety regulations and investigating breaches. He knew the law inside out and took his role very seriously. But he'd also been approachable, reasonable and had acknowledged the efforts made by Barrington Mining to make safety a priority. He and Hannah had enjoyed a mutually respectful relationship which had been maintained despite the recent rush of incidents.

But this new guy was over the top. It was like he had a personal vendetta against her. Or at least against her family. It was strange and more than a little disconcerting. She needed to keep the investigators who wielded the power of the resource regulator on side. They could do a lot of damage to her bottom line if they chose to play hard ball, not to mention her reputation and the reputation of Barrington Mining.

With an effort, she kept her tone even. "Look, Mr Hennessy. I don't know who you are or what beef you have against my family, but if we're done here, it's time you left."

The look he gave her was so self-assured it almost stole her breath. "Oh, we're far from done, Hannah Barrington. But that's it for now. Get me the rest of that paperwork ASAP." With another hard look, he pushed away from the desk and stood. "Until next time."

She didn't even bother to look up. "Good afternoon, Mr Hennessy. I'm sure you know the way out."

Hannah was still in a bad mood when she visited her parents for dinner that evening. Though they lived three hours' drive away from the Hunter Valley, she tried to catch up with them at least once every few weeks for dinner, along with the rest of her family. Her mother was a superb cook, and she usually enjoyed the time she spent with her parents and the chance it gave her to reconnect with them and with other members of her family.

Living so far away from most of her siblings, she didn't always know what was going on in their busy lives. Coming together regularly for a family dinner was one way she managed to keep in touch. An evening with her family almost always managed to put her in a good mood, but tonight, despite the sumptuous four-course dinner and accompanying wines, Hannah remained tense.

It's all because of him. Liam Hennessy. He's the reason I'm still in such a bad mood.

As she politely listened to her brother, Zac and his fiancée, Emily, share their wedding plans, including a lively discussion about the pros and cons of an indoor versus and outdoor celebration, her mind remained firmly fixed on the man who had the power to cause her real angst. At some point, she'd have to tell her father about the new investigator from the Resources Regulator. Any incident involving a breach of safety rules had to be reported to the regulator. That meant Liam Hennessy was in their lives for the near and maybe even distant future. Hannah usually took the time to brief her father on anything interesting happening at the mine or anything he should be made aware of. The arrival of Liam Hennessy fell squarely into that definition.

Great.

Something in her expression must have given away her disquiet. She started in surprise when her father leaned over and covered her hand with his.

"Perhaps you should come into my office, and we can talk about what's put that dark look on your face?" he suggested in a low tone.

Hannah closed her eyes briefly and drew in a deep breath. "Is it that obvious, Daddy?"

"It is to me," he said.

Pushing back his chair, he stood and excused himself from the table. Hannah followed suit. Together, they walked to the front of the house and into the room he used as his office The room was decorated with a masculine décor, with plenty of dark furniture and heavy drapes, but it had always reminded her of her father and it was the place where she felt closest to him.

He walked over to a sideboard and poured himself a glass of port. He turned to her. "Can I get you a drink?"

"Yes, please."

He handed her a glass and she took a sip. The sweet liquid slid easily down her throat and left warmth in its wake.

"So," her father said, taking a seat behind his huge, carved wooden desk. "What's going on?"

Now that the moment was upon her, Hannah wasn't sure where to start. Her father had put her in charge of the mine.

She didn't want him to think she wasn't capable of dealing with this unexpected complication. But he also had a right to know. Liam Hennessy might just prove to be a significant thorn in their side, and they could both do without that. But for now, she'd start with the easier stuff.

"Well, production's well up on our expectations. Coupled with the high coal prices, we've already met our quotas and we're only halfway through the quarter."

Her father nodded with approval. "Well done. That's what I like to hear. But that doesn't explain the frown on your face. What else is going on?"

She bit her lip. "I'm still having a bit of difficulty with some of the men. I've been there more than year. You'd think they'd accept me by now. At the very least, the fact I'm the mine manager should garner some respect."

"Did something happen?"

"Yes! I was down in the pit earlier today dealing with an issue. I addressed a group of men, asking questions to ascertain what had gone on. You should have seen them, Daddy! The way they looked at me! Like I was nothing!" she said, remembering the scornful look given to her by Joe Hammond. Even now, she burned with the need to wipe the smirk off his face.

"You have to earn their respect, Hannah," her father replied calmly. "These are tough men. They work hard. They're not used to having a woman in charge. They're not going to respect you just because you want them too."

"I know that, Daddy!" she cried. She pushed away from his desk and stood, overcome with anger and frustration. "But I work hard, too. Harder than most. I'm the first one to arrive on that mine site in the morning and I'm the last one on that shift to leave. I understand I might have been promoted well above my ability in the early days, but that was a long time ago. I've learned a lot since then."

Her father nodded. "You have and I'm proud of the effort you've put in. There isn't a piece of machinery or a section of the mine or a team you don't have extensive knowledge about, and I can guarantee that's made your job there a lot easier."

"Of course, it has. But there are still several employees who can't get past the fact that, not only am I a woman, but my father owns the mine. They think I'm Daddy's little girl and that's the only reason I'm in the position I'm in. It's infuriating! It's not like that anymore."

Her father sighed. "Would you like to me to address your employees? Would that make a difference?"

"No!" she immediately protested. And then in a calmer tone, "No. Thank you for the offer, Daddy, but that would only make things worse. You riding in on your white horse to rescue me would only reinforce their mistaken belief that I'm there not because I'm the best person for the job, but because I'm your daughter."

Her father shrugged. "Fair enough. I'm glad you see it that way. It shows me how much you've matured from the flighty girl who had no idea what she wanted to do with her life a year ago. Do I have to remind you how many careers you started and then lost interest?"

She looked away, feeling contrite. "No, Daddy."

"Hannah, look at me."

She reluctantly lifted her gaze. "I offered you the job at the mine to give you something to do, but I also knew you were capable of doing the job if you set your mind to it." He paused and then smiled at her. "You didn't disappoint."

She was filled with a rush of warmth. Her father didn't often hand out praise, and when he did, she knew he meant it.

"Thank you, Daddy. I appreciate your vote of confidence."

"Of course. I always had faith in you. Right from the start. The only thing you needed to do was to find that belief in yourself. And you've done it. You can hold your head up high and take your place beside any of my mine managers."

She flushed with pleasure. Hearing her father say those words did wonders for her confidence. Too bad some of the men derided her position at Strathwaylin. She'd ignore them, like she'd done in the beginning, and just get on with doing her job.

"How're we going as far as safety goes?" her father asked, changing the subject.

She compressed her lips and sighed. She'd almost forgotten about her nemesis. "There's a new investigator from the Resources Regulator. I met him today. Liam Hennessy. Have you heard of him?"

"No, what's he like?"

She sighed again and regained her seat. She reached for her glass and took another sip before responding. "He's rude and arrogant and overbearing. He drove all the way out to the mine just to tell me I hadn't submitted all the paperwork in relation to the latest safety breach. Something he could have easily done over the phone. What's more, he—"

"What do you mean, the latest safety breach? What happened?"

Her father's tone was harsh. Hannah swallowed another sigh. "There was a minor collision between a dozer and an excavator."

Her father exploded, as she knew he would. "What the hell? You call that a minor incident? How the hell did something like that happen?"

"I don't know, Daddy. But I'm going to find out."

Her father's gaze sharpened. "Was anyone hurt?"

"No, nothing like that. A miscommunication. The excavator bucket thought the dozer was clear of him. It turned out he wasn't."

"What kind of damage are we talking?"

"The cab of the dozer was almost completely crushed. I'd estimate three of four hundred thousand for that. Then there's the loss of production. Fortunately, we're ahead on our production targets and we've been able to secure the hire of another dozer. We were only down for a day."

"I guess it could have been worse," her father muttered. "At least no one was hurt."

His expression darkened and she could tell he was thinking about Evan Wilson's death. The man's family had been devastated. In a strange twist of fate, one of her brothers, Zac, had recently fallen in love with Evan's sister. They'd dated in high school but had gone their separate ways after graduation. Now they'd rekindled their romance. In fact, their wedding was only a month away. Apparently, they were both keen to make up for lost time. Hannah could only guess Zac and Emily had worked things out between them and in particular, that they'd come to terms with the details surrounding Evan's death.

She shot her father a look of reassurance. "You're right. We can be grateful no one was injured."

"I assume you reported it?"

She grimaced and sat back in her seat. "Yes, of course. I filled in all the necessary paperwork. Well, at least I thought I did."

"What do you know about this new investigator?"

"Not much. Only that he's a jerk. I've worked so hard over this past year to build up a good relationship with Michael Warren and now he's gotten a transfer." She scrubbed at her hair with irritation. "It's just that this Hennessy guy's so antagonistic. Like he's bearing a grudge. I'm sure I've never met him before, but he acts like I should know him. I can't figure it out. Are you sure you don't know who he is?"

"How old is he?"

"Mid-twenties. Maybe a year or two older than me."

"Where's he from?"

"I don't know. But he gave me the impression he knew a lot about us – the Barringtons."

Her father shrugged. "That's not hard. You only have to do a search on the Internet, and you can find out plenty. Not all of it's true, but that's the way it goes. And some of these people who work for the regulator – a lot of them aren't on our side. It's not just that it's their job to investigate and enforce safety, some of them take it personally, as if it's their duty to bring dirty coalminers to their knees."

He paused and then added, "There's nothing you can do about people like that, Hannah. The truth is, they're jealous of our success. They have a tiny amount of power over us and they're going to make damned sure they use it."

She reached for her drink and took another sip. "I'm not sure this Hennessy guy fits into that category. He didn't seem to care that we were rich. His aggressive attitude felt more personal than that."

"I don't know. Perhaps you'd have better luck asking your brothers and sisters. They might know of him."

"Yeah, I might do that. Maybe his beef isn't with me, but with one of my siblings? That might explain his nasty attitude."

"I'm sure you won't let him get to you, Hannah. More than that, you'll come out on top. There isn't a man on this planet who's a match for you when you put your mind to it." Her father winked. "The poor bloke doesn't stand a chance."

Hannah chuckled, her good spirits restored. For the first time that day, she looked forward to her next encounter with the rude and insufferable Liam Hennessy.

Bring it on...

Chapter Three

Liam chopped up the tomatoes like any moment he expected them to rise off the chopping board and attack him. All afternoon, he'd seethed with anger. It had put him in a filthy mood for the rest of the day and his bad mood had everything to do with Hannah Barrington.

"You should have seen her, Jac. It was like being sucker punched in the gut. I had no idea she worked at her father's mine. And not only does she work there, but she's the boss. Can you believe it? She sits behind a monstrous desk like a queen on her throne, lording it over everyone. She's as bad as she was in high school."

His older sister shot him a sympathetic look. "I can only imagine what a shock that must have been for you. It's been years since you saw her."

"Right. Not since I graduated from high school. I can't believe I'm going to have to deal with her now. I've never met someone more arrogant."

Jacqueline scooped up the diced tomatoes and dropped them into a hot frypan that already sizzled with onion and garlic. Liam had moved into her house in Muswellbrook temporarily while he looked for suitable accommodations of his own. Her house was situated in the Hunter Valley and was central to the mines that were now under his jurisdiction. Fortunately for him, she was still single and had a spare room.

"I never thought she was arrogant," Jacqueline continued in a conversational tone. "More like confident and proud. I think that's why she stood out. Most of us were desperately trying to cope with puberty, doing our best to blend in with the crowd. But not Hannah Barrington. Even though she was a few years below me, I still remember feeling envious of how she didn't seem to care what people thought. And of course, she was beautiful. That helped."

Liam grimaced. "Well, she's still beautiful, don't you worry about that. Not that I took much notice. I was so instantly mad when I saw her. As well as shocked. All those memories came rushing back. Ned..." Liam shook his head in an effort to hold the anger and sadness at bay. "Surely you remember what she did to him."

Jacqueline regarded him somberly. "The way I remember it, Ned had a lot of problems. Not the least was an abusive father and a drunken mother who never got off the couch."

Liam's anger ignited. It took all his self-control to hold onto it. "I can't believe you just said that!"

His sister continued to regard him calmly. "Is that really what you think? That it was all Hannah's fault?"

"It's not just what I think! It's the truth!" he cried impatiently, still aghast his sister might remember things differently.

She merely shrugged.

Liam forged on. "Come on, Jac! You were there! You know what happened!"

"It was a long time ago, Liam. Let it go. I've had a tough day at work. If you don't mind, I'd just like to cook dinner, chill out for a while, and relax."

The anger that held Liam's body taut dissipated. His sister worked long hours at the local hospital in the palliative care ward. It was a tough job, both physically and emotionally. Now that he looked at her more closely, he could see the dark shadows of fatigue beneath her eyes.

"Hey," he said softly. "You go and put your feet up. I'll finish this. How about I pour you a glass of wine? It looks like you need it."

She gave him a grateful smile. "Thanks, Liam. That would be great. You're right. I'm beat." With that, she took him up on his offer and after washing her hands and wiping them on the tea towel, she headed for the couch.

Seated on the couch with her legs tucked beneath her, Jacqueline sipped on her glass of red wine. It was true. She'd had a tough day. They'd lost two of their patients. Two elderly women who'd been struggling with terminal cancer for more than a month. In some ways, it was a blessing they were now free from pain. Still, it was always hard when they lost someone.

She'd been working on the palliative care ward for more than a year now. It was hugely demanding work, but she loved it. As Liam banged away in the kitchen, her mind went back to her years at high school. Both she and Liam had attended Broken High. The small rural town boasted a population of around five thousand, but it had a large catchment area for the high school. There were nearly four hundred kids that showed up every day. For all Liam's angst over high school, Jacqueline had only good memories of those years.

She'd also gone to school with the Barringtons. She was a year older than Liam. She'd had the Barrington triplets in her class. In particular, Trace. She remembered him as outgoing, confident, and good looking, like all of the Barringtons. She'd only had eyes for Ned. He'd been Liam's best mate. Too bad Ned had been so desperately in love with Hannah. He hadn't even noticed Jacqueline. She never held that against him. Most of the boys at Broken High had been in love with Hannah, including Jacqueline's brother.

Liam thought he'd been so clever at hiding the way he felt for the girl, but Jacqueline had always known. She'd thought it kind of tragic that two best friends were both in love with the same girl and even more tragic that the very same girl was unaware of their existence.

As the memories washed over her, she sighed and took another sip of wine. Such a sad and complicated world they lived in. At the ripe old age of twenty-six, Jacqueline was only too happy to wipe her hands of love. The small taste of it she'd had in her teenage years had burned her badly. No, she was happy being single. That way she only had herself to please. Right now, that felt pretty darn good.

Liam stirred the tomato, garlic and onion concoction and then added a generous dollop of tomato paste. He flavored the spaghetti sauce with salt and pepper and tore up some fresh basil and oregano. Dropping the herbs into the pan, he gave the sauce a final stir before setting the spoon aside and turning his attention to the pasta.

He hated arguing with his sister. They usually got on well. There was only the two of them now their parents had both passed away. Their mother a couple of years ago from cancer. Though she hadn't said anything to him, Liam was sure that was one of the reasons Jacqueline now worked in palliative care. Their father had died only two months ago from a heart attack. He'd been all of fifty-seven.

Their father's sudden death had been the impetus for Liam to make some changes in his life. One of those changes had been leaving his hectic life in the city for a quieter country pace. It was the reason he'd requested a transfer to the Hunter Valley. Only a two-hour drive north of Sydney, the Hunter Valley was the birthplace of Australian wines. Known for its exquisite varieties of semillon and shiraz, it was also renowned across the world as a leading gourmet getaway. For someone who liked to drink wine and cook, he was in paradise.

Though he hadn't yet had time to visit too many of the establishments on offer, he planned to do just that on his weekends off. A different place every weekend. That was his goal. And of course, being in the Hunter Valley meant he was also closer to his sister, which was important to him now that they only had each other.

He grinned ruefully. They were actually far closer at the moment than he'd anticipated. Right now, they were sharing a modest, two-bedroom house. Though he hoped to find a place of his own in the near future, so far, he hadn't found the time.

He sighed as he thought again of their recent argument. The thing that irked him the most was that he wasn't angry with Jacqueline. He was angry at Hannah Barrington. And angry at himself. He thought after all these years he was over her, but one look in her beautiful blue eyes and the feelings of love and hopelessness had come crashing back.

That was the real reason he was so mad – at her...and at himself. She was oblivious to how he felt—then and now—and all he wanted was to get over her. To put her out of his mind, once and for all. To exorcise her memory and move on. Except now she was here, on his new turf.

Even more alarming, they were likely to encounter each other on a regular basis. Not only when there were incidents, but it was also his job to enforce compliance of the regulations, along with a whole raft of other things. No matter how much he wished otherwise, it looked like Hannah Barrington was part of his life once again. That meant he had to work out some way of coming to terms with it and staying sane in the meantime.

Hannah tucked the tail of her high-vis shirt into the waistband of her work pants and adjusted her position in her chair. No matter that she was the mine manager and spent most of her days in an office, it was mine protocol that everyone on site dressed in protective safety gear, right down to their steel-toed boots.

Nathan sat across from her, similarly attired. They'd been going over the mine's safety protocols, tightening up the wording, making clearer the procedures that had to be followed every single day. It had been a week since their last incident. She'd finally started breathing freely again. Maybe their run of safety breaches had come to an end. She could only hope.

Still, she wasn't naïve enough to believe there wouldn't be another one. With more than one-hundred-and-thirty people on site at any given time and a large number of heavy earthmoving equipment engaged continuously on site, it was only a matter of time before something went wrong again. Especially going by their recent record.

"We need to make sure every incident, no matter how insignificant, is brought to our attention," Nathan said.

Hannah frowned. "Surely that's already happening?"

Nathan grimaced. "In theory, yes. It's supposed to happen that way, but I've heard on the grapevine that some of the contractors get a bit slack when it comes to reporting everything."

Hannah sat up straighter, alarmed. "But that's not their call to make. *Everything* must be reported. It states that clearly in the handbook. Every single one of those contractors and their employees are taken through each step of the safety protocols at their induction. They have no excuse not to comply. Which of the contractors aren't reporting properly? I need to speak with them."

Nathan held up a hand in a placating gesture. "Whoa, Tiger. I have no definite proof of anything. Only rumors. If you go charging in half-cocked and accusing them of breaching safety standards, we'll have a mass walk-out. We can't afford for the contractors to down tools for even a day, let alone anything longer than that. And where are you going to find fifteen dump trucks overnight? We need those contractors."

Hannah's anger refused to be mollified. "Then what do you suggest? That we turn a blind eye to what might very well be safety breaches?"

Nathan's tone remained calm. "No, of course not. Leave it with me. I'll make a few discrete inquires. See if I can find some evidence of wrongdoing. Any contractor deliberately ignoring the safety protocols doesn't deserve to be here, no matter how many machines they're supplying."

"In fact, the more machines they have, the greater the risk of something going wrong if they're ignoring safety protocols," Hannah muttered.

Nathan flashed her a smile that reminded her how attractive he was. "You're right." He winked. "That's why they pay you the big bucks."

Feeling slightly irritated by his comment, Hannah turned her attention back to the most recent incident.

"I submitted the additional paperwork to the Resources Regulator. I'm still waiting to hear whether they intend to launch an investigation. Let's hope they don't. How are we going with repairs to the dozer?"

"The mechanics and fitters have been working around the clock. There was a bit of a hold up on the glass, but I'm led to believe the dozer will be back in action in another week."

Hannah compressed her lips. "Then it's just as well I was able to source another one so quickly. Two weeks down is a lot of lost production time."

"Yeah." Nathan started scrolling through his phone.

Hannah felt a fresh wave of irritation. He was meant to be her second in charge and he couldn't have appeared less interested.

"Nathan!"

"Yeah?"

He didn't even bother to look at her. She clenched her jaw and tried to hold on to her temper.

"Are you listening to me?" she asked through gritted teeth.

This time he looked up and flashed her another smile. "Of course, I am."

"It doesn't look that way."

"Hey, you're concerned about contractors picking and choosing which incidents they report. I get it. I'm concerned too. All the incidents over the past year have involved contractors. For some reason, they don't seem to be getting the safety message. But I'm on it. You don't have to worry. I'll poke around and find out what's going on. Then we'll know how best to address it."

She sighed on a weary breath. "Thank you. In the meantime, I'd appreciate it if you attend the general communications meeting at the start of each shift for the next couple of weeks and reinforce the need for every single person on this site to be familiar with our safety protocols. We need to get on top of this."

Nathan reached across the desk and covered her hand with his. "You got it."

Hannah blinked from the unexpected contact. She looked at him in surprise. Nathan merely grinned and removed his hand.

"You've got this, boss. And you've got me here to help you. I'm there for you every step of the way. Don't forget that."

Another cheeky wink and he was gone, leaving her to ponder the wisdom of hiring such a good-looking offsider. It was downright distracting and right now, distracted was the last thing she could afford to be.

I need to keep my mind on the job. Now isn't the time to be preoccupied by a pair of teasing eyes and a cheeky grin... Best remember that next time that handsome devil's in my office...

A reluctant smile tugged at Hannah's lips. For all of Nathan's irritating inattentiveness, she couldn't deny she enjoyed working with such a sexy man. She knew from his HR record that he was single. In the time he'd been there, she'd heard no talk of a girlfriend. He was just the kind of guy she found attractive: Good looking, charming, sexy. Perhaps it was time to show him some interest. That is, if they managed to break the cycle of safety breaches and had enough time to focus on something other than the mine when they were at work...

The thought filled her with anticipation.

Down, girl!

The sound of Hannah's mobile phone ringing interrupted her musings. She pulled it out of her pocket and checked the screen.

"Nathan. What's up?"

"I'm afraid I have bad news."

His words and the grimness of his tone made her heart skip a beat. Tension of a different kind tightened her stomach.

"What is it?"

Broken Dreams is available now for preorder at your favorite digital retailer. It will be released in November, 2022.

Other books by Chris Taylor

The Munro Family Series (in order)

The Profiler
The Investigator
The Predator
The Betrayal
The Deception
The Negotiator
The Christmas Vigil (A novella)
The Ransom
The Defendant
The Shooting
The Maker

The Sydney Harbour Hospital Series (in order)

The Perfect Husband

The Body Thief
The Baby Snatchers
The Final Bullet
The Debt Collector
The Lab Test
The Stolen Identity
The Cliff-top Killer
The Likeable Fraudster

The Sydney Legal Series (in order)

An Accidental Murderer
At the Hand of her Father
A Woman Scorned
Lies and Deception
Ordinary Evil
The Ties that Bind
The Perfect Crime
A Toxic Inheritance
Malicious Love

The Craigdon Family Series (in order)

Callum
Joel
Isabella
Nicholas
Sophia
Flynn

Noah
Logan
Elizabeth

The Barrington Family Series (in order)

Broken Lives
Broken Promises
Broken Bonds
Broken Spirits
Broken Minds
Broken Vows
Broken Hearts
Broken Dreams
Broken Homes

The Fairfax Family Series (in order)

A Cattleman in Disguise
A Cattleman's Quest
A Cattleman's Daughter
A Cattleman's Secret Baby
To Catch a Cattleman
The Doctor and the Cattleman
To Rescue a Cattleman
A Cattleman's Heart
For the Love of a Cattleman

Bachelors and Brides Series (in order)

Matilda
Austin
Farrah
Benjamin
Verity
Denver
Ebony
Tyrone
Willow

Books by Chris Taylor
Writing as Bella Christian

This Is Where It Ends Series (in order)

Jessie's Story
Ryan's Story
Holly's Story
Sarah's Story
Veronica's Story

Love audiobooks? Check out Chris Taylor Books on audio
iTunes Amazon Audible

Join Chris Taylor's Facebook reader group/fan page and be
among the
first to receive news of book releases, read and review books

prior to release
and other amazing offers.

Join Now!

Acknowledgments

As usual, no book comes into being without a lot of help and support by my friends and family. A world of thanks must go to my editor, Nancy Cassidy. Thank you for everything that you do to make my stories even more amazing than I could ever dare to dream. To former Detective Superintendent Michael Kilfoyle, thank you for lending my story credibility. Any mistakes are wholly my own.

To Justin Mendez and all of the team at 100 Covers, thank you for the fantastic book cover. To my sister, Nicole Guihot and to my friend, Ally Thomson, thank you for your excellent editorial comments, proof reading skills and suggestions. I hope you like the final result.

To the fantastic writer organizations such as Romance Writers of Australia, Romance Writers of America and Romance Writers of New Zealand for all the help, support and encouragement they offer new and aspiring writers, including me.

To my readers, thank you for your support and love for my stories. Your encouragement and enjoyment make this journey all worthwhile.

And lastly, to my friends and family, especially my husband and children. Thank you for putting up with late dinners and even later conversations as I've emerged day after day from the sometimes scary but always enthralling world I've created on my computer.

About the Author

Chris Taylor grew up on a farm in north-west New South Wales, Australia. She always had a thirst for stories and recalls writing her first book at the ripe old age of eight. Always a lover of romance and happily-ever-afters, a career in criminal law sparked her interest in intrigue and suspense. For Chris to be able to combine romance with suspense in her books is a dream come true.

Chris is married to Linden and is the mother of five children. If not behind her computer, you can find her doing the school run, taxiing children to swimming lessons, football, ballet and cricket. In her spare time, Chris loves to read her favorite authors who include Richard North Patterson, Sandra Brown, Kathleen E Woodiwiss and Jude Devereaux.

You can find out more about Chris and get a free book when you sign up for her newsletter at her website:

http://www.christaylorauthor.com.au

Join Chris on Facebook at:
    https://www.facebook.com/christaylorauthor/